REBEL DAWN

ANN SEI LIN

WALKER
BOOKS

First published 2024 by Walker Books Ltd
87 Vauxhall Walk, London SE11 5HJ

2 4 6 8 10 9 7 5 3 1

Text © 2024 Ann Sei Lin
Cover illustration © 2024 Amir Zand
Map illustration © 2024 Tomislav Tomic

The right of Ann Sei Lin to be identified as author of this work has been asserted in accordance with the Copyright, Designs and Patents Act 1988

This book has been typeset in ITC Berkeley Oldstyle

Printed and bound by CPI Group (UK) Ltd, Croydon CR0 4YY

British Library Cataloguing in Publication Data.
a catalogue record for this book is available from the British Library

ISBN 978-1-4063-9961-5

www.walker.co.uk

MIX
Paper | Supporting
responsible forestry
FSC
www.fsc.org
FSC® C171272

REBEL DAWN

Also by Ann Sei Lin

Rebel Skies

Rebel Fire

Little star, do you
Remember being fire,
How it felt to burn
Your shining light, a beacon
To those long after your death?

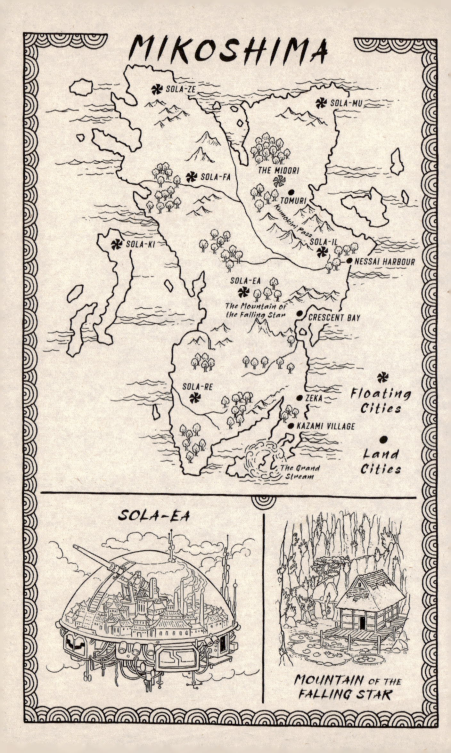

MIKOSHIMA
SOLA-ZE
SOLA-MU
THE MIDORI
SOLA-FA
TOMURI
Kumokiri Pass
SOLA-IL
SOLA-KI
NESSAI HARBOUR
SOLA-EA
The Mountain of the Falling Star
CRESCENT BAY
SOLA-RE
ZEKA
KAZAMI VILLAGE
The Grand Stream
Floating Cities
Land Cities

SOLA-EA

MOUNTAIN OF THE FALLING STAR

Prologue

When Tomoe was young, her mother had told her to stay away from soldiers. It was a warning all Sorabito parents gave their kids. The military were not bogeymen used to make children behave; they were real and vicious, and they prowled the sky cities like wolves.

For the most part, *"Stay away from soldiers"* was a sage piece of advice that had served Tomoe well.

At least, it had until today.

She and Sayo had found the military base quite by accident, tucked away in the middle of a forest, far from any towns or villages. What a tiny army camp was doing out in the middle of nowhere, surrounded by nothing but trees, Tomoe did not know, but she was not about to let this opportunity pass her by. She was hungry and tired, and she wanted to go home, to the *Orihime* – to the airship she loved. Army camps had food and fuel and, most importantly, vehicles that could take her back to the sky. Back to her airship.

Back home.

"It's quiet," said Sayo.

"Quiet" was an understatement. The camp appeared deserted. There was not a single soldier in sight, no guards patrolling the perimeter, or lookouts shouting at her to stay away from the cold metal gates.

"Do you think it's abandoned?" Sayo shuffled closer to Tomoe, their shoulders almost touching.

A week ago, Tomoe could not have imagined the military abandoning one of their camps, not even one as remote and hidden as this, but a lot had changed in such a short time.

A week ago, her father and Prince Ugetsu had declared that the sky cities would go to war against the empire. A week ago, Tomoe had watched Kurara fight a giant phoenix shikigami and crack open its core, unleashing a host of screaming, shadowy monsters across the land. The world was a different place from the one it had been before. In the grand scheme of things, an abandoned military base was not that strange.

Tomoe and Sayo had parted ways with Kurara soon after the fight – Kurara had wanted to stay on the ground, but Tomoe and Sayo had wanted to return to their airship. Though they had parted on good terms, Tomoe did miss having someone around who could kill a man with a playing card.

Turning her attention back to the army base, she peered through the gaps in the chain-link fence and said, "Let me take a look inside."

Alarm flickered across Sayo's face. "This sounds like another one of your bad ideas."

Another? What slander! What absolute, filthy slander!

"What are you talking about? All of my ideas are strokes of genius!" she said, to which Sayo merely sighed.

Tomoe was not going to let that stand. Sizing up the height of the fence, she backed away and made a running jump for it, leaping into the air and grabbing hold of the metal links. It rattled loudly beneath her weight. She waited for a moment until she was sure no one was coming then climbed to the top and dropped down onto the other side.

Still, the camp did not stir. There were no angry soldiers charging at her, no blaring warning sirens, not even a bullet to the head.

So far, so good.

"Stay here," she told Sayo. "I'll see what I can find."

"Oh no. There's no way you're going alone! I'm coming with you." Sayo scaled the fence as well.

Tomoe huffed, but she was secretly glad to have Sayo watching her back. There was no one else she would rather have by her side.

"I don't see anyone," Sayo said, dropping down from the fence onto the hard ground beside Tomoe.

The base really was empty. The commander's tent was deserted, and the barracks were all uninhabited. As Tomoe picked her way through the camp, she noticed scorch marks on the ground. Someone had lit a fire – a large one – in the middle of the training grounds, though now nothing remained but a dark mark on the stone pavement and a light coating of ash.

"W–who's there?" someone squeaked.

Tomoe and Sayo spun around, coming face to face with a thin, trembling man holding a pistol in one hand. The

gun was clearly aimed at them, but the man's hands shook so much Tomoe did not think he could hit them from even three feet away. He looked half dead. His soldier's uniform hung from his skinny shoulders like a tent and was marked with dirt and all sorts of stains she would rather not think about. The black circles under his eyes suggested he had not slept in days, his cheeks were sunken and an unhealthy grey sheen coated his skin.

"Who are you?" the man demanded.

"A–are you OK?" Tomoe raised her hands in the air, though she only did so to put him at ease.

"Wh–who are you?" he repeated.

"We were just passing by." It was a half-truth. "We noticed how quiet it was, so we thought we'd investigate. What happened here?"

The man stared at her with wide, bloodshot eyes, and shrieked, "The shadows!"

"Shadows?"

Tomoe and Sayo exchanged a worried glance. They were both thinking the same thing. They were both thinking of Kurara's fight against the phoenix shikigami Suzaku – and about the dark, ghost-like monsters that had come out of Suzaku's core after Haru had cracked it open.

"It happened at night, when everyone was getting ready for bed. They were – they were like nothing you've ever seen before. Like smoke shaped into human form, only their limbs were all wrong, and some of them were covered in eyes and mouths and—" The soldier dropped his pistol. It hit the ground with a clatter. "They came through the walls! Bullets

didn't stop them. Blades just went through them. Then they – those *things* crawled inside the men's chests and killed them! Everyone just fell down stone-dead."

"How did you survive? Is there anyone else left alive?" asked Sayo.

"It's only me! I noticed that the shadows were drawn to the lights, so I crawled beneath one of the bunks and kept still. I hardly dared to breathe. They disappeared when morning came, but by then everyone was … everyone was—"

"All right. Don't worry. You're safe now," Tomoe hurried to assure him.

"I burned the bodies. I had to! There were too many to bury. I burned them, and then I—"

"Look, why don't you come with us? We're taking an aircraft and heading towards the nearest sky city," said Tomoe.

Sayo shot her a sharp look, but Tomoe didn't see what other choice they had. Sure, he was technically an enemy, but it wasn't like they could leave the poor man here alone, literally jumping at shadows.

At the very least, her suggestion calmed the man down, but as he took another look at them, something in his expression hardened.

"You … you're Sorabito, aren't you?"

"So what if we are?" Tomoe had a bad feeling she knew where this was going.

Suspicion contorted the man's expression into something hateful and ugly. "I'm not going anywhere with you, sky rats!"

"Whoa there!" Tomoe held up her hands. "There's no need for—"

"You stay away from me, sky rats!" the man shrieked.

"Fine, then stay here!" Sayo spat before turning away.

Tomoe hesitated. In the back of her mind, she could hear her father crowing: *See? You offer a groundling a little kindness, and what do you get in return?* Disheartened, she hurried after Sayo.

"Wait, you can't take an aircraft! That's military property!" The man scrabbled for his pistol and aimed it at them, but his hands were still shaking too much. Tomoe doubted he could really stop them.

"Ignore him. He's just a bloody groundling," Sayo muttered beneath her breath, even as the man continued to shout after them.

"I *am* ignoring him. You're the one who keeps looking over your shoulder," said Tomoe.

Sayo said nothing, but her fists shook with anger. Dealing with stupid groundlings was nothing new. Perhaps it was so disheartening *because* it was nothing new. Tomoe took Sayo's hand and held it until her anger faded.

They did not have to search the camp for very long to find what they were looking for. As they slipped across the training grounds, they picked up a bag full of rations from a supply tent and then made their way to the aircraft hangar. Inside, they found a small brown qipak shaped like a wooden fishing boat. This was it – their ticket back to the skies. Tomoe glanced at Sayo – at her burning eyes and her jaw clenched so tightly she might break her teeth – and sighed.

She just wanted to go home.

ONE

WHEN Kurara closed her eyes, she could still see Suzaku. The phoenix's last moments played out over and over in her dreams – Suzaku wreathed in flames, Suzaku plunging into the water, Suzaku with its chest cut open as Kurara reached for its core. Surrounded by smoke and shadows, the phoenix screeched: *"THIS IS ALL YOUR FAULT! YOU KILLED ME! YOU KILLED US ALL!"*

Her fault. Yes, that was right: she had killed Suzaku. She had known that inside the phoenix's core lay a host of deadly shadows that, if unleashed, would spread across the land – and she had broken the core open anyway. Because she had wanted the Star Seed hidden inside Suzaku's core. Because the Star Seed was the key to saving the shikigami.

"YOU KILLED ME, AND I SHALL NEVER FORGIVE—"

Kurara woke with a jolt. Haru was crouched on the balls

of his feet, shaking her shoulder, but he backed away the moment she sat up.

"Are you all right, Rara?" A slice of pale moonlight cut across his face, illuminating his ink-black eyes.

"S—sorry, I had a … bad dream." A chill rolled down Kurara's spine, though whether it was from the dream or the weather turning colder, she could not tell.

"Is it Suzaku?" asked Haru.

"It's not Suzaku," she said. Which was half true. It was not *just* Suzaku that haunted her. It was the shadows that *had* been released when they cracked open Suzaku's core; it was learning about the destruction of the Star Trees, and the truth that shikigami were really humans who had been killed and turned into paper beasts for Crafters to control.

It was Aki. It was the enormity of knowing that she had lived far longer than she could ever imagine and had done so many terrible things. As Aki, she had killed the people of Kazami village, used their lives to create Suzaku, then escaped the horror of what she had done by shedding her memories and becoming Kurara – a clueless servant aboard a floating restaurant.

Even if she did not remember it clearly, she was still responsible for what she had done.

"THIS IS ALL YOUR FAULT! YOU KILLED ME! YOU KILLED US ALL!" Suzaku's voice still rang through her head.

Haru helped Kurara to her feet. The sparsely dotted trees did little to protect her from the wind. Now that summer was over, it was harder to sleep out in the open like this. She shivered and bundled her hands inside the sleeves of her kimono.

"Can I see it?" she asked.

She did not have to explain what "it" was. Haru stuffed his hand inside his inner pocket and pulled out the Star Seed.

Despite its name, there was nothing seed-like about it. In reality, the Star Seed was a bone-white rock in the shape of an eight-pointed star. It was rough and porous, like a pumice stone, with a certain heft to it that would have made it an excellent paperweight.

How strange that the key to shikigami freedom was such a small, unassuming thing. This lump of rock was supposed to bloom into a Star Tree, the sap of which could be used on shikigami cores to stop them from going mad. The shikigami would no longer need to rely on the bond with a Crafter to stay sane, and without a bond they could live free to do whatever they wanted – if only she knew how to turn a rock into a tree.

"Still no progress?" she asked.

Haru tucked the seed back into his pocket. "Nothing."

Ever since they had retrieved the Star Seed, they had both been wracking their brains for a way to make it bloom, though so far neither had come up with anything useful. They travelled without a clear destination in mind, moving from place to place in search of food and shelter and the vain hope that *something*, some idea about the Star Seed, would come to them.

"Maybe we should bury it somewhere and come back after ten years." Haru sighed.

"And in ten years it would still be a rock," said Kurara.

"How do you know that?"

Wasn't it obvious? Stones didn't just bloom into trees. There must be something else they had to do to it. Something special.

Haru frowned. "Maybe we should go home."

Kurara looked at him sharply. "Home?"

"After the Crafters cut down all the Star Trees and turned shikigami into obedient tools, we found a quiet little place to stay. A place where we could try to forget about everything. There are some old books and letters there. I don't remember what exactly, but there could be something useful. If we went back, maybe we might find some kind of clue."

Kurara stood a little straighter. This place, this ancient piece of her past, could hold the answers she sought. Answers about how to make the Star Seed bloom.

She opened her mouth to reply when a high-pitched whistle pierced through the air.

"Rara!" Haru dived for her, pushing her down as a flash of light shot overhead.

Kurara squeezed her eyes shut as the brightness burned with the intensity of a miniature sun. In the distance, she heard something go *BOOM!* as the ball of light crashed to the ground, followed by the distant caw of fleeing birds.

Seconds passed before Kurara peeled one eye open. The darkness had returned and the forest was quiet, as if nothing had ever happened.

"What *was* that?" said Kurara, breathless with shock.

Haru shook his head. "I don't know."

Kurara stared up at the night's sky. The flash of light had emerged from below the line of trees and curved through the air, until it had disappeared behind the horizon like the arch of a rainbow.

Or perhaps, the curve of a shooting star.

TWO

THE moment Kurara pulled herself to her feet and wiped the dirt from her clothes, she heard a loud rustling sound. A moment later, Himura burst through the bushes with a wild look.

"Himura!" Haru greeted him with a wide smile. It was difficult to judge whether Haru was just being his usual friendly self, or whether the bond that the two now shared was forcing him to act that way. A bond, Kurara reminded herself, they had formed without telling her first. "Did you see that light? Do you know what it was? Is that why you came rushing back?"

Himura looked at Haru the way a cat might look at a particularly energetic puppy – with alarm and barely concealed confusion. He turned his storm-grey eyes to Kurara as if to ask "What do I do with this?" Despite the bond between them, Himura seemed to find Haru overwhelming at best. Something that Kurara had no plans to help him with. In her opinion, the less time Haru and Himura spent around each other, the better.

"The fool came running back because he was worried." A voice echoed through their heads. With a quiet rustle, a snow-white snake emerged from beneath Himura's clothes, winding its way up his arm to cling to his shoulders. *"He was so worried he left the mushrooms we were foraging behind on the forest floor – not that he'll admit it. He'll have to go back and fetch them if you want dinner tonight."*

"I'll gladly admit that I was worried," said Himura, though the stiffness in his voice suggested otherwise. "There are all sorts of dangers out here – wild shikigami on the verge of losing their minds, trigger-happy imperial soldiers. It's only sensible to be on guard."

Mana simply laughed and poked Himura with its tail. The snake was a strange shikigami. It was not bonded to Himura, and yet it stayed with him, choosing Himura over even its own master, despite knowing what Himura had done to his previous shikigami, Akane.

It was unfathomable. This was *Himura* after all. Though he had technically saved her during the encounter with Suzaku, Kurara could not forget that he had sold her out to Princess Tsukimi. She could not forget that he had let Akane die.

Sometimes, she thought about telling him to leave, but each time she came close to sending him away, the words tangled in her throat. After what she had done to the people of Kazami, after she had killed Suzaku and cracked open its core, her hatred felt hypocritical.

"All right, but do you know what that light was?" she snapped.

"I don't know what it was, but I do know what it *wasn't*. It wasn't any kind of natural light," said Himura.

"Well, if it's nothing, then we should just go," she said airily.

Himura frowned. "Go? Go where?"

"Rara and I were talking about going home," Haru explained. "It's not too far from here. There's a place called the Mountain of the Falling Star. We lived on one of its peaks, and there was a village by the base." He pointed slightly north-west, to some distant point that lay beyond his fingertip.

"The Mountain of the Falling Star?" said Himura.

Haru looked vaguely embarrassed. "I'll give you three guesses why they named it that."

Kurara ignored Mana's cackling laughter. The name did sound significant. The Mountain of the Falling Star. Star Seeds and Star Trees. Surely, there was a link there. Perhaps Haru was right; maybe they would find something useful. After all, they had no other leads.

Himura's frown seemed permanently etched onto his lips; the exact degree of his displeasure evident in the angle of its curve. "You want to leave now? It's the middle of the night."

"And I'm not sleepy," said Kurara. "So let's go."

"What's the rush?" Mana flicked its forked tongue at them. *"You young folk are all the same – always quick to run into things without thinking. Some caution—"*

"And how many shikigami will die while we wait?"

19

snapped Kurara. "How many shikigami like you will be forced to do things they don't want to do by masters who don't care a bit about them? Every moment we delay is a moment that could be used to save the shikigami!"

Every night that passed, Suzaku was inside her head, screaming at her, blaming her for what had happened between them. If she did not make the Star Seed bloom, everything she had done would be for nothing. She would have killed Suzaku for nothing. Unleashed the shadows for nothing. All the suffering she had caused would be meaningless.

"Your haste will not save anyone; it will only make you reckless," Mana replied coldly.

"Now, now, let's not fight. Maybe we could get a *little* sleep and leave at dawn." Haru came between the two of them, his hands raised in a pacifying gesture.

"We can leave now," said Himura, surprising everyone around him. "I don't mind travelling in the dark. But … I have a proposal."

Kurara's eyes narrowed. She trusted Himura about as far as she could throw him, which wasn't very far without ofuda. If he was agreeing with her, that made him doubly suspicious in her eyes.

"We should stop at Zeka," Himura continued, regardless of the daggers Kurara was shooting at him. "It's the closest city to our current location, and if we're going to do this, we should be prepared for the long journey. I have money; we should use it to buy the supplies we will need."

"And what *do* we need?" asked Kurara sourly.

Mana snorted. *"Winter clothes, for one. Food too.*

The weather is turning colder, and as the days pass, it will become harder to find things to eat in the forest. We may be all right now, but I assure you that you do not want to go foraging in the dark once the days grow shorter."

Kurara huffed. Eating and drinking were inconveniences that did not trouble shikigami like Mana – the type of shikigami that had been created for war. It was the only thing Kurara envied about their bodies.

"All right then. Let's go to Zeka."

THREE

HIMURA pulled off the white bracelet he usually wore around his wrist. It unfurled and broke apart into hundreds of tiny pieces of paper that twisted through the air. Like many Crafters, Himura's mastery over ofuda – over the paper in his control – had been honed by years of training. With a click of his fingers, his ofuda cascaded upwards, like a waterfall falling in reverse.

In a matter of seconds, an origami wolf stood before him, large enough to ride.

"We should travel by ofuda," he said. "We can cover more ground this way."

"Again?" Kurara groaned. As much as she loved paper and the thrill of creation, it took far too much effort to hold her ofuda creatures together and support her own weight at the same time.

"You could use the practice."

"You don't want to be all strength and no stamina now, do you?" said Mana.

"All Crafters have their strengths and weaknesses." Kurara glowered at the snake. Some were better at shape-changing than others; some fought best at close quarters with paper weapons. Kurara didn't see why Himura should expect her to be great at everything.

"Yes, but you're not just a Crafter, are you? You're a shikigami too. One of the very first ever created," said Himura pointedly.

"That doesn't give me some sort of magical ability to control ofuda better than anyone else," said Kurara.

Still, she pulled back the left sleeve of her kimono to reveal her white, paper arm. Upon her command it unravelled into more than a dozen pieces of paper and swirled together into a wolf with white eyes as blank as a marble statue. With a jump, Kurara hoisted herself onto its back, pulling Haru up as well.

———————o———————

They travelled for hours, bounding over tree roots and moss-eaten stones, past old pines and weathered oaks with browning leaves, until the forest fell away to reveal open fields. It was a relief when Kurara finally caught the first glimpse of civilization.

Zeka was a maze-like city connected by long, meandering stone steps that zigzagged between floating gardens and buildings built upon tall, thin stilts. Spiralling staircases led to wide docking platforms for airships, and steep wooden stairs connected houses together. Tall grey walls surrounded the entire city, hiding the ground level from view.

By the time they reached Zeka, the sun had fully risen. A crowd of people had gathered outside the gates, lining up to enter, though from the looks of things no one was getting in. Even from a distance, Kurara could hear angry voices and the wail of crying children.

As they approached the crowd, it was clear that they were all villagers; some with donkeys saddled with heavy bags, others driving carts full of children and the elderly. Their eyes were bloodshot and ringed with purple, as if they too had travelled all night just to get here. They stared at Kurara with suspicion, but no one said anything as she made her way down the line.

Slowing her steps, Kurara managed to catch snatches of gossip. Even in the daylight, the villagers' whispers floated through the air like lingering ghosts.

"... completely destroyed," she heard someone mutter. "All of them dead."

"We never had any warning."

She suppressed a shiver, wondering what they were talking about.

At the front of the line, a pair of military police stood before the city gates, bellowing, "Turn back! No one is permitted to enter Zeka!"

"You can't do this!" someone shouted. "We're citizens of the Emperor! We're guaranteed protection!"

"Good citizens are obedient! Do what we tell you and leave!"

The line grumbled and shifted with displeasure, but no one turned back.

"What's going on?" Haru turned to the nearest villager.

"You're not from around here, are you?" A man with a round, red-tipped nose leaned over the side of his cart. Both his legs were bandaged and bleeding. His family sat at the back of the cart, huddled together, murmuring softly to one another. Something about their gaunt cheeks and haunted eyes set Kurara on edge.

"What do you mean?" asked Haru. "What happened?"

The man's face suddenly drained of colour and his eyes grew distant, as if he'd been transported somewhere else. "A curse! Monsters! Demons! Yuurei!"

"Yuurei?" said Kurara. The people nearby suddenly averted their eyes. Some muttered what sounded like a prayer.

The man nodded so vigorously Kurara was afraid his head would snap off. "That's what we call 'em. They came at night. Crawled through people's chests and killed them. We couldn't do anything! All the other villages have been attacked too! Every settlement south of here."

South. Where the ruins of Kazami stood, silent beneath the ground. Where the paper remains of Suzaku's body lay strewn across an empty crater. Kurara glanced at Haru. Was he thinking the same thing? Remembering that storm of wailing shadows that had emerged from Suzaku's broken core?

"Yuurei." Guilt churned through Kurara's gut. If these were indeed the same monstrous shadows that were once inside Suzaku, then this was her fault. The only reason those things were free to roam across the land was because of her;

because she had wanted the Star Seed inside Suzaku's core, despite knowing that retrieving it also meant releasing those monsters into the world.

"This is all your fault." Suzaku's voice echoed through her mind. *"You killed me. You killed us all!"*

"Why don't they just let you in?" Haru asked while Kurara's mind whirled.

"They think we're lying and were sent here by Prince Ugetsu to cause trouble for the empire. Or, worse, that we're Sorabito spies. Everyone is on edge. Because of the war, you know."

At the front of the gates, the military police shouted, "You have five minutes to leave – or we will *make* you leave!"

The crowd recoiled. More guards appeared on the wall, armed and ready to fire as they stared down at the line of villagers below.

Kurara wanted to shout at them to let the villagers in, but Himura caught up to her before she could open her mouth.

"You'll only make things worse if you cause a scene here," he hissed as he tugged at her sleeve. "Let's wait and come back when it's quieter."

Although Kurara wanted to protest, she knew that he was right. If she provoked the guards, they might open fire into the crowd. Reluctantly, she let Himura drag her away, her heart still pounding. Despite her anger at the city guards, she had learned something far more important.

The shadows they had released from Suzaku's core had found their way towards civilization and they were killing everyone they encountered.

FOUR

HIMURA followed the others as they retreated to a shaded area at the top of a nearby hill, where the trees and bushes offered shelter and a good view of the surrounding land. He glanced over the rolling fields towards the city of Zeka. The last time he had been there, he had let Rei slip loose, but he had also met Mana. He wondered what his life would be like if he had never come here; if he had stayed on the *Orihime* with his books and nightmares. Strange how one small decision could change so much.

And now here he was, in the company of three very different shikigami. Everything that had happened so far felt like a dream. All he knew was that he wanted to keep travelling together regardless of how much Kurara glowered at him.

No, perhaps it was *because* of how much Kurara glowered

at him. He needed to prove to her that he was different now, that he wasn't like the Crafters of old who had slaughtered people, killed other Crafters and turned them into shikigami. Who had abused their power and treated those very same shikigami like tools.

If he could help free the shikigami, then maybe he could forgive himself for what he had done to Akane.

He still had nightmares about it. The burning library. The shaking walls. Ordering Akane into the flames.

"I love you, Master." Akane's last words haunted him.

"What are they going to do now?" Kurara wondered, looking down at the line of villagers outside the walls.

Himura shrugged. "Move on to the next city and hope their welcome will be kinder. Zeka was attacked by Sohma not too long ago; it's no wonder the city is on edge."

"But this is my fault," Kurara protested. "I should do something."

"No, it isn't," said Haru. "I'm the one who cracked open Suzaku's core."

"But I was the one who told you to do it." Kurara knew Haru would never say no to her. That made it her fault, didn't it?

"Because you knew that we had no choice!" Haru protested. "If we wanted to free the shikigami, we needed the Star Seed from inside Suzaku."

"What is done is done." Mana slithered to the ground. *"What is important now is to decide what we will do about it."*

"Making the Star Seed bloom is our goal." Himura glanced down at the lingering crowd. "*Not* helping a bunch of displaced villagers. *Not* dealing with these yuurei things."

"Just because ensuring the Star Seed blooms is my *main* goal," Kurara said with a ferocity she only seemed to use when speaking to him, "doesn't mean I can forget about everything else. If we can do something to stop those shadows from attacking people – those yuurei, or whatever – then we have to try. We have to figure out what exactly these yuurei want."

"I don't think they *want* anything, Rara," said Haru. "They just exist. And cause trouble."

"But they have habits. We already know that they're attracted to lights, to fire."

"They also attack people," said Himura.

"Right, but why?" Kurara asked.

Haru made a sound as though he was pondering her question. His fingers drew spirals in the ground between the blades of grass.

"You know the answer already, don't you? Just tell us," grumbled Kurara.

"I don't *know* the answer, Rara. I have a theory."

Before Kurara could ask him what it was, Himura spoke up. "A shikigami is a paper creature with a Crafter's soul trapped inside it. To make a shikigami, you need to bind the soul of a Crafter to their ashes. Those ashes are put into a paper ball, which becomes a shikigami's core. When the core is broken, the soul inside escapes and is corrupted by the outside world, which turns that soul into a yuurei."

"And Suzaku had multiple souls inside it. So when its core was broken, multiple souls escaped and became yuurei," said Kurara.

Himura nodded. "The dead do not belong in the living

world. They desperately want to pass on. That's why they flock towards fire – the only thing that could destroy them if they were still shikigami."

"But then why do they go for people's chests as well?" she asked.

"Souls can't exist in the living world without some kind of protection. They don't realize people aren't shikigami, and they are looking for a core to hide in. It's nice and cosy inside a core," said Haru.

"So these shadows – these yuurei – they want to die by fire. Or return to a core," Himura finished.

Kurara flicked away a pebble near her shoe as she scowled. Himura knew she was upset about the way he and Haru had come to the same conclusion together, as though the bond they shared had allowed them to operate on the same wavelength.

"But the fire doesn't kill them, and humans don't have cores, so what's the point of them trying?" she muttered. All it did was cause immense pain and even death.

"I don't think they're self-aware enough to realize that. They're more like mindless moths drawn to a light," Himura said.

"So how can we help them pass on?" asked Kurara. "If they break out of a core, couldn't we seal them back inside?"

No one said anything. Although the image of stuffing a yuurei back into its core was an odd one, Himura doubted Kurara would appreciate it if he laughed.

"Great. More questions without answers," Kurara huffed.

"Perhaps it is best to leave things alone. When you Crafters meddle with things, you often make things worse," said Mana.

"I'm not just a Crafter, I'm a shikigami too," said Kurara.

If Mana had shoulders, Himura was sure the snake would have shrugged. *"And you think you are more powerful simply because you are unique. Simply because you were created differently from the rest of us* normal *shikigami. The rest of us tools."*

Kurara's eyes narrowed.

Himura was baffled that the two were not on better terms. He had thought that all shikigami would like Kurara by default, the way Akane had grown instantly attached to her.

Then again, Akane had loved everyone.

"Rushing in won't help. If you wish to truly save anyone, you must be smart," Himura said.

Kurara glowered at him, and Himura did his best not to be hurt by her frostiness.

I know you don't trust me, he wanted to say, *but I don't want to hurt shikigami any more and I'm sorry for what I've done. I don't want to fail you the way I failed Akane.*

But no amount of apologizing would bring Akane back or erase the way he had treated Kurara when he first discovered that she was a shikigami too.

On the surface, he seemed perfectly calm, but anxiety chiselled away at his nerves. He knew that Kurara was having nightmares. That she still felt the weight of Suzaku's words resonate within her even now. The Star Seed and the freedom of the shikigami rested on her shoulders, and yet she was still ready to take on all of the world's ills and fight against every injustice she came upon.

A person could snap under the weight of that stress.

Himura knew all too well what desperation felt like. It might drive a person to do something reckless. To do something they would regret.

He felt his bracelet tighten around his skin, almost digging into the bones of his wrist. He would keep a better eye on her.

Interlude

The sky is the sea
In my grief I sank below
An ocean of clouds

– from *Life in the Skies: 100 Sorabito Poems*
(banned by the Patriots Office)

Tomoe loved being close to the clouds. On the ground it was like she struggled to breathe, like the earth was a living thing sapping the strength from her legs. Now that they were back in the sky, she finally felt calmer. Like she belonged here.

The qipak they had taken from the military hangar cut through the air like a boat cruising through the waves, and Tomoe lay back and watched the clouds stream by. As the weather turned colder, the stars seemed brighter, the autumn constellations painting a carousel of images against a dark blue canvas.

"We're a few hours away from Sola-Re." Sayo put the

aircraft into cruise, left the controls as they were, and clambered over to where Tomoe was sitting.

The *Orihime* was docked at Sola-Ea, but they did not have enough fuel in the qipak's tank to take them that far. They were going to refuel at Sola-Re, the place where Tomoe had been born. The Unbreakable Lily, some called it, because of the long petal-shaped sheets of metal that would fold over the dome like a flower whenever the city was under attack.

She took a deep breath. Returning to Sola-Re felt like picking a scab, but they had no choice. There was nowhere else they could stop.

"Let's hope the docking guards let us land." Sayo dug through the dwindling rations they had stolen from the military base.

"It would be good to get a feel of what's going on in the sky since Prince Ugetsu declared war." Tomoe unwrapped a military-issued rice ball. The sky cities had always been under groundling control, but with the war waging on, Tomoe suspected that at least one or two cities had kicked the military out.

"Information is valuable, sure. But the most important thing is to find someone who can sell us enough levistone to fill our tank. Without fuel, we'll never make it back to the *Orihime*. No offence, but I don't want to be stuck on Sola-Re," said Sayo.

"No offence taken." Sola-Re was a miserable place filled with memories of her father. Tomoe didn't want to be stranded in the city either.

They ate in silence, washing down the rice balls with army-issued flasks of cold, watery tea.

It had been years since Tomoe had been to Sola-Re, but she could still picture its maze-like streets, the building stacks that towered so far above the ground some parts of the city were covered in constant darkness, the shipyards where she used to play and the colourful air trawlers that dotted the sky every morning, each one with large nets set out to catch the schools of migrating sky fish that passed by.

Her heart skipped as they flew closer. Sayo guided the vehicle into the docks, through long metal tunnels and down onto a free landing spot between the rows of other colourful airships. A man with a long, jagged scar down one side of his face hurried towards them. He looked like someone who had spent more time wrestling bears than helping ships land, but he was dressed in a dock worker's usual blue-and-gold uniform.

"Identification papers?" His rolling vowels and sing-song cadence were the unmistakable markers of a Sorabito accent.

"We don't have them," said Tomoe, "but we fly with a hunting ship called the *Orihime*. If you could—"

"Wait, I know your face." The scarred man squinted at her with his one good eye. He suddenly brightened. "You! You're Rei's daughter, aren't you?"

It was as if the man had slapped her. There was only one way that he would know who she was.

"Are you a member of Sohma?" Tomoe did her best not to break any teeth as she clenched them together into a tight grin.

Sohma was her father's band of Sorabito rebels – heroes of Sorabito liberation to some, but Tomoe knew that beneath the veneer of noble freedom fighters, her father and Sohma were nothing but Sorabito purists and terrorists. They did not want peace, but a world where the Sorabito were on top and the groundlings grovelling below them.

"Of course I'm part of Sohma!" The simpering fool grinned. "Sola-Re was the first of the cities we liberated."

Liberated, Tomoe wanted to scoff. In the corner of her eye, she saw Sayo give her a warning look.

"Hey, shall I call your father?" the docking guard asked.

"He's here? Is he in charge of Sola-Re now? What about the mayor and the military police?"

"Dead, of course," the man replied quite happily, oblivious to the shocked looks on Tomoe's and Sayo's faces. "They put up a fight, but in the end they were no match for the might of Sohma."

Tomoe glanced at Sayo. It had been a long time since she had felt so utterly out of her depth. They had only been gone from the sky for a few months at most, and yet it felt as though the entire world had changed. It made her long for the safety of the *Orihime* even more. For friendly faces and familiar ground.

"Shall I call for your father?" the guard offered again.

Tomoe shook her head. "No, I… Don't bother. I'm just… I'm going home."

Home. The word sank through her bones. Home was the *Orihime* and its simple corridors. It was the crew she loved

– and who let her cheat at shogi. Home was the soothing hum of levistone boilers.

"Shame! Delivering his daughter might have got me into Rei's good books." The man shrugged and Tomoe thought about stabbing him in the gut. He signalled for the other docking guards to open the gates to the city. There was a loud clunk as a bolt slid back, and the cogs of the giant gates began to turn, pulling open the large metal doors to Sola-Re.

Sayo took her hand and squeezed it tight. "It's fine," she whispered. "We'll be fine."

Tomoe held on to Sayo's hand like a raft in a storm. Taking a deep breath, she nodded. No matter what happened, or what awaited them inside the city, they would face it all together.

FIVE

AS Himura had predicted, the villagers moved on in search of another city. Children wailed and the adults shouted curses at the soldiers guarding the wall as they went. Kurara knew she should be glad that things had ended without bloodshed, but it was a cold comfort. The villagers were only travelling because they were fleeing from the shadowy monsters she had released.

She was none too pleased with the way their discussion had gone that morning, or Himura's half-hearted attempts to comfort her. A part of her wanted to leave with the villagers, but Haru convinced her that they still needed those supplies they had come to the city for. Kurara tried to tamp down her irritation as they waited until nightfall to sneak into Zeka.

As soon as the sun dipped below the sky, she and the others began picking their way through the long grass to the eastern side of the city. Reaching the walls was easy. Torches were lit along the top of the walls, creating oceans of shadow between the pools of light.

"I'll go first," she said as her paper arm crumbled away. The squares of ofuda merged together, and she rolled them out into a long spiral of rope. Taking a step back, Kurara swung the rope around her head once and then threw it into the air.

The paper rope sailed upwards and wrapped itself around the stone battlements. She gave it a tug to check that it was secure then wrapped the rest around her hand.

With a click of her fingers, the length of rope shortened, pulling her upwards to the top of the wall.

"Hurry! I think the guard patrol is coming back!" Haru hissed.

Once Kurara had hauled herself over the wall, she threw the rope back down. Both Haru and Himura made short work of climbing up the wall and then dropping down onto the other side, using ofuda to cushion the fall.

"Gods, that was cool! Didn't it feel like we were ninjas?" Haru grinned.

Rolling her eyes, Kurara grabbed his hand and tugged him away from the walls before anyone could spot them.

Zeka was not a glamorous city. At least, not any more. Signs of the war were everywhere. Collapsed buildings lay as conspicuous as missing teeth. Some of the floating gardens were beginning to sink, and the plants looked as though they had not been tended to in months. Propaganda posters lined every wall. One showed paper monsters attacking children. In another, the shadow of a Sorabito ship loomed over a cowering family.

In the rubble of one building on the main square someone had painted the words:

BLOOD IN THE SKIES
SHALL RAIN TO THE GROUND

The words were slightly faded now, but beside them, someone else had painted the words *SKY RATS!* and a series of other insults that got more vulgar as they went on.

"Mana and I were here a while ago. People were rioting. The crowd was so angry the military police could barely contain them." Himura pulled a face.

"*There was some trouble with Sohma, and the Patriots Office was burned down,*" said Mana.

Unease filled Kurara's gut. Ruined stalls lined the edge of the square; bolts of fabric had been trampled against the cracked flagstones, crates of fruit left upturned and rotting. She shook her head. This was no time to worry about the war; they had their own mission to fulfil.

"First things first." She turned back to the others. "We'll need food and winter clothes. Soap too."

Himura nodded. "The market should still be—"

Mana interrupted him with a sudden, painful hiss.

"What's wrong?"

The snake groaned. Its coiled body twitched and shuddered.

"*Oda,*" Mana whispered. "*Master Oda is dead!*"

The others jumped. Oda. Grave-keeper Oda. The woman who had tried to kill Himura. Mana's master.

"H–how do you know that?" asked Haru, eyeing the snake cautiously.

"*What a foolish question! I can sense it, of course! The bond between us is broken!*"

"But how did Oda die?" They had left her in Kazami, alone but safe inside her little underground cavern.

"*She was an old woman. Maybe it was old age. Maybe she fell into a pit somewhere and died.*"

Perhaps, but Kurara had a bad feeling that something more sinister was at play.

"Then you don't have a bond any more," said Himura. He sounded calm, but there was a tightness around his eyes that betrayed his anxiety.

"*It is newly broken. You can relax, child. I am not about to lose my mind this instant.*" Mana waved its tail.

Kurara frowned. She had seen shikigami lose their minds before – the slow descent into madness, the sudden spurts of violence – it was never pretty. "The rate is different from shikigami to shikigami, we don't know whether—"

"Bond with me," Himura interrupted her.

Kurara looked at Himura sharply.

"*No, thank you,*" said Mana.

"It's only temporary. Once the Star Seed blooms, you can be free."

"*I believe that I politely declined.*"

"Why would you? I told you, it would only be temporary!"

"*Do I need a reason to say no? What will you do? Force me to bond with you?*" Mana replied frostily.

Himura clicked his tongue in annoyance. "Fine! You can always change your mind," he grumbled, as if he expected Mana to eventually come around – once the snake had really thought about it.

Kurara's eyes narrowed. Himura had said that he regretted ordering Akane into the fire. He had admitted that he was wrong about shikigami being nothing more than tools. Yet how could he expect her to trust him when he jumped at the first chance to have another shikigami under his control?

She was lost in her own thoughts when a shrill scream pierced the night air. Kurara whipped around, but she could not tell what direction the sound had come from.

A moment later, she heard more shouts and the sound of feet pounding against the stone roads. Was it an attack? Maybe Sohma rebels?

Then she looked up. It was hard to tell what was wrong at first – the sky was so dark and overcast that Kurara could hardly see anything, but the longer she gazed into the night the easier it became to spot something moving below the clouds. Something swirling faster and faster, gathering above them.

A swarm of yuurei.

SIX

THE yuurei's glowing eyes dotted the darkness. Their wide mouths revealed rows upon rows of bone-white teeth. Writhing limbs made of inky shadow were almost invisible against the night's sky.

It did not take long for the entire city to notice them. The air echoed with screams as frightened city folk and military police rushed into the streets.

As the yuurei swooped through the city, Kurara heard the crowds begin to run, heard the shouts of the police trying to fend off the swarm. Then came the gunshots. The sheer terror as the police realized that their weapons could not stop the shadows. Kurara wanted to yell at them that it was useless, that they were better off fleeing than trying to stand and fight, but the mere sight of the yuurei had her too frozen to speak.

"Look out!" Haru cried as the shadows dived straight towards them.

Like a waterfall, they streamed down into the square and flooded the area, forcing Kurara and the others to split apart in order to avoid them.

"Do not let them touch you! Make sure they cannot reach your core or your heart!" Mana clung to Himura's sleeve and bellowed.

"Haru!" Kurara tried to reach for him, but it was no good. A hurricane of writhing shadows kept them separated. There was no way she could pass through it. Just coming into contact with the yuurei caused excruciating pain.

"Don't just stand there! Run, you fools!" Mana's voice echoed from somewhere behind the wall of darkness.

With no other choice, the three of them split off in different directions. Kurara ran as fast as she could out of the square and onto a busy road, where dozens of other city folk were fleeing for their lives. Soon, she was swept up in a stream of screaming citizens, and carried away by the crush of their bodies.

When the yuurei moved in a swarm, it was impossible to tell where one began and another ended. All Kurara could see was a shadowy mass of spider-like limbs, a gnashing array of too many mouths and teeth.

The city bells began to ring, tolling a warning that echoed through the night. All around her, people fell as the yuurei swooped into their chests and through their hearts. Some screamed in agony; some were completely silent when they hit the ground, though Kurara did not want to think about why.

Her foot snagged against something large and soft as she ran, sending her sprawling to the ground. People stampeded past without sparing her a second look. Picking herself up, Kurara glanced behind to see what had tripped her over.

It was a body.

She shrieked and scrambled away from it, suddenly, sickeningly aware of the other bodies scattered on the ground, their eyes wide open and mouths agape like dead fish that had drowned on dry land.

A military policeman raised his pistol and shot at the oncoming swathe of darkness, but the bullet went straight through the yuurei. Another man held aloft a burning torch in the darkness and waved it frantically in front of him.

"Away! Stay away!" he screamed, swinging his torch, but that only had the opposite effect on the shadows. The yuurei nearby abandoned whatever they were doing to circle the man. There were other small lights around the city, but the yuurei seemed especially drawn to the open flames.

With a terrified whimper, the man dropped the torch and fled. The shadows did not give chase. Instead they lingered around the flame like moths.

While they were distracted, Kurara used the opportunity to get out of there. She commanded her ofuda to swirl around her arms and shoulders, forming a pair of large paper wings, and took off into the sky.

The fires only kept the yuurei distracted for a few minutes before they were on the move again. Like vultures, they circled the tops of the city and swooped through the walls of buildings, through stone and wood and paper, and into the places where the remaining people were hiding.

Kurara scanned the streets for Haru or Himura, but they

45

were nowhere to be seen. A small stream of shadows took notice of her lingering in the air and raced towards her. With a cry of surprise, Kurara shot off as fast as she could, ducking and diving beneath the city's large stone staircases and around the floating gardens.

I need to fly faster than this! She cursed as she pulled further away from the ground. No matter how hard she tried, the yuurei continued to tail her. While each beat of her wings made her arms ache and her shoulders groan, the shadows were catching up fast.

Mana and Himura were right. I really do need to work on my stamina.

She dropped back to the ground, using her ofuda to cushion her fall, and found herself in the same ruined city square as before. Bells rang through the hollow night. Shots of gunfire peppered the air. It was useless, all useless. There was no stopping the yuurei.

But there has to be a way! A familiar pang of guilt echoed through her. It was her fault that the yuurei were free. She had to find a way to stop them.

What did she know about yuurei? They were the souls of shikigami that had been twisted and corrupted by exposure to the world. Souls were not supposed to dwell in the land of the living, Haru and Himura had said.

A cannonball hit a nearby bell tower, sending a shower of stone falling over the buildings below. Kurara jumped out of the way as a cloud of dust filled the air. Some fool in the military had got their hands on a cannon somehow, but no amount of cannon fire would kill the yuurei. It would only cause more injury and destruction to the city they were supposed to protect. This was getting out of hand. She had to do something, and fast.

If a yuurei came out of a broken shikigami core, was there a way to put one back? To put them all back?

Kurara froze. It hit her. The sealing circle. The one that Crafters used to make shikigami. The sealing circle allowed someone to bind a person's soul to their own ashes.

Yuurei were souls – twisted and corrupted, yes, but souls nonetheless.

And if yuurei were just souls, couldn't she use the sealing circle to bind them to a person's ashes again?

First, she had to draw the sealing circle. Jumping into action, she rummaged through the wreckage for something she could use. After what felt like an eternity, she came across a half-empty ink pot. Unscrewing the lid, she drew a wobbly circle and an eight-pointed star over the flagstones.

Next, she had to lure the yuurei into the circle. The yuurei were attracted to fire. She remembered the man waving his torch about, unwittingly calling all the shadows to him. The fire would only keep them distracted for a few minutes, but a few minutes was all she needed.

Dragging as much wood as she could manage from the wreckage in the city square, she piled it up into a bonfire at the heart of the sealing circle.

The screams continued to ring in the distance, people shouting out in terror.

This is your fault! All your fault! A voice that sounded suspiciously like Suzaku echoed through her head. Gritting her teeth, Kurara did her best to ignore it as she stacked the pieces of wood still higher.

Once she was certain the mound was tall enough, she struck two bits of rock together until they created sparks that caught against the bonfire. Flames quickly roared up the tangle of wood, dancing in the night air.

No sooner had the flames reached the top of the mound than the sky above swirled with shadows and a sudden feeling of dread washed over her.

The sealing circle bound souls to ashes of the dead, but she had forgotten one key thing.

Where was she going to find a person's ashes?

SEVEN

THE yuurei began to swarm overhead, gathering like storm clouds.

What was she supposed to do now? It was too late to run.

Did she have to use human ashes? Did the ashes have to belong to a Crafter? The bonfire's flames would create ash as it devoured the wooden heap, would that be good enough?

She was running out of time. The yuurei were only getting closer. She had to try. Placing her hands together, Kurara concentrated on the flames and chanted.

"All that lives shall die. As cicadas at the end of summer, as mayflies before the autumn moon, all that lives shall die. All that lives shall die and be reborn. From this day forth, your name is Shiki. May you contain all that is divine within you."

She clapped her hands together.

"May you be worthy of your name!"

Nothing happened.

Yuurei swirled above her. The flames would not keep them occupied for much longer. Kurara panicked. Why had the sealing circle failed? Maybe she had to use a person's ashes after all, but where would she find something like that?

The answer hit her like a bolt of lightning.

One of the steps to make a shikigami was to bind a person's soul to their dead ashes. Those ashes were then put inside a paper ball to form a core.

Kurara could use her own ashes! The ashes inside her core. She could use them to bind the yuurei.

There was no time for debate. She had to act now. As the shadows dived towards her, Kurara clapped her hands together as if in prayer.

"All that lives shall die. As cicadas at the end of summer, as mayflies before the autumn moon, all that lives shall die. All that lives shall die and be reborn," she chanted again, as fast as possible.

"Rara, what are you doing?" A shout drew her attention away from the yuurei for a split second. Kurara jerked her head towards the source to find Haru and Himura racing towards her.

"Stay back!" she shouted. Every shikigami had ashes inside their core, and if either Haru or Mana entered the circle, the yuurei might get sucked up into their cores as well.

Haru did not stop. In fact, the sound of her voice only made him run even faster.

"Himura, hold him back!" Kurara clapped her hands together one last time.

"Stop!"

The next thing she knew, Haru had slammed into her with all the force of a speeding qipak. Kurara landed with a painful thud, the stones biting into her arm as she rolled across the ruined ground and out of the circle.

Haru slammed the palms of his hands together and roared, "May you be worthy of your name!"

"No!" Kurara staggered to her feet.

What appeared next could only be described as a vortex of light and wind as the yuurei were sucked into the middle of Haru's chest. The wind roared. A huge ring of light rippled out from the middle of the circle, blinding her for just a moment.

When Kurara could finally see again, it was dark, the streets were quiet, and all the yuurei were gone.

They had disappeared inside Haru, bound to the ashes inside his core.

Kurara scrambled into the circle, and grabbed Haru by the shoulders. Her hands shook.

"Haru, what in the seven hells have you done?"

She was pale, furious. Her eyes darted back to Himura as he approached.

"Did you order him to do this? To push me out of the circle?" she snapped.

Himura jerked back, reeling as if she had punched him. "No, I never... I didn't—"

"Stop, Rara." The weak thread of Haru's voice pulled her attention away from Himura to Haru's pale face. "I did it for you. To protect you."

Kurara gave him an outraged look.

Haru grinned at her then fainted on the spot.

Himura caught him before he could hit the ground. Within seconds, Kurara was at his side, her hands fluttering over Haru, unsure of what to do. She hardly knew what string of panicked questions were spilling from her lips as Himura arranged Haru's body so that he was lying on his back.

"Give him some space!" snapped Himura, and it was only because she was so terrified that she did not gut him with a piece of ofuda right there and then.

Haru was almost as pale as the paper he was made of. His body jerked and his expression twisted into one of pain.

"Is he going to be OK?" She couldn't lose Haru again, not after everything they had been through.

Mana slithered out of Himura's sleeve and onto Haru's chest. *"He's adjusting to having so many souls inside his core. Suzaku survived all those years with an entire village's worth of souls inside its core. Something like this shouldn't kill him."*

"Shouldn't" was not exactly a comforting word. Like saying "It *shouldn't* explode", or "It *shouldn't* be painful".

"*Shouldn't* die" wasn't the same as "*won't* die".

"But Suzaku was *created* with multiple souls inside it! Haru can't handle that kind of thing!" Kurara reached for Haru's hand, squeezing it tight. Was it her imagination, or were his fingers colder than usual?

Mana flicked its tail against her wrist.

"Let him rest."

"But—"

"You will only tire yourself out fretting over something you can do nothing about, and then what good will you be to anyone?"

She glared at the shikigami as if Mana had just eaten her last red bean bun.

"But why did he pass out in the first place?" asked Himura.

"What a foolish question!" Mana's tongue flicked out of its mouth. *"A shikigami core is meant to house a single soul. How would you like it if you suddenly had a dozen other souls squirming inside that core of yours?"*

Kurara tensed. Was that what was happening inside Haru's core right now? Were there dozens of yuurei – dozens of souls – squirming and screaming inside him?

Her head shot up at the sound of pounding feet approaching the square. The military police must have come looking for the source of the mysterious light.

"Let's move!" Himura hauled Haru into his arms and hurried out of the square.

Cursing beneath her breath, Kurara ran after him.

EIGHT

KURARA followed Himura and Mana through the narrow streets. Himura avoided the main roads and scurried down winding alleyways lined with tall, crooked buildings. Broken toys and trampled clothing lay on the road, soaking into the puddles of water from a burst pipe. Kurara could hear people shrieking and sobbing. The further away from the town square they ran, the quieter and emptier the streets became.

Beneath a shadow of a large staircase, they found an abandoned shop with its windows smashed in and sloppily boarded up with long planks of wood. It was a small, double-storey building, tall but narrow, with a sliding wooden door and sagging walls. Graffiti on the doors proclaimed that the owners were *Sorabito lovers!*, *Traitors!* and *Flying rats!*, each badly scrawled accusation seemingly angrier than the last.

Inside, the shop was dusty and empty. Himura wiped

the worst of the dirt from the counter using his sleeve and laid Haru down.

The ceiling light was not working, and Kurara could not find any lamps or candles. She rifled through every cupboard and searched every shelf there was, but all she found were some old sheets of dried seaweed and a few battered boxes of stale senbei.

"Kurara," said Himura.

"What?" she snapped, slamming shut yet another empty cupboard.

"Sit down. You're making too much noise."

Kurara scowled, but she sat down in the corner of the shop floor, taking an angry bite of senbei.

It tasted like cardboard.

Haru remained lying on the shop counter, still as a statue.

———————o———————

She tried her best to sleep. The abandoned shop was not exactly the most comfortable place to spend the night, although they were at least out of the wind and the worst of autumn's chill. Lights from the street broke through the gaps in the boarded-up windows, illuminating Haru's soft figure. The sound of distant wails rang through the night. Himura slept close by, hunched against the foot of the counter, his head falling against his chest as he snored.

Kurara lay there, staring at their slack faces. Himura was an unwelcome intruder in a world that had long consisted of just Haru and herself. Long before Suzaku, long before the sky cities, it had always been the two of them. Her and

Haru. Haru and her. They had always been together, and they always would be. The bond Haru had with Himura would not change that. These yuurei that he had absorbed would not change that. She wouldn't let them. She would not let anyone take Haru away from her.

At last, she closed her eyes.

In her dreams, she saw flashes of Kazami, of herself standing upon a mountain of ashes. Human ashes. Those ashes transformed into Suzaku, who burned before her eyes as it screeched at her, *This is all your fault! You will never be forgiven!*

She awoke with a gasp.

"Nightmare?" Himura's voice startled her.

She turned to find him sitting on the floor near Haru, looking at her with an unreadable expression.

"Where's Mana?" She changed the subject.

"Hunting," said Himura. "Mana finds it boring to watch us sleep. It went to fight some rats."

That made sense. Unlike Kurara and Haru, shikigami like Mana had no need for food or rest – they had been made for war, after all. To be convenient tools.

With a sigh, Kurara took a piece of paper from her arm and let it spin on the tip of her finger.

"I have nightmares too," said Himura, like he was admitting to something shameful. "About Akane mostly. But sometimes about you too."

Kurara sucked in a sharp breath. This was the first time

either of them had mentioned Akane since Kazami. The name still stung like an open wound. Sometimes, Kurara could not believe that Akane was gone; she half expected the fox to pop out of the bushes at any moment and start running circles around them.

"I'm surprised you even remember Akane. You've replaced one shikigami with another, haven't you?"

There was no real bite to her words, but Himura flinched nonetheless. *Good,* she thought. *He should be hurt; he should be ashamed.*

"Are you talking about Mana or…?" He turned his head to where Haru was fast asleep.

Kurara said nothing. Her feelings for Himura were a tangled, painful thing.

He was trying to be better.

Nothing he did would ever be enough.

"Mana isn't like that. We don't have a bond," said Himura. "And the fact that we don't have a bond is going to be a problem. Now that Oda is dead, Mana's mind will start to slip."

"But it *feels* like Mana is yours, doesn't it?" Kurara hissed. She had seen the way Mana clung to Himura, the way the snake teased him by flicking its forked tongue against his ear or thumping him across the back with its tail.

"No," said Himura tightly. "Mana isn't a replacement for anyone. Neither is Haru."

Kurara scrubbed her hands over her face. She did not have the energy for an argument. Whatever forgiveness Himura was fishing for, she was wholly uninterested in giving it.

"What did you dream about?" asked Himura, bringing the conversation back to the reason she'd woken up in the middle of the night.

"You know, the usual. Suzaku."

"The usual?"

Kurara pursed her lips. She had not meant to reveal that her nightmares were a common occurrence.

Himura shook his head. "I … I won't say it gets better, but you learn to cope. I know you blame yourself for breaking open Suzaku's core, but you had two difficult choices, and you did the best you could."

Unlike me. He did not say it, but Kurara could tell he was thinking it. To send Akane into the flames or not. To sell out Kurara or not. Those were not difficult choices for anyone who had not been motivated by greed and an unhealthy need for knowledge above all else.

But had she really made the best choice? Was it really as simple as Himura said? Maybe if she had tried harder, if she had been stronger, she could have found another way to get the Star Seed from Suzaku's core without destroying the phoenix shikigami.

"We've wasted so much time here." Kurara wanted to tear her hair out, to punch something, to scream – anything that might help her deal with the growing anxiety bubbling beneath her skin. What if Haru didn't wake up? What if he went mad?

They should never have come here.

"It's not been that long," said Himura. "You're under a lot of stress because you think you're the only one who can help the shikigami and you have to help them right this second."

"Don't I?" she snapped.

"Not alone, no."

Kurara turned away from him.

"By the way," said Himura, "what exactly did Haru do to make all the yuurei disappear like that? I think I can guess, but everything happened so fast."

"Do you remember the sealing circle Crafters used to make shikigami? After they killed and burned someone, they'd use the circle to bind the soul to the dead person's ashes."

"And then pour those ashes into a paper sphere to make a shikigami core," said Himura.

Kurara nodded. "Yuurei are just corrupted souls, so the sealing circle works on them too. They can be bound to someone's ashes again."

Only she had meant to bind the yuurei to her own ashes, not Haru's. Never Haru.

Reading the anguish on her face, Himura said gently, "If you hadn't done anything, those yuurei would have killed a lot more people. You saved a lot of lives tonight."

"None of this would have happened in the first place if we hadn't broken open Suzaku's core."

Himura sighed. "What's done is done. Get some sleep." He tried to smile at her. "You'll be all right this time. No nightmares."

NINE

HARU woke with the rising sun. Himura heard him groan as he sat up. He nudged Kurara, knowing that she would want to be awake for this.

Kurara's eyes snapped open. Before he could speak, she was at Haru's side in an instant, helping him swing his legs over the edge of the counter and sit up.

"Oh Gods, my spine!" Haru groaned, arching his back like a cat. "Why am I sleeping on a wooden counter?"

"Haru." There was a hard edge to Kurara's voice that reminded Himura of the way Captain Sakurai used to speak whenever he caught the crew sneaking open a barrel of sake.

"I'm fine, Rara. Sorry I worried you." Haru fended off her concern with a sheepish smile.

He did indeed look much better than the night before. The colour was back in his cheeks, and his eyes were as bright and sharp as ever, though his hair was slightly more unruly than usual.

Himura frowned. There were several souls inside Haru now, just like Suzaku. Surely, he could not be as "fine" as he claimed. But Himura didn't want to press him. Now that they shared a bond, he was careful to avoid giving Haru anything that might seem like an order. He was all too aware that it was his blood on Haru's core, and that the more time they spent together, the more Haru would agree with his opinions. If he were a better man, he would leave Haru and Kurara alone, but he could not bring himself to do it. He wanted to remain with them, to help them, so that one day he could look at himself in a mirror and not hate the person he saw reflected back at him.

I'm not like that any more. I understand now that shikigami are people too, Himura wanted to say. Though sometimes it felt like the only person he was trying to convince was himself.

"It does feel weird," Haru admitted. "Most shikigami only have their own soul inside their core, right? Having all those yuurei – all these different souls – inside feels … uncomfortable. Like getting sand stuck between your toes. But I'm not going to lose my mind any time soon if that's what you're worried about. After all, I have a bond, don't I, Master?" He turned to bat his eyelashes at Himura.

"Don't call him that!" Kurara snapped.

Himura pursed his lips. Ever since they had started travelling together, he had tried not to talk to Haru that much, not that he would know what to say anyway. Haru was his opposite in almost every way – he was sunny but mischievous, too talkative for his own good, with a smile that made Himura feel he was being mocked in some subtle way.

"Are you able to stand up?" he asked.

Haru pushed himself off the counter and onto his feet.

"Ta-da!" He did a little twirl. Nobody clapped.

"A perfect bill of health," Mana hummed approvingly.

"And I've been telling you all that I'm perfectly fine! Well, no, I'm *starving* actually. Please tell me you have food, Rara."

Kurara wordlessly handed Haru an open box of senbei.

"There is one thing that worries me." Haru seized the box and began cramming rice crackers into his mouth. "I remember how many yuurei escaped from Suzaku's core, and the amount that showed up last night wasn't all of them. I'm sure there are more out there than just the ones I absorbed."

"If there are, you're not going anywhere near them!" said Kurara.

Haru smiled sheepishly.

No one said anything. Perhaps no one *wanted* to say anything. Himura felt Mana slither up his leg and around his shoulders, before giving his arm a protective squeeze.

"You still have the Star Seed, don't you?" said Kurara.

"Safe and sound." Haru nodded and pulled it out of the inner pocket of his clothes.

"Let me hold on to it."

"Why? Don't you trust me?"

Kurara shuffled her feet against the dusty floor. "I do. I just … feel better holding it."

Haru gave in and handed the seed to Kurara, who glanced at it once, checking it over for damage, before tucking it behind the folds of her obi.

"We mustn't lose sight of what we're here for," said Himura. "We only came to grab some supplies before moving on to the mountain."

"The Mountain of the Falling Star," Haru reminded him, as if Himura could ever forget anything with such a ridiculous name.

Mana suddenly shuddered against his shoulders, its coils twitching as if it had just been zapped with electricity.

"Are you all right?" Worry blossomed between Himura's ribs.

The snake dropped back to the floor and slithered away. *"It is nothing,"* it hissed. *"I am perfectly fine."*

Himura squeezed his eyes shut for a moment. He thought of Akane, and all the thoughtless orders he had given his previous shikigami. *Be quiet. Come here. Shut up. Stop fidgeting.* How many times had he trampled over Akane's will without ever realizing it?

But things were different now. Himura wouldn't abuse his power. Not any more. He would be careful. He would not be a bad master.

"You can always bond with me," he offered. He had to try again. Himura had no desire to see Mana's sharp mind wither away into insanity, to watch as the snake became angry and violent.

"Hmph! I do not need you to tell me what I can and cannot do! I will do whatever I like, just as I always have." There was a challenge in the snake's tone, daring him to say otherwise. Himura had never met such a stubborn shikigami. He bet Mana had been a force to be reckoned with as a human.

"Don't do anything stupid, Mana."

"Stupid? Ha! It is the privilege of the old to do whatever foolish thing one wishes," Mana cackled, but Himura did not find anything funny about it.

You frighten me when you speak like that. I care for you, he wanted to say, but he did not know how to begin admitting those feelings to himself, let alone anyone else. He had not known how terrifying it was to care about someone else until he realized it was too late.

"Boy." Mana's voice pulled him from his thoughts. "*Stop thinking so much.*"

Interlude

Born of earth and sky
There is still stardust in me
Clouds sing in my veins
I am a Sorabito;
Who dares tell me otherwise?

– from *Wooden Sparrows*
(on the issue of Sorabito nationality)

Tomoe had not visited Sola-Re for years. Now that she was back, she did everything she could to avoid thinking about her parents.

It was a task easier said than done. Everywhere she looked, there were shops her mother would bring her to when she was young, street corners where she and her sisters played, noisy workshops that she would hang around so she did not have to go home to her father. The entire city reminded her of who she had been before she had left home, before she had joined the *Orihime* – an

angry little girl powerless to stop her father's violence.

She pushed the feeling aside. The important thing right now was finding someone who would sell them levistone to fill their aircraft's engine, but on that front things proved surprisingly difficult. All the levistone in the city had been claimed by Sohma to further the war effort. Even the vendors on the black market had nothing to sell. Tomoe was starting to feel desperate. If they did not find fuel soon, they would be stranded here, with no way back to the *Orihime*.

"There's one last seller I want to check," said Tomoe.

Sayo opened her mouth and Tomoe knew she was going to suggest that they go to her father. His rebels had taken all the city's levistone reserves for themselves after all, but the idea of asking her father for anything was like swallowing hot oil. She was irritated that Sayo would even *think* of going to him.

"One last seller," she snapped.

Sayo pressed her lips into a thin line, the way she always did whenever she disapproved of something but didn't want to say so. Her pointed silence irritated Tomoe even more. "Let me just check in with this guy. I know he won't let me down," she insisted. This last one would have the levistone they needed, she was sure of it.

The city was strangely normal. If Tomoe didn't know better, she would never have guessed that there was a war going on. There were more people about than she expected – shoppers heading towards their favourite food stalls, traders flogging their wares, waitresses calling to passers-by to come

inside and have a cup of tea. It did not feel like they were at war. It did not feel like anything was different at all.

Except … the military police had been replaced by Sohma rebels dressed in blue-and-white uniforms, there were no groundling merchants anywhere to be seen and the Patriots Office was a blast site full of flattened rubble and scorched debris.

As they made their way through the city hub, they passed murals of brave Sorabito fighting grotesque human-shaped maggots; underneath one were the words: *Fighting for freedom against the groundling worms.* Another depicted a man cutting off the head of a demonic child. Below, the caption read, *When the divine blood of the sky mixes with the mud of the earth, it produces devils.*

Tomoe looked away, queasily.

The building stacks of Sola-Re towered over her so high they almost touched the glass dome. Looking up at them had once filled her with awe, but now she only felt tiny and insignificant, like an ant in a jungle of trees.

She and Sayo climbed the steps leading up the side of a building stack to the fifteenth floor and made their way along a wooden plank that connected one rooftop to the next.

They picked their way past washing lines, over rooftops, and across pipes skirting along the sides of buildings. Iron-rung ladders and sheets of corrugated steel created paths through the sky, connecting the higher floors of one stack to the floors of another. From up here, Tomoe had a better view of the city: its iron foundries and scrapyards in the

distance, the large metal chutes spewing steam into the sky. The smell of molten metal hung in the air, more pungent than she remembered.

"Here it is." Tomoe pushed open the door to a cramped auto-part shop.

"Tomoe!" The old man sitting at the shop counter grinned as she entered. "Well, aren't you a sight for sore eyes? Why, the last time I saw you, you weren't even tall enough to reach my knee!"

Plastering on the biggest smile she could manage, Tomoe made her way towards the counter with Sayo in tow. "Yoichiro, how are you? Listen, I need—"

"I don't have any levistone for you."

Tomoe raised her eyebrows in surprise. "How'd you know I was going to ask that?"

"Because that's what everyone and their mother has been asking for the moment they step through my door. Lots of people want to leave the sky cities, but the ships aren't taking them and they ain't got the levistone for their qipaks."

"Oh." She had not realized how much hope she had pinned on this last place having what she needed until reality decided to kick her in the gut.

"People want to leave?" said Sayo. Tomoe shot her a sharp look. Of course people wanted to leave. Sohma were in charge!

"Well…" The man's eyes darted about the shop, as if he was afraid of spies hiding in the cardboard boxes scattered around him. "Not everyone likes the changes Sohma have made."

"What kind of changes?"

The man looked taken aback by her question. "I—I don't pay attention to this stuff! The city is ours now. A Sorabito city run by Sorabito. What do I have to complain about?"

Tomoe sensed his hesitation. If Sorabito were also trying to leave the city, things could not be as peaceful as they seemed.

"What about the groundlings?" she asked. "Where did they go?"

"Booted off or killed. Who cares?"

"Even if they were innocent civilians?"

He shook his head. "Listen, Tomoe, you're a sweet girl, but you've always been a bit soft. There ain't no such thing as an innocent groundling. Did any of those groundlings ever stand up for us when the military police pushed us around? Did they say anything when the military police raided our stores and took our stuff? If they couldn't be bothered to help us in need, I can't be bothered to help them—"

"Is there really no way off the city?" Sayo cut in before Tomoe could go off about how an eye for an eye left everyone with eye patches.

"Apart from getting kicked out and falling to your death? Well, there is one option, but nobody's fool enough to take it."

"I'm a fool! I'd gladly take whatever 'it' is," said Tomoe.

The man looked to the shop door then cupped a hand around his mouth and gestured for them to come closer.

Glancing at one another, Tomoe and Sayo leaned in.

"The only people who have levistone are Sohma, right? Well, word is a bunch of their ships are leaving for Sola-Ea.

Apparently, the empire is building a cannon powerful enough to shoot down a sky city. Sohma are heading to Sola-Ea to destroy it!"

A levistone cannon. That did sound dangerous, but Tomoe was more concerned about the people of Sola-Ea caught in a war they never asked for. She worried for the *Orihime* and its crew, stuck on that sky city, unable to flee.

The old man shrugged. "So you see why it's a fool's errand. Who wants to stow away on a ship heading right into a war zone?"

A determined grin spread across Tomoe's face.

She and Sayo had flown through a storm of angry sky whales and set fire to wild shikigami. Compared to that, what was a hail of bullets or a barrage of battleships if it meant she could see the *Orihime* again?

"Well," she said, "I think that sounds like a brilliant plan!"

TEN

NOW that everyone was awake, the first order of the day was to get the supplies they had come here for. Kurara and the others cautiously stepped outside the abandoned shop and into a city still reeling from the yuurei attack. The streets were a mess, the ground painted with rubble and blood, and everywhere she went worried city folk whispered to each other:

"What were those things?"

"They were demons! Obviously we've angered the Gods somehow."

They were yuurei, Kurara wanted to say as she followed Haru and Himura in search of someone – anyone – willing to sell the things they needed.

"Don't worry, Rara." Haru nudged her shoulder.

"I'm fine," she ground out stiffly. It was Haru that she worried about. Haru, who had just absorbed a ton of yuurei into his core and was still grinning like an idiot as they made their way down the very streets where so many people had died.

"You can't lie to me, Rara. Unclench that jaw of yours, or you'll shatter your teeth."

"You're one to talk. How are you feeling?"

"I'm fine."

Kurara did not like the tone Haru was taking with her. "Ah, so we're both fine, are we?"

"Yes," he said flatly.

"Good." She sniffed.

"Good!"

"Double good!"

"Children…" Mana's exasperated voice emerged from the depths of Himura's sleeve. *"Please do not make a scene."*

Kurara sighed as Haru peeled away to gawk at a collapsed bell tower, which had fallen across the road. She wanted to scream. Since when had it become so hard to be honest with each other? She knew Haru cared about her as much as she cared about him, but perhaps that was why the truth snarled in their throats and choked on the way out.

Hardly any of the stores were open, but Himura found a handful of shops – run by a few hard-knuckled, scowling men – that were still operating despite the destruction around them. As Kurara took a look at the slim selection of dried meats and bags of rice, she overheard more whispers:

"Did you hear? Prince Ugetsu and the Emperor have sent soldiers to fight each other all along the midlands of Mikoshima."

"There've been a lot of bandits cropping up as well. It's too dangerous to leave the city now."

It seemed that the yuurei were not the only danger out there. Of course, when the land was in turmoil, there would be soldiers and bandits aplenty. Kurara added them to her list of things to worry about. As if her list wasn't already long enough.

"Come on." Himura's approach jolted her from her thoughts. He heaved a heavy cloth bag over his shoulder, full of the things they had come for. "I have our supplies. We can leave now."

That was blissfully fast. Kurara was only too glad to leave the city and never come back.

"I'll go and fetch Haru then," she muttered and hurried down the line of shops towards the bell tower where she knew Haru was dawdling.

The main street was partially blocked by debris. Along the rubble-lined road, she found Haru near the broken tower, sitting on the misshapen lump of metal that had once been a bell.

"A dying star fell from the heavens," he sang beneath his breath. It was a lullaby every shikigami knew.

"It's time to go!" Kurara offered him a hand.

Haru jumped. "O−oh!" Instead of accepting her help, he slid off the side of the metal bell himself. "Sorry, my mind was miles away!"

Kurara fought back the uncontrollable wave of suspicion that swept through her. Haru was acting strangely. Something was wrong, her gut whispered. Something was wrong with him.

As if sensing her thoughts, Haru held out his hand.

"Come on," he said. "Let's go."

It was a peace offering. Gingerly, she reached for him when a sudden beam of light arched overhead.

Like a shooting star, the light soared through the clouds, so bright it turned the sky around it pure white. The people in the street screamed and ducked as it flew over them. Kurara had to squeeze her eyes shut until it curved over the edge of the horizon and disappeared out of sight.

"That light again!" she cried.

"Ah, the shopkeepers told me about that." Himura made his way towards them. "That would be the new weapon the Emperor is building on Sola-Ea. A levistone cannon capable of shooting down the sky cities. What you're seeing are the test shots."

Sola-Ea. Just before Tomoe and Sayo parted ways with them, Himura had told her that the *Orihime* was docked at the city of Sola-Ea. Kurara did her best to keep her emotions from her face, but she was sure that the others saw the flicker of fear in her expression anyway. Would the crew of the *Orihime* be OK? What about Tomoe and Sayo?

"Hmph, that foolish contraption is none of our business." Mana snorted.

That was right. Between reaching the mountain and finding a way to make the Star Seed bloom, they had enough on their plates. She didn't have time to worry about other people. Still, this cannon felt like a scorpion sitting in the corner of her room – even if she ignored it for now, it would one day scuttle up and sting her when she least expected.

"I agree with Mana. There's nothing we can do about

some cannon up in the sky. We should just keep going forward. Onwards to the Mountain of the Falling Star!" Haru pointed north-west, towards their destination.

Kurara's gaze snapped back to him. Before the shot of light, she had thought that he was acting strangely, but now she was not so sure. Maybe it really was nothing. Maybe she was still spooked by yesterday's events and just reading too much into everything.

"Himura?" She wanted to ask him if he had noticed anything odd about Haru.

"Yes?" he said.

Kurara hesitated. She could not bring herself to share her worries with him. After all, she had trusted him once, and he had betrayed her to Princess Tsukimi.

"Nothing," she mumbled. "It's nothing."

ELEVEN

THEY spent the next few days covering as much ground as they could, stopping only to eat and sleep, while watching out for yuurei. Himura had bought warm blankets and winter capes that made the nights more bearable as they made their way across the country. They didn't linger in any one place for too long, and for the most part their journey was peaceful, unhindered by soldiers, bandits or shadows.

Perhaps it was a little too peaceful. Kurara kept one eye on the Star Seed and the other on Haru, sure that something was due to go wrong at any moment.

Sure enough, a few hours later, the clouds rolled in and the sky unleashed a torrent of rain that turned the ground to mud and made their travels difficult. When they tried to use ofuda, the ceaseless rain made their paper soggy and difficult to control. When they walked, the mud stuck to their boots, turning each step into a battle against the elements. Kurara cursed as they climbed past clumps of swaying bamboo that grew so thick they formed towering walls of greenery. Her sleeves were heavy with water and the cold damp seeped through her boots and into her socks.

"I wish you were big enough to ride," she grumbled at Mana, who was hiding, comfortably dry, inside Himura's sleeve.

"You would make this poor old shikigami carry you? For shame! These old bones ache in this rain." Mana chuckled and hid itself further inside Himura's clothes.

"You don't have any bones!" Kurara argued, but that only made the shikigami laugh even louder.

Bloody snake! She clicked her tongue. Walking through endless mud was not pleasant. Her socks were damp, and each step was accompanied by an awful, wet squelch.

"A dying star fell from the heavens, and from that star…" Mana sang while the rest of them struggled against the mud.

"Come on, Rara. Keep up!" Haru tromped through the muck like a boy on an adventure. He knocked a stick against the bamboo as he went, shaking water from the leaves, much to Kurara's irritation.

"He's full of energy," muttered Himura.

Was that a pointed comment? Kurara wondered. Did Himura suspect that there was something off about Haru too? That Haru, as Kurara feared, was just putting on a mask of excitement to cover up what was really going on inside his core? She shuddered at the thought.

"Are you cold?" Himura loosened the fastenings of his cloak, but before he could hand it to her, Haru gave a shout of joy and burst into a run.

As the land rose, the walls of bamboo gave way to a small clearing at the top of the hill, from which Kurara could see the land unfurl around her for miles.

"There it is! Our home!" Haru pointed to the mountain looming in the distance.

The Mountain of the Falling Star was so tall it pierced the grey clouds. They still had a few hours to go before they reached its base, but from the top of their hilly vantage point Kurara's gaze swept across a landscape burning with red maples and golden ginkgo trees. If she squinted, she could make out a path through the forests and across the rolling fields to the foot of the mountain.

Home. The word was a hollow echo in her chest. The mountain, the blazing maples, the faint mist veiling the fields – it was a landscape like any other landscape; the sight didn't bring forth any particular feeling in her. The only thing she cared about was whether they would find some clue about the Star Seed there.

"*I can see a village.*" Mana slithered out of Himura's sleeve to point its tail towards the small wooden houses scattered around the hills in the mid-distance.

"Excellent." Himura nodded. "We'll take shelter there and wait for the rain to end."

Kurara's hopes of finding a warm, dry inn that served a good meal and hot tea were dashed the moment they entered the village. The buildings were all abandoned. Piles of chopped wood lay bundled up beside the homes, but all the windows were dark and empty. There was no one out in the paddies tending to the rice either, no one walking down the dirt paths or playing in the fields.

Haru grabbed her sleeve. "Rara, look!"

A man was lying face down in the middle of the path. As they rushed towards him, they were both assaulted by an overpowering stench.

The smell was so foul Kurara could not even begin to describe it. Slapping a hand over her nose and mouth, she braced herself and made her way towards the man.

Haru was quicker. He kneeled beside the villager and gently turned the man over, checking for signs of breathing.

"He's dead."

With such a rancid odour, Kurara could have guessed as much. "Another yuurei attack?" She trembled.

"No, judging from his wounds, it was good old-fashioned steel and gunpowder that did this," Himura murmured.

There were more corpses scattered further throughout the village. Bodies lying slumped against the walls of their homes. Discarded weapons and fallen flags littered the ground between the bushes and buildings. What little grass there was stood in dried, yellow patches, dirtied by blood.

Kurara's stomach turned at the sight. Whoever did this could still be around.

"We shouldn't stay here," she said.

"What, and leave all the bodies?" Haru looked appalled. "At the very least, we should give these people a proper send-off."

"If Tomoe and Sayo were here, they'd say the best way to deal with the dead is to leave the bodies for the birds."

According to the Sorabito, birds would carry the souls of the departed to where they needed to go. How could the birds reach your soul if you were six feet underground?

"Yes, but these people aren't Sorabito," said Haru.

Kurara looked away. What about the Star Seed? What about getting to the mountain? There was no time to waste on the dead. She was about to list all the reasons this was a terrible idea when Himura said, "I'll help you build a pyre. Mana, could you go with Kurara and look for a spot to make camp?"

Kurara tried to protest when Mana gave a sudden hiss. "*Shikigami!*"

TWELVE

AT first, Kurara didn't understand what Mana was talking about. Then she noticed the white lumps scattered around the village. Heaps of paper that had once been shikigami.

Her breath stuttered in her throat.

"What about the cores? Are the cores still intact?" she asked. Shikigami could not truly die unless their cores were destroyed. As long as they were still in one piece, they could be brought back, just as Princess Tsukimi had once brought Haru back.

Himura crouched next to the nearest mound of paper. With a grimace, he peeled away clumps of wet ofuda. "Gone." He shook his head. "Likely stolen. Shikigami cores are valuable. Even if you can't do anything with them yourself, they fetch a pretty price."

Kurara cursed beneath her breath. She hated the thought

of those cores being taken to be traded with like a handful of coins.

"We should go," she muttered.

"But the bodies," said Haru.

"Fine, we'll burn the bodies! But be quick about it!"

Between the three of them, they pulled together a halfway decent pyre. Himura and Haru handled the bodies – Kurara could not bring herself to go near them – and she stacked the wood for the bonfire. When the flames sprang to life, panic welled up in her chest.

Fire reminded her of Haru's body turning to ash, of shikigami burning, of Suzaku wreathed in flames as it screamed at her, *"It's all your fault!"*

"Shut up!" she hissed.

"Are you going mad?" Mana slithered over to her with an amused look on its face.

Kurara jumped, embarrassed to be caught talking to herself. She did not know how to deal with Mana. She had never met a sane shikigami she hadn't got along with. A part of her had just assumed that, since she was a shikigami too, she would hit it off with any and all shikigami she met.

Mana was doing an excellent job of proving otherwise.

She shook her head when she noticed something rustling in the bushes nearby. A large mound of grass rose up, revealing a man camouflaged in a hat and cloak made from woven leaves.

Kurara almost jumped out of her skin.

"Who are you?" Her ofuda spun around her in a whirlwind of paper.

"Whoa, whoa!" The man raised his hands in the air as Himura and Haru rushed over. "I mean no harm."

"Were you spying on us?" said Himura.

"Spying? No! Well, maybe yes. Maybe a little bit," the man said sheepishly. "The villages around here have been battered by both the Emperor and Prince Ugetsu's men. The land is crawling with both their soldiers, and every time their armies fight each other, they get innocent people involved. I thought you were Crafter dogs, serving the empire. I was ready to give you a piece of my mind, but you're not, are you? You burned the bodies, tried to give them a decent send-off. Who are you lot?"

Kurara glanced at Haru and Himura. For a moment, the three of them were united in their shared caution.

"Travellers," said Haru. It was a half-truth.

The man seemed impressed. "Rather bold of you to be travelling, what with all the chaos in this country. Bandits! Soldiers! Wild shikigami and yuurei—"

"Yuurei?" said Kurara, dread mounting.

"Surely you've heard of them. Those shadowy things that come and suck the life out of you. They've been spotted around these parts."

Kurara was becoming very familiar with the sting of guilt. It seemed wherever she went she only met people who were suffering as a consequence of her actions.

That's why it's so important that the Star Seed blooms! she told herself. How could she justify such suffering otherwise?

The man peered at her from beneath the brim of his hat. His face was as weathered as a stormy cliff, his skin lined with wrinkles and crow's feet, and his beard peppered with white. It was a face that had seen much tragedy.

"What happened to the shikigami here?" Mana slithered towards him.

The man flinched. It was not often people saw a shikigami, let alone talked with one.

"Well, they were killed in the fighting. Same with all the villagers and the soldiers."

"And their cores?"

"You probably won't believe me if I told you, but … it was a bunch of sky rats."

"You mean you saw a *Sorabito*? Here?" said Kurara.

"Bloody scavengers. I've heard rumours that other Sorabito have been spotted around other battlefields too, stealing cores. Like damn vultures, they are."

Kurara gave the man a frosty look. He was polite to them now, but she wondered how quickly he would change his tune if he knew that she and Himura had once lived with a crew of Sorabito.

She glanced at Himura and Haru. The Sorabito believed the ground was impure. As valuable as shikigami cores were, it was hard to believe they would want to pick through the muddy battlefields and unclean earth in search of them.

"It's getting dark. Come with me to my village. You'll be safe there," the man offered.

Kurara opened her mouth to refuse when Haru cut in front of her with a cheery, "We'd be glad to!"

"Haru!" she hissed.

"He's giving us a warm meal and a roof out of the rain,"

Haru whispered back. "We should take whatever help gets us to the mountain faster."

Kurara frowned. She didn't see how a warm meal and a dry place to sleep would make them any faster.

"Don't mistake the man's offer for kindness. He only did so because we are Crafters. Likely, he believes our presence will protect his village should bandits or soldiers attack," Himura muttered beneath his breath.

"You don't know that for sure!" said Haru, but he turned to Kurara anyway and shrugged. "It's up to you, Rara. I'll go along with whatever you want to do."

Kurara glanced at the sky. A levistone cannon. Sorabito stealing shikigami cores. Battles across the country and yuurei roaming the wilds. Why did it feel like the walls of the world were closing in on her?

The sun was setting earlier and earlier. Even now, the miserable grey sky was beginning to darken. A warm, dry place to spend the night didn't sound bad after everything they had been through, but did they have time for a detour? Every second they wasted was a second she could spend working towards saving the shikigami.

"Where is this village?" she asked.

"Over that way. About five miles north." The man pointed to a spot in the shadow of the mountain.

It was on the way to their destination.

Satisfied, Kurara nodded.

"Lead the way."

THIRTEEN

"HERE we are!"

Himura winced as the man gave a booming shout. The small, run-down village was barely more than a handful of huts and a stable. Each house was so closely built next to its neighbour they seemed to grow out of one another. Trees pushed through what little gaps they could find as the land sloped up towards a small terrace of rice paddies.

On the edge of the settlement stood several large torches, each about twelve feet tall, burning brightly.

"What are those for?" Himura asked as they passed them by.

"Oh, those?" The man grunted. "The yuurei are attracted to fire. These torches are made to distract them while the other folk run."

So the villagers were smart enough to notice that the

yuurei had patterns to their behaviour. How fascinating. Himura had to stop thinking of the villagers as mere country bumpkins.

"Does it work?"

"We're alive, ain't we?" the man spat. "Though the ones running with the torches often don't survive."

"The ones running with the torches?"

"When the yuurei appear, one or two good men hoist the torch poles outta the ground and run off with them, and the yuurei follow. It gives everyone else time to flee, though the men holding the torches hardly ever come back."

As they entered the village, people stopped to stare. Beneath the waning sun they looked as pale as ghosts. In the distance, Himura could hear people singing as they went – a low, mournful song.

They were met halfway by several men dressed in grass-woven cloaks and leaf hats, and armed with farming tools. Their faces were rough and scarred, skin pale beneath the dirt and sweat, hair shorn so close to their heads that their scalps looked almost blue.

An old woman with a piece of cloth tied around her nose and mouth pushed to the front. Only her flint-like eyes, narrowed in suspicion, were visible above the cloth.

"And who are these lot?" she demanded.

Their guide made introductions and explained the situation. The villagers seemed relieved to have Crafters around, though they were less keen on having three extra mouths to feed.

"Well, I suppose I better prepare your beds then," the woman huffed.

"And a bath too, if you can wrangle one up!" Haru added with his usual charming smile that set the villagers' nerves at ease.

The next thing Himura knew, he and the others were ushered inside a large broken hut at the end of the street, which opened into a single room, more like a meeting hall than anything else, full of long tables and a cooking pit that had been dug out of the floor.

Something was boiling in a huge brass pot suspended over the pit on an iron tripod. A man doled out food into crude clay bowls and all but threw them at Himura and the others.

"So, Crafters, are ya? All three of ya?" Their guide took off his hat and placed it on the table.

"That's right. We're a travelling band of circus performers," said Haru.

"Oh, really? How's business?" the man asked, and Himura was not sure whether to be offended by the fact he had believed Haru's lies.

The old woman had lured Kurara away with the promise of a bath and clean clothes, leaving Himura and Haru alone with the men of the village. Himura could feel Mana curled up around his forearm, refusing to come out. Meanwhile, Haru was entertaining the men with the absolutely-true-don't-question-it story of how he and Kurara had once saved the princess of a distant kingdom from a horde of giant squid monsters.

The villagers' stew was simple but hearty, made mostly of badly chopped root vegetables tossed together with some salt. Himura ate slowly, relishing the feeling of a full stomach.

He was ready to call it a night and head to bed without a much-needed bath when he heard Haru's pained hiss and the loud clatter of chopsticks hitting the floor.

"Tell me what's wrong." The words were out of Himura's mouth before he could stop them. Had that been too direct? Did that sound too much like an order?

"Nothing." Haru shook his head. With a forced grin, he turned to the other men inside the hall and bowed. "Gentlemen, I think I need a bit of fresh air."

Himura frowned as he watched Haru beat a quick retreat. Mana tapped its tail against his wrist, urging him after the boy. Not that he needed telling twice. He waited a moment then followed him through the door.

———o———

Away from the echoes of laughter inside the hall, the village was as quiet as the grave. In fact, Himura was sure that he was next to a few graves. Piles of rock, arranged carefully in artistic mounds, dotted the dirt roads, perhaps marking where people fell during a yuurei attack. It was near one such pile that Himura found Haru.

"I'm fine," Haru said before Himura could even speak.

He certainly *seemed* fine, but Himura knew better by now than to rely on appearances. Besides, there was a seed of nagging doubt he couldn't quite shake that told him that Haru was very good at faking being OK. He thought of the way the boy's body had jerked on the ground in Zeka; how pale he had looked when he had fainted. Something was wrong, though he could not quite put his finger on what.

He could order Haru to tell him how he was really feeling, but that felt too invasive. Shikigami were people too; they should be allowed to have their privacy. Himura was not going to abuse the bond he had. He was going to be kinder. Better.

"*I love you, Master.*" Akane's voice drifted through his head. If he focused on it, he could see the fox's face as it was consumed by flames. He could smell the smoke and feel the heat of the fire lick up his arms.

Nothing would bring Akane back – both the fox's body and core had been burned to a crisp – but he could decide how he treated other shikigami.

"I felt a little pang of pain. I've had paper cuts that hurt worse than that," said Haru, shrugging. He made a motion as if to kick the small pile of stones then, realizing what they were, quickly stepped away from the grave marker.

"*And what about your core?*" Mana poked its head out from Himura's sleeve.

"What about *your* sanity?" Haru retorted.

"*Don't take that tone with me, child. I've not lost my mind yet.*"

"I think I'm older than you."

"*Older, but not wiser.*"

"Do you have something to hide?" Himura interrupted their bickering. He did not need a reminder that Mana was still refusing to bond with him.

"Why don't you *order* me to tell you? I'll spill all my dirty little secrets to you, if you just say the word." Haru's smile was cutting – all teeth and no humour.

It was a low blow, aimed with the intention of hitting

his every insecurity. It made Himura wonder how Haru managed to see through him so effectively. He flinched, but he was not about to back down.

"I'm not going to order you to tell me, but as … as someone who worries about you, I wish that you wouldn't lie to me. I wish that you would trust me enough with the truth. I'm concerned about you. As your … *friend*." His voice quivered over the last word. Were they friends? Could one be considered friends when there was also a blood bond in the equation?

Haru glanced up at the Mountain of the Falling Star looming overhead. It was so close they could not see the peak beyond the clouds. The carpet of ginkgo trees layered the slopes in gold that shone in the moonlight.

"…Fine."

Taking a deep breath, Haru opened the front of his kimono and bared his chest. Carefully, Himura ran his finger from the end of Haru's collarbone down to the bottom of his ribs, slicing open the paper skin, and eased the two folds apart. Haru hissed and scrunched his eyes closed but otherwise stood still.

With Haru's chest open, Himura had a window to the inside of the boy's body. He had seen all of this once before – the paper organs, the threads of ofuda in lieu of muscles – but they never ceased to fascinate him.

Himura zeroed in on the core, hanging suspended inside Haru's chest where his heart would be. There was the dent where Haru had met some kind of accident long ago – an accident Kurara claimed had taken away his ability to use ofuda. The blood markings where Himura had bonded with Haru stood starkly against the white paper ball.

"See? There's nothing wrong." Haru tried to close his chest, but Himura stopped him.

There, slicing through one of the blood markings, was a long, thin cut. It was not particularly deep, but bits of paper around it were flaking off.

The wound had not been there before when they had formed their bond, Himura was certain of it. It was something new, something caused by absorbing all those souls. Suzaku had been created to contain many souls, but Haru had not, and his core was suffering for it.

Would it get worse? Would Haru's core eventually crack inside him, and if it did, would the yuurei be released into the world again?

"Haru," Himura began.

"Don't tell Kurara." Haru could not meet his eye. "This is my secret, and I'll share it when I'm ready. *Please*."

He sounded beyond exhausted, his voice tinged with the kind of bone-deep weariness Himura could only imagine. Haru looked both too young for such burdens and impossibly ancient – a strange contradiction as tangled as the souls twisting inside him.

"Don't tell Kurara," he repeated.

Himura swallowed around the lump forming in his throat. Keeping secrets was a stupid, reckless thing that would only end in more hurt and betrayal.

"I really think this is the kind of thing she should know."

"I will tell her. Just not today. I'll tell her when I'm ready."

And when would that be? Himura held his tongue.

Not for the first time, he marvelled at how easy life was when he could just order his shikigami to do his bidding, when he directed others on what he considered the "right path", with no concern for their feelings or wishes. But shikigami were individuals with thoughts of their own; if he was to respect that, he had to accept their bad decisions too.

Even if he could see the train crash coming from ten miles away.

"Fine. I'll keep my mouth shut. I promise."

"*Foolish!*" Mana hissed. "*All of you are fools.*"

Interlude

Praise be to Sohma!
No more shall the rotten worms
Eat away our lives

                       – Sohma rallying cry

The last thing Tomoe wanted was to be within five feet of a Sohma rebel. They were murderers and blood purists the lot of them, blocking less violent attempts towards Sorabito independence and generally exhibiting the same terrible behaviour they accused groundlings of. What aggravated Tomoe the most about Sohma was the sense that they did not want life for the Sorabito to be better as much as they wanted to be right.

Under normal circumstances, she would have stayed well away from any gathering of such rebels – a decision that had served her well so far – but these were not normal circumstances. The only people who had the fuel to travel were from Sohma, and the only way to leave the sky city

was on a Sohma airship. The fact that they were heading to a war zone, to Sola-Ea where the empire was building a levistone cannon, did not bother her. The *Orihime* was stuck on Sola-Ea anyway, and this was the only way home.

The only way back to the ship and the people she cared about.

As it turned out, stowing away on a ship was no easy feat. First, Tomoe had to find out where Sohma's ships were stationed. Then it was a matter of sneaking into the dock and onto the right airship. When they finally made it inside the right docking bay, there were several Sohma vessels preparing to leave.

Tomoe recognized each and every one: they were regular merchant or transport ships that had been stolen by Sohma, with extra cannons attached to the deck, as if that was all they needed to make them into battleships.

The vessels stood like a row of slumbering beasts, attended to by men and women busy loading each ship with supplies. Crates and casks stood stacked to one side, waiting to be loaded. Boys struggled up the gangplanks carrying boxes filled with everything from dried meat to cannonballs. The smell of levistone oozed from dirty barrels loaded onto metal trolleys.

"That one." Sayo pointed to the largest of the airships. Tomoe glanced at the name painted on the side of the hull: the *Kujiraza*.

It was a monster of a vessel, with a huge, bulging underside that looked like the baleen plates of a whale's mouth. Before Sohma had taken it over, it had been a levistone transporter,

armed to the teeth with cannons and lookout towers and all sorts of smoke screen launchers to protect it from shikigami and bandits looking to steal its precious cargo. Tomoe had heard of the *Kujiraza* before, but it was not until she was hiding there, in the shadow of its hull, that she realized how massive it actually was.

Such a splendid aircraft had no business flying straight into a war zone, but as far as ships went, the *Kujiraza* was an ideal target for stowaways; its size would provide more hiding places and blind spots to avoid detection. It was just a matter of sneaking on board without anyone noticing.

Tomoe remained crouched in the shadows of the ships, watching the deckhands move the cargo. Her attention came to rest on a large canvas sheet stretched across a metal trolley, covering whatever was underneath from view.

"Follow me!" she whispered to Sayo, before dashing across the docking bay floor, darting from one shadow to the next, until she reached the trolley.

Lifting the canvas cover, she found at least a dozen wooden casks. Tomoe almost laughed. *Someone* on board was trying to smuggle a load of wine onto the ship. She supposed even Sohma needed to let off some steam once in a while.

"Tomoe!" Sayo hissed, the urgency in her voice reminding her that they should not linger in the open for too long. "The both of us can't fit under there."

"Sure we can, we just need to squeeze in." Tomoe pushed the casks so that there was less space between each of the

barrels and more room for them, drawing her knees up to her chest so she could fit on the trolley.

Sayo hesitated, her cheeks reddening, but Tomoe grabbed her by the hand and pulled her beneath the canvas.

It took some effort, but they managed to both cram themselves against the wooden barrels. Crushed tight, they waited in miserable, uncomfortable darkness until at last it was their turn to be loaded onto the ship. Tomoe's heart pounded as she peered between the folds of the sheet. The trolley wheels rolled over the deck, down a long ramp and into the hallway of the ship.

Eventually, they were parked next to a stack of crates. Footsteps faded. Somewhere behind them a door swung shut, and they were left in the darkness of the *Kujiraza*'s storage room.

Tomoe waited, ears straining for the slightest sound, then threw off the canvas and uncurled her cramped legs. Light in the hallway spilled beneath the door, illuminating just enough for her to pick out the vague outlines of the shelves and barrels that crowded the room.

Sayo jumped to her feet and stretched out every muscle in her body. Their eyes met and even in the darkness Tomoe could make out the wicked curve of Sayo's mouth, pulled into a victorious grin. Something about her delight sent a thrill down Tomoe's spine. Sayo was usually so gloomy and quiet, seeing her so triumphant was like watching a rare flower bloom.

She laughed.

They had made it.

FOURTEEN

WHEN Kurara woke, it was already mid-afternoon. She stretched like a cat, yawning as she pushed off the raggedy blankets that the villagers had given her to make the ground a bit more comfortable. She had not dreamed of Suzaku all night, and, for the first time in weeks, she felt well-rested. Hopeful. They would find a way to make the Star Seed bloom as soon as they reached the Mountain of the Falling Star. She was sure of it.

After a hurried breakfast of vegetable stew with Haru and some of the other villagers, Kurara licked her spoon clean and prepared for a long day of walking.

The village looked even worse in daylight. Men and women were already about, tending to what little scraps of land had been set aside to grow crops. It was a depressing sight. Kurara wondered if things had been better before the war. If things would get better once the fighting was over.

As they made their way past the huts, the man who had brought them to the village stopped sweeping his front porch. Despite how friendly he had been, Kurara could not bring herself to like the man. His comment about Sorabito "sky rats" still needled at her.

"Hey, there!" he called to them. "I heard you're going to the mountain. The folk here say there's a God living inside there and that if you listen closely you can hear a voice whispering. Course, with the yuurei and the war, we've been far too busy to make the trip. When you go, say a prayer for us, will ya?"

"Sure. We'll let them know that you're really, really sorry you've been slacking on your worship," said Haru.

The man laughed, though there was a note of unease beneath at the thought of them leaving so soon. Himura had been right; the man was only so friendly because he hoped they might stay and protect the village from soldiers or bandits.

"And your friend – the one with the snake shikigami? He ain't going with you?"

Kurara shook her head. In a rare display of consideration for others, Himura had offered to stay behind to let her and Haru make the journey to the mountain alone. Though she had not said so, she was glad that Himura was not coming. It had been just the two of them living near that mountain for so many years, it felt right that just the two of them would return there together now. Like they would somehow have better luck finding a clue to make the Star Seed bloom if they went together, without Himura.

"We'll be back for him later," said Haru.

The man nodded. "Be careful now – there've been

imperial soldiers spotted around the area. It's best not to get tangled up in their business."

"We'll keep an eye out. Thanks!" Haru waved goodbye with the enthusiasm of a child sent on his first errand.

The moment they stepped out of the village, a loud *boom* echoed through the air and a bright white light arched across the sky.

The levistone cannon. Kurara wondered when the test shots would end and the cannon would begin firing at targets for real.

She wondered if Tomoe and Sayo were doing well.

"A dying star fell from the heavens," Haru sang as he led her through the forest and towards the shadow of the mountain. Golden ginkgo trees had shed their fan-shaped leaves on the ground, creating a yellow path along the forest that crunched underfoot. Sunlight melted between the leaves. It was a gloriously dry, if cold, day.

"What do you remember about our old home?" Kurara asked as she tried to keep pace with Haru's long, confident strides.

Haru said nothing.

"Haru, are you listening?"

"I am. Go on," he said, though he sounded distracted.

"I was asking you a question. Do you remember anything about our old home?"

Haru did not respond immediately. His mind seemed a million miles away.

"Haru!"

"Huh? Well, there isn't much to say. We hid there after the Crafters cut down all the Star Trees. There was a village at the foot of the mountain that we would visit from time to time, but that's about it."

Kurara frowned. She wanted to know more about their life. About Haru. She had been so distracted with worries about Haru's core, with the need to hurry up and make the Star Seed bloom, that she had not paid as much thought as she should have to Haru's feelings.

"I know, but … was it hard living there?"

"It's never hard being with you, Rara."

She shook her head. "You say that, but I don't have any memories of the Crafter war. I don't really remember when the Crafters started cutting down the Star Trees. Or when they started turning shikigami into tools for war. Everything is hazy. But you remember all of it, don't you? And you're … OK?"

"OK" was a clumsy way to phrase it, but Kurara didn't know how else to ask Haru how he felt about their past. The sheer, crushing weight of history. The enormity of their long, immortal lives.

When Haru smiled at her, it was with a fond gentleness. "Thanks for worrying about me, Rara, but it's not so bad. Not when I have you—"

Kurara didn't have a chance to respond. Haru broke off at the sound of footsteps marching through the undergrowth.

"Get down!" She grabbed Haru's wrist and yanked him to the ground.

They lay beneath the bushes, listening closely as the footsteps grew closer and closer. Heavy boots marched in lockstep. Kurara shrank further back as a group of soldiers appeared beneath the trees, armed with a katana on one hip and a pistol at the other.

"What are they doing here?" she hissed as the men passed uncomfortably close to their hiding spot.

"I don't know. A patrol maybe? They're not heading in the direction of the mountain. Let's just wait—" Whatever he was about to say was cut off by a sharp, pained gasp of breath.

"Haru! What's wrong? Are you feeling all right?"

Haru waved off her concern. "I'm *fine*. Let's wait for them to leave."

Kurara held her tongue. There was a lot she wanted to say, but she suspected Haru would only tell her that she was imagining things.

It felt like an eternity passed before the soldiers moved on. Kurara didn't want to leave their hiding place until she was sure there wasn't a single soldier within hearing distance.

The presence of the military felt like a bad omen. Like something terrible was about to happen if they didn't reach the mountain as fast as possible.

"Let's go," Kurara whispered.

───────o───────

They arrived at the foot of the mountain by the afternoon. Though it was still early, the sun was already bleeding into the horizon, turning the sky into a hazy watercolour of orange and pink. A fine carpet of emerald grass grew between the trees, scattered with large boulders that had shaken loose from the mountain.

"This is it!" Haru ran through the long grass, towards a bunch of lumpy shapes half eaten by moss. He seemed back to his usual self, but Kurara's unease still lingered.

Tearing her eyes away from Haru, she turned to stare at the ruins. If she used her imagination, she could picture the village that had once stood here. The stumps of buildings lay dotted here and there among the trees. Cracked foundations of old homes and bits of wall remained standing, though they were completely overtaken by vines and weeds. If she looked closely, she could just make out bits of broken toys lying tangled in the grass, and dolls so worn and weathered that their faces had completely rubbed off.

Was this home? Kurara had expected her chest to swell with emotion, for her eyes to tear up and her chest to pound, but as her gaze swept over the ruins, she did not feel anything in particular. This was just another village that had been abandoned to nature. When she thought of home, she thought of the *Orihime* and its sunny hallways, the way the crew would abuse the voice-pipes to serenade the entire ship with Sorabito ballads. She thought of the mess hall with its rows of tables and chairs screwed down in perfect lines, the gurgle of rain falling into the rain catchers, and the churning hum of the engines lulling her to sleep.

She thought of Haru. They had always been together, twin satellites orbiting one another in a never-ending cycle. When this was over, maybe they could join the *Orihime* together. Or maybe they could find somewhere quiet to settle down and watch the world turn.

She shook her head. Thoughts of the future could wait until the Star Seed had bloomed.

"A dying star fell from the heavens, and from that star grew a tree…" she heard someone sing. Kurara turned to Haru, but he was picking his way through the long grass and not paying any attention to her.

She remembered the villager had mentioned people

around here worshipping an ancient God. Could that God actually be a shikigami? Was there one around the mountain, maybe buried somewhere beneath the ruins? Is that what she was hearing?

"You probably don't remember, but this was where we were found and taken to the *Midori*. Wow, this really takes me back!" Haru grinned.

"So this is where we lived?" Kurara scanned the ruins in search of something familiar, something that might jog her memory.

Haru shook his head. "This was a village that popped up nearby. We would visit it from time to time, but our actual home was just a little further on." He pointed towards the giant mass of the mountain. The slope was so steep it seemed almost a vertical wall covered in golden trees. "Up there. There's a hidden path along the mountainside."

She followed Haru up the slope and through the undergrowth. Vines and bushes grew thick and wild, tangling around her ankles as if nature itself was fighting her with every step. The path was so steep at times that Kurara had to crawl on her hands and knees for fear she would fall backwards and tumble right back down the mountain.

Eventually, the incline flattened into a hidden clearing among the trees. When Kurara looked to her right, she spied a small wooden house in front of a dried-up lotus pond. A bolt of familiarity jolted through her. She remembered that house – the feel of the tatami mats beneath her feet, the creak of the wooden floor, the soft rustle of paper.

"Home, sweet home," said Haru cheerfully, as the shrivelled lotus flowers dropped their heads into the empty pond.

FIFTEEN

"THIS way," Haru whispered.

Kurara followed him to the house. The porch creaked beneath her weight as she stepped up and slid open the battered wooden front door. Inside, the main room was filled with dusty furniture and scattered belongings. The tatami mats were old and worn, the reeds poking against the soles of her shoes. Yellowed books and bits of paper lay strewn about the room, and the faint smell of damp filled the air.

"So this is where you and I lived after … everything."

After all the Star Trees had been cut down during the Crafter war. After Aki had killed the people of Kazami, hidden the Star Seed inside Suzaku's core and then retreated here to have her memories wiped.

Hazy recollections stirred inside Kurara as her gaze swept across the room. There was a profound emptiness to this place. It was like visiting a gravesite; the person she had been when she lived here was gone. Everything she had felt back then, everything that she might have held dear was gone too.

Everything except for Haru. He was the thread connecting it all together – her past, present and future. Kurara felt the sudden urge to grab his hand and hold him tight. If this place had ever been home, then it was only because Haru had made it so.

"So there are some old books here that talk about the Star Tree, right?" she asked.

"I think so. I can't quite remember which. Just grab whatever book looks really old. And boring." Haru crouched in front of the scattered papers, gathering them up into a neat pile.

Kurara wasn't sure whether to take offence at that; doubtless, any book about the Star Trees would be fascinating. With a click of her fingers, a selection of letters rose from the ground and floated towards her. She plucked one at random, turning the piece of paper over, but the ink was so faded she could not make out anything written there. Another piece of paper simply said: *Grow radishes in spring.* And another: *Something is eating the radishes. FIND OUT WHAT!*

There was nothing about the Star Trees or the Star Seed in any of the papers she could find. The notes were all about planting crops or sketches of the local wildlife, and the books were a mix of poetry and fiction. The high hopes she had had this morning were beginning to dwindle. Why had she ever thought this place might hold any answers?

The last book she selected was a slim leather tome bound

with string. When she opened it to the first page, Kurara instantly recognized Haru's spidery handwriting.

> **We decided to take shelter at the Mountain of the Falling Star. Long ago it was from the peak of this mountain that Crafters witnessed a once-in-a-millennium meteor shower. Stars fell and left large scars across the land. They fell and killed many people. Seems like a bad omen to make a home near a place named after a tragedy, but it's isolated and quiet and humans hardly ever come this way.**

It was a journal. Kurara paused. It felt odd reading Haru's words from so long ago; familiar yet just odd enough to feel uncanny. She turned the page, the paper surprisingly heavy, and scanned the next entry.

> **We plant crops and try not to think about the war. About our failures. I mentioned this place being the site of the first meteor shower, and Aki says the shikigami lullaby is actually about that very same event: A dying star fell from the heavens.**

The pages continued, detailing their time living on the mountain, but she couldn't bring herself to delve any further. This was Haru's diary; these were his innermost thoughts and feelings during a time Kurara barely remembered. It did not feel right to continue without permission. As she closed the book, she heard Haru choke.

"Are you all right?" She hurried over.

"I'm fine!" Haru wheezed. "My chest just hurts a little."

Fear beat through her like a war drum. This did not look like a *little* pain. It looked like something was trying to tear through him from the inside out.

"It's your core, isn't it?"

"No—"

"Don't lie to me!" she yelled. She could clearly see that there was something wrong. Didn't he trust her? Why did it feel like she cared about him more than he cared for her?

"I was going to tell you," Haru mumbled.

"Oh, really? When?"

"Today, actually. Himura—"

"*Himura* knows?"

Haru winced. "He said I should tell you."

"Oh, well if *Himura* says you should!" Hurt made her bitter. Why had Haru told Himura and not her? Was their relationship so fragile that a simple blood bond between Haru and Himura could overtake the years of friendship they shared?

"I'm sorry. I shouldn't have tried to keep it from you. You've always been the most important person to me." Haru looked well and truly miserable. "It's my core. I feel the yuurei squirming inside me. My core wasn't made to handle so many souls inside it. It's … peeling."

"What do you mean by 'peeling'?" she snapped. "Your core isn't a bloody potato!"

"I mean," Haru winced, "some of the paper on my core is flaking away."

Bristling anger gave way to a sharp and terrible fear.

A core was a shikigami's heart. If it broke open, Haru would … he would die, and all the yuurei he had absorbed would spill out into the world again.

But what would that matter without Haru?

"It's not bad!" he rushed to assure her. "There's, like, a small cut on the surface of my core, but you can barely notice it! It's not like my core is going to break apart!"

Guilt was a dagger in her lungs. Haru had pushed her out of the sealing circle and used his core instead to bind the yuurei. It should have been her. She should have bound the yuurei into her core instead. This was her fault.

She jolted as Haru's hand closed around her own, the warmth of his skin a faint comfort for Kurara's frayed nerves.

"Don't blame yourself. I did this to myself, and I don't regret it for one second. It was the right thing to do – if I hadn't sealed the yuurei, they would have massacred everyone in the city," he said softly.

Kurara kept shaking her head, as if she could change the reality of things if she just kept denying it. They had to fix this, though she had no idea how. Why wasn't Haru panicking as much as she was? If their positions were reversed, she would want to find some way of removing the other yuurei from her core as soon as possible.

"We didn't come here for this anyway." Haru sighed. "The Star Seed is more important. Let's concentrate on that. Did you find anything?"

"How can you even think about the Star Seed when your core is damaged?" she cried.

"Rara!" Haru replied with a fierceness he seldom

displayed. "You're overreacting. I told you, it's fine. Now, tell me what you found."

Biting back her unease, she allowed her gaze to rest on the small leather book she had been reading. She plucked it from the floor, dusted off the cover, and stepped towards the porch. Maybe some fresh air would help her thoughts.

"I found your journal." She leaned against the creaking wooden doorframe.

A slight blush coloured Haru's cheeks as he took it from her.

"I didn't read all of it," said Kurara.

"What *did* you read?"

"Just the first two pages. Something about moving here and how the Mountain of the Falling Star got its name."

"Oh, yeah. It was named after a rare meteor shower," said Haru. "A bunch of stars fell all across the land and..."

"And bloomed into trees?" A thought hit her like a speeding hovercraft. "'A dying star fell from the heavens, and from that star grew a tree.' The shikigami lullaby is about that meteor shower! The Star Seed – this rock – is a meteorite!"

"...OK." Haru kept looking at her like she had grown an extra head.

Kurara wanted to tear her hair out. How could he not understand what a monumental breakthrough this was?

She was right. She had to be. It fitted too perfectly to be anything else.

"The shikigami lullaby says that 'A dying star fell from the heavens, and from that star grew a tree'. In your journal, you mention a bunch of stars falling across the land. They're both talking about the same event," she tried to explain. "This Star Seed, this rock, is one of those falling stars. Perhaps the lullaby is actually a clue about how to make it bloom."

"What do you mean?"

"I think that in order for the Star Seed to bloom it has to fall 'from the heavens' like the song says!"

Haru did not seem as convinced.

"Is it really that simple? How far does it have to fall? From the top of a mountain? From above a sky city? From the edge of space? Is it even possible to fly that high?"

Kurara's hopes deflated. That was a good point.

Tying the book to her obi with a paper rope, Kurara began to pace up and down the porch. As she looked out across the clearing, a shadow darted across the corner of her vision.

"Did you see that?" She froze.

Haru blinked up at the bushes and trees. "See what?"

"A shadow."

"Do you think it's a yuurei?"

Before she could reply, something whistled through the air and struck the roof of their home, bursting into flames.

"Rara!" Haru threw himself at her. Together, they flew off the porch, their bodies tumbling to the ground as the house caught alight, the flames quickly spreading from the roof down to the rest of the home.

Kurara barely had time to stumble to her feet as a huge paper tiger came barrelling towards them.

Her mouth fell open.

A shikigami.

SIXTEEN

THE shikigami towered over her, engulfing her in its shadow. It was a gnarled, beaten thing, pitted with scars that ran down its body, almost as numerous as the stripes on its back. When it roared, its voice seemed to shake her very core.

What was it doing here? How had such a beast managed to wander across the mountain?

"Stop! We don't want to hurt you!" Kurara raised her hands, hoping that there was enough of the tiger's mind left for it to listen to reason. There was something awfully familiar about the beast, though she could not put her finger on where she had seen it before.

"There you are!" a shrill voice called out to her.

A figure emerged from behind the tiger holding a hand-carved bow and carrying a small quiver of arrows on her back. She walked towards the shikigami without fear and placed a hand on its muzzle.

The woman looked as wild and untameable as the tiger. Her hair was a tangle of knots. Three long, jagged scars ran from her left eye to the right side of her mouth, as if something had clawed at her face. It looked like a new injury; the skin around the wound was still puckered and red. Kurara did not think the woman was a Crafter. After all, Crafters could usually sense one another, but there was no telltale shiver of electricity skittering across her skin when she looked into the woman's eyes.

But if she's not a Crafter, then why does she have a shikigami? Just who in the seven hells was this strange person?

The wild woman's face lit up.

"Ah, my little shikigami. It's good to see you again."

Again? What did she mean by that? Kurara stared long and hard at the woman's bedraggled hair, at her deeply scarred face and dirt-stained clothes – there was something familiar about her. That haughty look, that imperious tone… Where had she seen them before?

No, it couldn't be… But there was no other explanation she could think of. Kurara swallowed around the hard lump in her throat.

"P–Princess Tsukimi?" How was this possible? The last time Kurara had seen the princess, it had been at the crater after the yuurei had spilled out from Suzaku's core. What was she doing *here*?

Kurara's eyes darted to the tiger shikigami.

"…Ruki?"

Why was the tiger following Tsukimi around? Ruki's

master was dead and, without a bond, the tiger's mind was in danger of unravelling.

"We had a bet. One that I lost." Ruki's voice rumbled through her mind, slow and painful, like a metal rake through gravel.

"Ruki and I had a little fight. That's how I got this." The princess gestured to the scars on her face. "But as you can see, I came out triumphant. Now Ruki serves me."

"Until I am no longer in possession of my senses."

That seemed like it could happen very soon. The tiger was quivering, as if the strain of holding itself together was beginning to overwhelm it.

"Why are you here?" Kurara asked. "What do you want with us?"

"My dear shikigami, you have an awfully high opinion of yourself, don't you? What makes you think I want anything from you?"

It was astounding how, even filthy and scarred, the princess still carried herself with such confidence.

"Because you chased us around half the bloody country!" Kurara seethed.

Tsukimi laughed, and Kurara had the deeply unsatisfying feeling that the princess enjoyed her irritable responses. Like a child cooing over a hissing kitten.

Haru stepped in front of her, using his body to shield Kurara from Tsukimi's piercing gaze. "Don't lie. Tell me, how long have you been following us?"

Princess Tsukimi stared at Haru like a butcher trying to work out how to best carve up a pig. "My dear, if you want to know something, you really should learn how to ask nicely."

Behind them, the fire crackled as it consumed their old home. The house might not have meant much to Kurara, but Haru had cared about it. It was one of the few things he had left of his old life; one of the few things that he had shared with her when she was still Aki. Kurara did not think she could hate the princess any more than she already did.

Haru ground his teeth together as he glowered at the princess. "We saw some soldiers earlier. They were looking for you, weren't they?"

Princess Tsukimi shrugged. "The soldiers want to drag me to Sola-Ea, where my father is holed up. I expect he wants me to help him fight my oaf of a brother – and I will, but just not yet. As much as I'd like to see my brother choke, I have more important things on my mind at the moment."

"Like what?" said Kurara.

"I'm so glad you asked me that, my dear shikigami!" Tsukimi's face lit up. "You see, we have a common goal."

"No, we don't!"

"Ah, but we do, my dear. The Star Seed!"

Kurara froze. "How do you know about the Star Seed?"

Princess Tsukimi's smile morphed into a smirk. "I paid a certain Grave-keeper a visit. Honestly, I wasn't very impressed with Oda. In the end, she had a few interesting tales, but that's all."

Something about the way Tsukimi spoke about the Grave-keeper struck Kurara. She remembered Mana mentioning Oda's death.

"You killed Grave-keeper Oda." So the princess was the reason why Mana was slowly losing its mind.

Tsukimi's smile was unshakeable. "There's no use

worrying about a dead woman. Let's talk about how we can make the Star Seed bloom, shall we?"

Kurara could only stare at the princess. Why would Tsukimi want that? The Star Seed would give shikigami their freedom. Wasn't that the opposite of what the princess wanted?

Sensing her confusion, Tsukimi continued, "I often asked myself why normal people cannot bond with shikigami. A shikigami is the soul of a dead Crafter tied to ashes and trapped within a ball of paper. The dead need a link to the living. They need the blood of a living Crafter … but I'm alive too. Why is *my* blood not good enough?" There was a note of bitterness in her voice.

Oh boo-hoo, Kurara wanted to say. *So you can't force a shikigami to obey you. So what?*

"The Star Tree is special though!" said Tsukimi. "Its sap does exactly what the blood of a living Crafter does. Even if the Tree is cut down, the sap still works. If I can combine my blood with the sap, perhaps I can control shikigami. After so many years, I might finally get the one thing I want – the very thing I *deserve*: my own shikigami!"

Kurara would have punched the woman if she wasn't so sure that Tsukimi would shove her fist through Kurara's chest and rip out her core if she tried. Of course, the princess did not want the Star Seed to bloom because she cared about the freedom of others. Tsukimi never did anything unless it was for herself.

"And if you're wrong – and combining your blood with the sap doesn't let you control a shikigami?" asked Haru.

Tsukimi's eyes glittered darkly in the shadows cast by

the crackling flames of their home. "We can cross that bridge when we get there."

Kurara scoffed. "You'd chop down the Star Tree, wouldn't you? If your experiments with the sap don't give you what you want, then the Star Tree is a failure – and you get rid of failures."

The princess said nothing, but her smile was as sharp as a blade.

SEVENTEEN

PRINCESS Tsukimi sighed. "I suppose it was foolish to expect a creature like you to understand. You do not *negotiate* with a dog; you train it to obey."

Kurara opened her mouth when Ruki suddenly lunged at her.

"Rara!" Haru shoved her out of the way.

As they slammed into the ground, Princess Tsukimi shot an arrow at their feet. Kurara barely managed to roll out of the way when Ruki lunged at her again. The tiger opened its jaws wide, as if to swallow her, but instead Ruki snagged the back of Kurara's clothes in its mouth and hauled her off her feet.

"Rara!" Haru tried to jump after her only to end up crumpled on the ground, clutching his chest tight.

"Haru! Are you all right? Is it your core?" Kurara

struggled, but she could not worm free from the tiger's grip.

"Oh my, is there something wrong?" Tsukimi gave a shrill laugh as she towered over Haru, who lay curled up on the ground.

Kurara's paper fingers sharpened like knives, cutting through the back of her kimono. She hit the ground with a heavy thump and rolled out of the way of Ruki's paw as it came crashing down.

Princess Tsukimi prepared to fire again. Her arrows were strange, and unlike anything Kurara had seen before. A small tube was attached to the shafts, likely filled with gunpowder, with a small strip of ignition paper, which, if pulled, would create a spark that slowly travelled up the tube to the gunpowder inside.

When Tsukimi fired, the arrow hit the ground in a burst of flames. "Come now," she said. "Is it wise to keep fighting me? One stray little ember and the both of you will be nothing but cinders."

Fire spread across the grass at an alarming speed, torching the trees and bushes around them. Kurara jumped to her feet and hauled Haru up. They had to get out of here.

"Rara, stop!" With a pained shout, Haru fell to his knees again, breathing heavily.

"Is it the yuurei?"

"I feel them … all shouting. It's like they're pushing at the walls of my core trying to make room!"

Kurara sucked in a sharp breath. Haru's situation was worse than she had thought.

Princess Tsukimi made her way towards them, through the blazing grass.

"Why can't you leave us alone?" Kurara snapped. "Your brother is waging war across the country, and you have time to waste on us? Go and fight him instead!"

"Oh, I will. I won't just fight him. I'll kill him, and then my father too. But first I will make the Star Seed bloom and obtain a shikigami of my own." Tsukimi leered at her. "And you and the boy will be the first of your kind that I bring under my control. It wouldn't do to have anything but the most extraordinary shikigami serving me, after all."

"Our lives are not something for you to toy with!" Kurara screamed. "The Star Seed is not yours!"

"STAR SEED?"

A voice rang through Kurara's head with such force she thought her skull might split open. She clapped her hands over her ears, as if that might block out the sound. That voice … it was not Ruki. But, if it wasn't Ruki, that could only mean one thing.

There was another shikigami nearby. But where was it? Kurara scanned the clearing, yet all she could see was their burning house and the dried-up pond.

The folk here say there's a God living inside there, Kurara remembered the villager mentioning as she and Haru left. *And that if you listen closely you can hear a voice whispering.*

The voice sounded like the one she had heard at the foot of the mountain, the one that had been singing the lullaby.

The ground shifted. Tremors shook the land, dislodging large boulders from the mountainside. The earth swelled beneath her feet, lifting Kurara and the others into the air. Rivers of soil cascaded off its body as a giant paper toad rose from the depths of the earth.

"*WHERE IS THE STAR SEED?*" The toad's eyes swivelled around in its paper sockets, its gaze coming to rest squarely on Kurara.

"Holy skies!" Kurara struggled to keep her balance on the shikigami's mud-caked back. Haru had to grab her to keep her from falling off.

A hint of recognition lit up the toad's paper eyes. "*AKI.*" It leaned its humongous body forward, lowering its head as far as it could without grazing the ground. "*THERE YOU ARE, YOU LITTLE TRAITOR.*"

EIGHTEEN

HIMURA wondered what Kurara and Haru would find in the ruins of their home. He wondered if they would return by sundown, triumphant and with the solution to making the Star Seed bloom. In truth, he would have liked to have gone with them, but he knew that Kurara had wanted to be alone with Haru and he was gracious enough to know when to take a step back. This was their home, after all. Who was he to interfere with that?

Instead, he remained in the village, busying himself with mending a tear in his knapsack and gathering supplies. He tried not to think about his conversation with Haru the night before or the thin cut on Haru's core, the peeling paper that threatened to grow into a crack. Perhaps it was good that he had decided not to accompany them to the mountain after all. Himura did not know how he was going to keep this from Kurara.

He was just about done repacking everything into his knapsack when he noticed that his sleeve felt suspiciously light. At some point during the day, Mana had disappeared without telling him.

"Mana?" He stood up and slipped out of the main hall.

The village was quiet. Perhaps too quiet even for Himura, who had never dreamed he would miss the rowdy hallways and gossiping crew of the *Orihime*.

"Mana!" he shouted as he made his way down the village steps and towards the fields. "Mana, where are you?"

"Oh, stop your hollering! Here I am!"

Himura turned to find the snake resting near the muddy rice paddies outside the village.

"What are you doing here?" he asked.

"Hmph! Can I never get away from you? Must you always cling to me like a baby?" Mana flicked its tongue at him in a rude gesture.

Himura's face fell. "What's the matter? Is something wrong?"

"'Is something wrong?' he says!" the snake sneered. Something *was* wrong. It was not like Mana to speak so scornfully. The shikigami was harsh, yes, with a wicked sense of humour, but never cruel.

"Is it the bond? Or rather, the lack of a bond? Do you feel your mind slipping? I'm happy to—"

"How many times must I say that I do not want a bond with you!"

Himura's cheeks flushed with anger. Why was the snake still refusing him? He was just trying to help. "Is it the bond as a whole that you object to, or is it just *me*?" Would Mana be happy bonding with another Crafter? With someone who wasn't Himura? Someone who had not sent their first shikigami into the flames?

"This is not about you. I told you, I never wanted a bond with anyone," said the snake tersely. *"If I lose my mind, then so be it. At least it will be my own choice. At least it will be honest. I want something honest."*

Himura didn't understand what the shikigami meant. A bond would save Mana. As a friend, shouldn't he intervene when he saw someone he cared about driving themselves towards destruction? His hand itched with the desire to hold the snake down and cut it open, to reach inside Mana and force his blood onto its core. If Mana lost itself, and he could have done something to save it, he would hate himself for the rest of his life.

But… He wavered. Wasn't there dignity in choosing one's own end? Who was he to take that away from Mana?

As Himura stood mired in his own thoughts, a sudden tremor shook the ground beneath his feet. An earthquake? In the fields, the villagers stopped tending to their crops and looked up. The ground shook again, stronger than before. Himura glanced at the Mountain of the Falling Star. Something was … rising from beneath the mountain slope.

The next thing he knew there was a giant *boom* and the sound of something crashing to the ground. A massive cloud of dust rolled towards the village like an oncoming tide.

The villagers' yells turned to screams as a sudden darkness swept over the land. Yuurei? No, this was different. Himura whipped around just in time to see a giant paper toad launch itself into the air.

"What in the seven hells?" Mana voiced exactly what Himura was thinking.

The toad was mountainous. It could easily flatten the entire village in a single leap, and it was coming this way.

"Run!" Himura shouted.

The villagers did not need telling twice. They dropped their tools and scattered into the forest.

The sensible thing to do was to flee with them, but instead Himura pulled his bracelet from his wrist and unravelled his ofuda, forming a large paper falcon. The toad had emerged from the mountain, and he had an awful feeling that meant Kurara and Haru were involved.

Mana darted up his leg and into his sleeve as Himura mounted the falcon and flew towards the shikigami.

"STAR SEED! WHERE IS THE STAR SEED!" the toad bellowed.

Its voice was so loud Himura almost lost control of his ofuda. Concentrating on keeping the falcon together, as he drew closer, he noticed a woman and a tiger shikigami standing on the toad's back, next to Kurara and Haru.

"Magnificent!" Himura heard the woman shout. "I can't believe a creature like you was sleeping under the earth all this time!"

Was that Princess Tsukimi? A quiet curse slipped out from between Himura's lips. He should have known that *she* was going to turn up at some point. The princess was not the kind of woman who would just give up and die quietly in a corner. Tsukimi was a hurricane in human form, promising destruction to all those who came into contact with her.

"Himura!" Haru waved to him, beckoning him to bring the falcon closer.

Tucking the bird's wings in tight, Himura dived towards

the toad's back. "Can you jump?" He stretched out his hand.

With a running leap, Haru dived across the space between the toad and the paper falcon. Himura caught him and pulled him up, his arm straining under Haru's weight.

The movement caught Tsukimi's attention. "Not so fast!" she shouted as Himura reached for Kurara next.

The princess pulled her bowstring back and shot right at him, the arrow igniting as it flew through the air.

Himura yanked the falcon out of the way to avoid the flames. Haru clung to the wing, screaming as he held on tight.

"Where in the seven hells did that shikigami come from?" Himura yelled.

"Underground!" cried Haru. "It was buried beneath the mountain and the princess woke it up!"

"STAR SEED! WHERE IS THE STAR SEED?" The toad pounded its feet against the ground like a toddler demanding something sweet. The earth around it shook and cracked under the pressure, causing large chasms to open up beneath its body.

The princess fired another arrow and a small explosion erupted across the shikigami's back. The toad reared back in pain as the flames burned a small hole in its back, but it was covered in so much mud that the fire quickly died out without spreading to the rest of its body.

Enraged, the toad jumped through the air. Himura swerved out of the way as it landed in the forest, crushing several miles' worth of trees. Kurara and the princess could only hold on for dear life as the shikigami shook itself again and leapt away.

Interlude

What is done is done
And with your empty hands
You learn to build boats

– from *Conversations with Yōkai*
(banned by the Patriots Office)

Stowing away on the back of a ship was not as exciting or glamorous as Tomoe had thought. Despite the stories of plucky young heroes sneaking onto airships in search of a better life in the sky, it turned out that stowing away consisted mainly of hiding, sitting in the dark, hiding, pilfering scraps of food and hiding some more.

Within days of setting sail, it became clear to Tomoe that they could not remain in the storage room. There were just too many people popping in and out for things, too many people moving crates about and reorganizing the shelves, each time coming dangerously close to their hiding spot.

They needed to be somewhere safer.

"The engine room, really?" Sayo curled a hand over the metal railing, assessing their new surroundings with a critical eye.

"What's wrong with it?" asked Tomoe. She had led them through the vents, down to the bottom of the ship on purpose. The air stank of levistone and machine oil, but there were plenty of nooks and crannies to hide in and the sound of the churning engines would drown out any noise they made. It was an ideal spot. If only Sayo could appreciate her brilliance.

"It's loud. How am I supposed to get any rest? And what about food?" Sayo grumbled.

They were standing on one of the metal walkways hanging above the engine room floor. The boilers below gurgled louder, like children clamouring for attention.

"We can still make trips to the storage room. But this place is far more private. There's less risk we'll be discovered here. We won't have to hide every ten minutes."

As if the universe was conspiring to prove her wrong, the morning bell rang, and a gangly boy with messy brown hair burst into the room and made his way across the main floor. Sayo grabbed Tomoe, pushing her onto her stomach so that they were both lying flat against the walkway. The cold metal pressed against Tomoe's skin as she peered over the edge.

The boy was worryingly young for someone serving aboard a Sohma ship heading for a war zone. He looked like one strong gust of wind could knock him off his feet. Tomoe hated the idea that her father might have had anything to do with his recruitment.

She watched as the boy started off the morning by pulling the large pipe from a hatch in the floor and siphoning fuel into the engines.

No, you're doing it wrong! Tomoe wanted to shout. He wasn't paying attention to the pressure dials or the gauges. Couldn't he hear the pipes gurgling in protest? The levistone was being pumped too quickly, putting too much strain on the boilers. If she had to endure this for much longer, she would jump down there and show him how it was done.

Fortunately, the engine room door opened before she could do anything stupid, and a burly man almost twice the boy's size marched inside, frowning as he passed the boilers.

"Hey, boy, where are last night's cylinders?"

"By the machine." The boy scrambled to hand them over.

"Is this all?" The man took them, unimpressed. "Rei won't be happy with this."

"Well, I–I..." the boy stuttered, his eyes widening with the kind of fear Tomoe recognized all too well. She was not surprised to hear that her father was around – they were heading to war; there was no way he would sit this one out. Knowing that he was close, that they were on the same ship, however, made her uneasy, like someone who knows there's a viper waiting for them in the grass.

"Do double the amount tonight." The man turned around and slammed the door shut.

The boy's sigh was just audible over the thrashing engines. He left the boilers and headed to the other end of the engine room, where several large tables stood covered in sheets of metal. The boy picked up a piece and fed it into

a strange machine lying next to the tables and turned the crank. A loud gurgling sound escaped the machine as it took the metal sheet and spat out what looked like a perfectly shaped soup can.

What in the bloody skies was he doing? Was the boy really spending his time making empty cans? Curious, Tomoe crawled closer to the edge for a better look, but as she shimmied closer, the end of her braid caught on the metal walkway, tugging sharply at her scalp. A yelp of pain escaped her lips.

"Who's there?" The boy looked up.

Before Tomoe could so much as squeak, Sayo grabbed her by the shoulders, dragging her away from the edge. They lay there, perfectly still, listening to the sounds below.

After a beat, Tomoe heard the creak of the hand-crank turning again, the clang as another cylinder dropped onto the ground next to the machine. After about three cylinders hit the ground, the boy turned to leave, his footsteps echoing against the floor. A moment later, the door opened then slammed shut.

The sound of gurgling boilers resounded through the empty engine room.

Tomoe sat up.

"That was close!" She freed her hair from where it had snagged against metal. "Oh no, my hair!" She grimaced as a few strands came loose from her scalp.

"You're being dramatic. Your hair is fine!" Sayo scowled.

"Really? You mean it? How does it look?" Tomoe turned her head this way and that so her braid swished through the air.

"Same as it always looks." Sayo reached out to brush a few strands from Tomoe's face.

Tomoe caught Sayo's hand with a huff. She wasn't fishing for praise – OK, maybe she was a little – but would it kill Sayo to give her a proper compliment every once in a while? She had smuggled them on board the ship, she had found a way to sneak into the engine room. She deserved a little credit.

"Anyway, I thought you said this place would be safer!" said Sayo.

"It is! The walkway is only used when something goes wrong with the pipes crawling up the walls, and that's rare. People don't usually come up here."

"I do." The boy appeared behind them, from a door she had not noticed. "I come up here all the time."

Tomoe shrieked.

The boy gave an awkward cough, as if he was embarrassed to have surprised them. Instead of attacking them or alerting his crewmates, as one would normally do, he gave a stiff bow. "Hello. How do you do? I'm Shuichi. Kazeno Shuichi."

Well, this was unexpected.

Tomoe and Sayo exchanged confused glances. Did the boy not realize that they were stowaways?

"Sorano Sayo," Sayo said with a grunt. Her hands were curled into fists, ready to throw a punch at any moment.

"Don't mind her," said Tomoe hastily. "She always makes that face. Kazeno Shuichi, was it? That's my city name too, because, you know, I'm also from Sola-Re…" She floundered. As if the boy didn't know that Sorabito names were based on the city they were born in. "I'm Kazeno Tomoe."

The boy – Shuichi – smiled weakly.

"So why did you decide to sneak aboard the *Kujiraza*? You do know where we're going, don't you?"

Sayo tensed, ready to pounce.

"I, uh…" Tomoe blinked. She was prepared for hostility, she was prepared for suspicion, but she didn't know what to do when faced with the boy's open curiosity. So he knew they were not meant to be here, but he had not reported them yet. She could work with this. There were ways to buy the boy's silence.

"Find the vein and stab deep." Her father's voice floated to the top of her mind. It was one of the first things he had ever taught her: when you knew what someone cared about, you had a way to influence and control them.

Tomoe just had to find Shuichi's vein.

"Well, we… We want to fight! Sohma said we were too inexperienced to join the crew, but what we lack in knowledge we make up for in enthusiasm. We want to, you know, crush groundling worms, feed their bones to the dogs, spit in their general direction!"

"Oh." Shuichi's reply was less enthusiastic than she had expected.

"Don't you want the same thing? Aren't you a member of Sohma?" Sayo asked.

The boy flinched. "I care about the sky cities and our people. I want to fight for the glory of the Sorabito."

It was a nothing answer that avoided the real question, but that told Tomoe just as much about Shuichi as a proper answer would. The boy had opinions and loyalties of his

own, and they did not appear to be wholly with Sohma.

Interesting. Tomoe gave him another once-over, taking in the boy's scrawny form.

"And why are you stuck down here by yourself, shovelling levistone and making these ... soup cans?" she wondered.

Shuichi flushed. "The cylinders aren't for soup."

"They do look important," said Tomoe, partly to soothe the boy's pride, but partly because she remembered the other man shouting at Shuichi to hurry up. Surely, no one could get that angry over regular soup cans. They were obviously important.

Find the vein and stab deep.

"Let's make a deal." She stood a little straighter. "I used to work in engine rooms. I can monitor the boilers for you so that you can focus on these cans. In return, you have to keep us a secret."

The boy's eyes darted to the work he had yet to do. Tomoe could tell that his mind was made up before he even opened his mouth.

"Deal."

NINETEEN

THE giant toad continued to hop through the forest, crushing everything in its path. Each leap took Kurara further and further away from the Mountain of the Falling Star, and from Haru and Himura, who had long since fallen behind. Though the toad was not completely mad, Kurara didn't think it was totally sane either. Its mind seemed to flicker in and out of awareness, one minute completely forgetting that Kurara and the others were there before remembering and screaming.

Kurara glanced back at the trail of destruction it had left in its wake – at the dead animals and broken homes of what had once been a village, at the flattened trees and crushed earth. If she flew away now, she might be able to make it back to Haru. She could not leave him with Himura, not when there could be problems with his core. She should jump now.

But the toad knew her. The last shikigami that had known her had been Suzaku. Had she done something terrible to this shikigami too?

"Well, this is quite fascinating! I rarely meet shikigami as large as this one!" Tsukimi marvelled as she moved closer to the toad's head.

"TRAITOR! COWARD!" The toad lashed its tongue at them.

Kurara ducked behind one of the shikigami's warts. "Who are you?" she cried. "What do you want?"

The toad did not reply.

"Hey, can you hear me? Can you tell me your name?" Kurara tried again, lowering her voice to sound as soft and gentle as possible.

"ENTEI." The shikigami's voice rumbled through her head like a thunderstorm.

"My name is Kurara."

"NO LYING! I REMEMBER YOU, AKI!" Entei roared. *"WHERE IS THE STAR SEED?"*

"You remember me? What did I do?"

"THE STAR SEED WAS MEANT TO GIVE US OUR FREEDOM. DURING THE WAR, YOU SAID YOU WOULD HELP ME! BUT INSTEAD YOU HID THE STAR SEED AND DISAPPEARED! YOU WASTED ALL OF OUR TIME AND NOW MY MIND IS SLIPPING—"

The toad cut itself off as if it had forgotten she was there again. Kurara had no idea how many years Entei had spent underground, lying in the darkness as it tried its best to preserve its mind, but being out in the world again, speaking with people, was clearly having an ill-effect on its sanity.

"It's all your fault!" Suzaku screeched inside her mind.

Guilt was a familiar beast. Aki had hidden the Star Seed inside Suzaku and run away. How many shikigami had lost their minds because of that? How many had been killed by hunters while they waited for freedom? And how many more would suffer while she failed to make the Star Seed bloom?

"I'm sorry!" she cried. "But I know how to make the Star Seed bloom now. You can have your freedom. It's not too late. We can stop and talk about this!"

Like a wind-up toy marching forth on rusted gears, the toad made a displeased sound and continued to hop onwards. Had it even heard her? Could it still make sense of the words coming from her mouth?

"Do you really know how to make the Star Seed bloom?" said Princess Tsukimi.

"Of course I do!" She balled her hands into fists.

A dying star fell from the heavens, and from that star grew a tree. The Star Seed would fall from the heavens and bloom.

"Then why haven't you done anything yet? Is it because you don't have the guts for it? Are you afraid?"

Kurara gave her a puzzled look. Why would she be afraid of making the Star Seed bloom?

Sensing her confusion, Tsukimi's lips slid into a smirk. "You *don't* know how to make it bloom."

"I do!"

"No, you *think* you do, but you don't."

Kurara glowered at the princess. She should not believe Tsukimi's lies. The princess was just trying to unsettle her.

"'A dying star fell from the heavens, and from that star

grew a tree.' The answer is in the lullaby. *That* is how you make a Star Seed bloom. It has to fall from the heavens."

Laughter burst from Tsukimi's throat. When she looked at Kurara, it was with a smug, haughty expression that Kurara wanted to punch right off the princess's face.

She seethed. How humiliating it was that Princess Tsukimi might know things that she didn't. It wasn't fair! After all, *she* was a shikigami, not Tsukimi. This concerned *her* people.

"You really don't know anything, my little shikigami," the princess said. "The fall doesn't matter. Only one thing does. Nothing is gained without sacrifice."

What does that mean? Kurara wanted to snap, but Ruki's warning growl alerted them of just how far Entei had carried them.

They were no longer in the forest. The toad hopped over fields and large swathes of wetland, covering miles within a single leap. On the horizon lay a glittering line of dark blue water, stretching beyond a strip of golden sand. Directly ahead of them stood a city, sprawled along the edge of the shore like pebbles scattered across the beach.

Entei continued forward, heading directly towards it. At this rate, it was going to barrel straight through the city, flattening whatever and whoever got in the way before crashing right into the sea.

"Ah, that's Crescent Bay. Beautiful place. A shame we're about to flatten it," said Tsukimi.

Kurara raced to the top of the toad's head. "Stop! Don't go that way!"

The shikigami didn't respond.

With trembling fingers, Kurara pulled the Star Seed from the folds of her clothes. "Look! I have the Star Seed right here! If you stop, I'll give it to you!" she lied as she waved the seed in the air, right between the toad's eyes.

Still Entei said nothing. They were already close enough to the city that every time the toad leapt, tremors vibrated all the way to the stone walls. Distant alarm bells rang through the streets. At the very least, no one could be caught off-guard by the massive shikigami barrelling its way towards them.

This was why normal people feared shikigami. Why the Crafters of old had thought of shikigami as such effective weapons. With one step of its massive webbed feet, it could crush a dozen men. Roads would crack beneath it. Buildings would fall. Lives would be ruined.

"Entei?" shouted Kurara. "Can you hear me? Snap out of it!"

"Enough! You're only wasting your time on this beast." Princess Tsukimi drew an arrow from her quiver, pulled back the string of her bow and aimed the shot for the space right between the toad's eyes.

Once again, the flames did not catch hold and were quickly extinguished by the wind, but the toad screamed and leapt even higher, landing with a massive thud that caused the surrounding land to crumble and split into chasms. Ruki hissed as the impact sent them lurching into the air for just a moment until gravity slammed them back down against the toad's body.

"Stop that! You're not helping!" Kurara staggered to her feet.

"Stop? Why, I've not had this much fun in years!"

Princess Tsukimi reached behind her back to draw another arrow from her quiver.

With a flick of her fingers, Kurara sent a piece of sharpened ofuda flying towards the princess. Ruki moved to block her, but the piece of paper swerved around the tiger and cut through the straps of Tsukimi's quiver. Arrows spilled out of the case, rolling down the toad's back and clattering to the ground far below.

Princess Tsukimi's expression darkened, but before Kurara could find out what the princess would do to her, Entei crashed through the city walls and all hell broke loose.

TWENTY

FROM the top of Entei's head, Kurara had a perfect view of the destruction below. The toad flattened shops and homes, crushed animals and people beneath its webbed feet. The city was not prepared to deal with a wild shikigami, especially not one this size. Entei paid no attention to the pots and pans hurled at its back or the bullets shot into its side.

"Stop!" Kurara screamed. She could not bring herself to look down at the broken streets any more, at the people left crushed against the road.

"You shouldn't have taken my arrows. Now look what you've done!" Princess Tsukimi shook her head as the toad barrelled onwards, straight through the very middle of the city.

Kurara glowered at her, even though she knew the princess was right. There was only so much her ofuda could do against a shikigami of Entei's size. What she really needed was fire and a lot of it, like the gunpowder arrows she had cut from Tsukimi's back.

By the time Entei reached the harbour, the workers and sailors had fled, leaving their catches to be crushed into a fine pink paste.

"There is no stopping it! Let it run itself into the sea!" Ruki growled as Entei shouldered its way through a line of warehouses, knocking them to the ground.

Kurara was not sure whether that would do any good. If Entei rammed into the water, it could cause a tsunami that would claim even more lives.

There was nothing for it. Holding the Star Seed high above her head, Kurara used her ofuda to pull herself onto the roof of the nearest building. She wasn't even sure this plan would work – it had not worked when she had tried it earlier – but she could not think of anything else to do. If she could just lead the toad away from the city, at least she could save some lives.

"Entei! Look, I have the Star Seed! This is what you want, isn't it? Well, come and get it!" she hollered.

This time, the toad took notice and turned its broad head towards her.

"GIVE ME THE STAR SEED!" Entei thrashed back and forth with such violence, Tsukimi and Ruki were flung to the ground. The tiger caught Tsukimi as she fell, saving her from becoming a bloody splatter on the floor.

Tsukimi howled with laughter as she landed on Ruki's back.

"Oh, this is fun, isn't it?" she cried as Entei's tongue

lashed out from its open mouth, striking the ground in front of Tsukimi's feet and almost flattening her like a fly. Still, she shrieked with joy, as if she were a child playing a game of catch.

Kurara was so distracted by the princess she didn't notice Entei's tongue hitting the building that she was standing on until the ground was suddenly knocked out from under her feet.

She had not been ready for that. As the building came down, Kurara barely had time to cushion her fall, using the ofuda in her arm to create an inflatable mat to catch herself. Haru's journal slipped free from the paper rope that kept it tied to her obi. It tumbled across the broken ground and landed in front of Tsukimi.

"Give that back!" Kurara staggered to her feet as Tsukimi scooped it up. That was Haru's. The princess had already burned his home down – what more did she want to take from him? Tsukimi smiled like a snake slowly coiling its way around Kurara's throat. When she opened the journal and flicked through the first few pages, that smile only widened.

"I'm surprised," said Tsukimi. "You don't know how to make the Star Seed bloom, and yet the answers are right here. On the first page."

"What?" Kurara sucked in a sharp breath. She had already read the first few pages of the journal and found nothing useful. Was Tsukimi just messing with her? Or had there been something she had overlooked?

There was no time for an explanation. Entei lifted one webbed foot over their heads and tried to crush them all like ants. Kurara and the others scrambled out of the way, but the aftershocks of the impact rippled through their bodies, making Kurara's teeth rattle.

Without warning, a high-pitched whistle screamed through the air, and something struck the toad's side and burst into flames.

"Keep shooting!" someone yelled.

A squad of military police rushed towards them.

"Wait!" Kurara's cry was drowned out by the sound of a dozen hand-held cannons going off at once. Flames burst to life across the toad's warty hide, eating into its back, its legs, its broad face.

"Kill it!" the men screamed, and Kurara could only stare, helpless, as they opened fire once again.

Should she stand back and let the soldiers burn Entei to cinders? It had killed so many people, but it didn't really know what it was doing. It was not the shikigami's fault that it was losing its mind.

With a shriek, Entei reared onto its back legs and dived into the water. The sea rose in response, a tidal wave cresting over the harbour towards them. Ruki snatched the princess up just in time and jumped to safer ground. Seconds later, the water swept over Kurara. She tumbled through the flood, head over heels, her hands flailing for something, anything, to stop her being dragged out to sea. One hand held the Star Seed close to her chest; the other found the edge of a broken wall and she held on tight until the water receded, leaving her shocked and spluttering.

The military police were nowhere to be found. Perhaps they had drowned and their bodies had been pulled by the current into deeper water. Maybe they had been knocked back into the rubble. Either way, they had not stopped Entei. Just when Kurara thought the toad was gone, its head broke the sea's surface and it clambered back onto the harbour again.

Both the fire and water had significantly weakened it, yet the toad's sheer size still made it a threat.

"GIVE ME THE STAR SEED!" The pain seemed to have lifted the fog from its mind. Entei's eyes were clearer than before; its voice was stronger and more alert.

"I grow tired of this noisy beast." Tsukimi picked up a hand cannon that had not been swept away by the waves and pointed it at Entei.

The toad screamed at her, lashing its tongue in her direction with surprising speed.

Tsukimi pulled the trigger, but the gunpower had been too damaged by the water to ignite. What should have caused an explosion to the toad's face burst into nothing more than a few pitiful sparks.

"Princess!" Ruki shouted as Entei's tongue wrapped around Tsukimi and yanked her away.

The princess only had time to give an outraged shout before she was pulled into Entei's mouth and swallowed whole.

Kurara's breath stopped dead in her throat.

She could not believe her eyes. Princess Tsukimi had been … eaten!

Most shikigami were hollow on the inside, though. It was likely Tsukimi was still alive in Entei's belly. Kurara didn't know if that was a good thing or not. As long as the princess was alive, she would continue to hunt Kurara and

Haru down. She would never let the shikigami have their freedom.

A shout pulled her attention towards the main road. Another group of furious men were making their way towards the harbour, weapons in hand.

"Seize her! She's the Crafter that did this!" the military police shouted as they charged at Kurara.

Entei roared at the police until they began shooting. At the first sign of fire, the toad took fright and ran. In a single bound, it leapt over their heads, its body flying clear above the roofs of the few buildings that remained.

"Wait!" Kurara staggered to her feet.

"Hands in the air! Don't move! You're under arrest!" the men yelled.

Kurara could only watch as Entei disappeared towards the horizon, carrying Princess Tsukimi away with it.

Go after them! Go after them now! a voice in her head urged, but she was surrounded by military police pointing their guns at her. She could not fight them off without causing more harm, and there was no way she could catch up to Entei on her own either. Even Himura, riding his paper falcon, had not been able to keep up with Entei's strides.

Seven hells, what about Haru and Himura? Where were they now?

Reluctantly, Kurara slipped the Star Seed into her obi and raised her hands above her head. The smell of death was already thick in the air. Sirens echoed in the distance between the wails of young children and the screams that still rang through the city, each one like a knife between Kurara's ribs.

TWENTY-ONE

RUKI snapped at the men when they tried to get close. Its hackles were raised, almost daring them to come any nearer.

"Order your shikigami to stand down!" the police cried.

Ruki isn't my shikigami. Kurara pursed her lips. She knew they would not listen, no matter what she said.

The military police were armed with hand cannons – the same type they'd used to try and set Entei on fire – and Kurara did not want to see another shikigami burn. She hurriedly pressed a hand against Ruki's trunk-like legs, leaning in to whisper, "Calm down. These people will burn you if you don't do as they say. Just come with me; I'll get you out of this mess."

The tiger seemed to understand that it would not get far by running away now. The police were so spooked, all it would take was one wrong twitch and they would open fire.

Once Ruki backed down, one of the men grabbed Kurara's wrists and bound her hands together with rope.

There was no point trying to argue her innocence. Everyone had seen her and Tsukimi riding on top of Entei's head. Whether the police had recognized Tsukimi, Kurara did not know. Not that it mattered anyway – the men had someone they could blame for the destruction they had witnessed.

Without another word, the police dragged them back through the city to the remains of their military headquarters – or at least to what Kurara assumed had once been their headquarters. Everything except the support pillars had been blown away by Entei, leaving only a metal hatch leading down to the underground prison intact.

Someone shoved Kurara through the hatch. She struggled down the stone steps leading into a small underground cavern filled with iron cells. The prison looked more like a dungeon than a jail; a single burning torch flickered against the grey stone walls.

There were no other prisoners, yet the military police stuffed both Kurara and Ruki into the same cell with barely enough room to lie down.

"Hand over your ofuda." An officer stuck his hand out towards Kurara.

"You want my arm?" Kurara's hands were bound behind her back. She turned around and wriggled her paper fingers. She could just hear the jokes Haru and Tomoe would make if they could only see her now. Something about lending the officer a *hand* or being dis*armed* by the military police.

The officer paled at the sight. He needed to take away her

147

"weapon", but obviously did not want to carry away a human arm, even if it was made of paper.

With a sigh, Kurara let her left arm crumble away into dozens of tiny paper squares. The ropes slid off and she kicked them away. Before the man could shoot, her ofuda folded together into a small braided bracelet.

"Here. Does this make you feel better?" she spat as she dropped it into the officer's hand.

Without so much as a thank you, the man slammed the metal door shut and marched back upstairs, leaving her with only Ruki for company.

As soon as he was gone, she turned and punched the stone wall with her remaining arm. The pain that shot through her knuckles was a welcome distraction from the riot inside her mind.

She didn't care that the military police had taken away her ofuda – that didn't matter when she was made of paper. No, what bothered her was everything that had happened before she had been locked up. Everything was going wrong. The yuurei in Haru's core. Princess Tsukimi's sudden appearance. Entei's rampage. It felt like there were a million fires burning all around her; a million emergencies pulling her in different directions all at once.

Her mind was a carousel whirling from one failure to the next.

She had released the yuurei from inside Suzaku – it was her fault they were now roaming the land and killing people.

She had failed to stop Haru from absorbing the yuurei at Zeka – it was her fault his core was peeling away.

She had not been able to stop Entei rampaging through

the city – it was her fault that so many people were dead.

For all the time and effort she had spent travelling across the country, she had done nothing except release a bunch of yuurei into the world, damage Haru's core and watch as a giant toad crashed through a city. For all her good intentions, Kurara couldn't shake the feeling that all she had ever done was make things worse for other people.

"Damn it! Damn it all!" She pounded her fist against the wall again and again until at last she slid to the ground and curled into a ball, every tense muscle in her body sagging. Her only comfort was that she had managed to keep hold of the Star Seed, despite Princess Tsukimi's and Entei's attempts to take it from her.

Ruki knocked its tail against the iron bars of the door. The sound of ringing metal jolted her out of her thoughts.

Kurara glanced at the tiger, taking in its battered frame.

"Are you all right?"

The tiger didn't reply.

"You're not going to talk?"

"*Talking*," Ruki said slowly, "*makes my mind slip further. I am trying to hold myself together.*"

Kurara bit her lip. She could not believe she was about to suggest this.

"Himura is a Crafter. If we can make our way back to him, you could bond with him."

"*No*," said Ruki.

"Why not?"

"*Because I do not want another master, even though it means that I will eventually lose my mind. I want the freedom of having my own thoughts. The freedom to choose my own end.*"

That sounded a lot like something Mana would say. Kurara wondered how the snake was doing. If Himura had convinced Mana to bond with him.

"Can I at least fix those wounds?" Her eyes trailed over the countless gashes and rips all over Ruki's body. They would not heal without help.

There was a pause. After a moment, Ruki nodded. Kurara stepped forward, rolled up her empty sleeve and grabbed a handful of paper from the stump of her elbow. She laid the sheets over Ruki's side, covering the wounds. Drawing a deep, shuddering breath, she concentrated on merging her ofuda with the rest of the shikigami's body, stretching the paper around the wounds so it could cover the gaps. She knitted together Ruki's paper fur to form long, puckered scars. It was not the prettiest work Kurara had done, but once she was finished, there were no holes or gashes left.

"What will you do now, Ruki?" she asked.

"I am … unsure what to do next. I made a deal with Princess Tsukimi to obey her orders. However, she left me no instructions about what to do if we were ever separated. She has never told me to go after her."

"Then you're free."

The tiger shook its head, as if the thought of freedom was too strange to consider. *"Perhaps I shall find somewhere quiet where no one will bother me. But what about you? What will you do?"*

"I'm…" Kurara cut herself off.

What was she going to do?

Entei had carried her far away from Haru and Himura.

She had to go back for them. What if the condition of Haru's core worsened and she wasn't there to help him?

But the things Princess Tsukimi had said bothered her. Kurara thought she knew how to make the Star Seed bloom now, but Tsukimi had sown doubts into her mind.

"The fall doesn't matter. Only one thing does. Nothing is gained without sacrifice," the princess had said. What had she meant by that? What about Haru's journal? Tsukimi had mentioned something about answers in the very first pages, but Kurara had read the first entries and she couldn't remember anything that might be useful.

Maybe the princess was just trying to mess with her. A dying star fell from the heavens, and from that star grew a tree – the answer was right there, in the lullaby. Kurara just had to get out, go back to the Mountain of the Falling Star and hurl the Star Seed off the highest peak.

Then the Star Seed would bloom.

Then the shikigami would be free.

Then Suzaku would stop visiting her dreams to tell her that everything she had done had only caused more pain.

Despite the depressing conditions of the jail cell, Kurara's spirits lifted.

Soon. Everything would be over soon.

TWENTY-TWO

HIMURA had long since lost sight of Kurara and the giant toad. No matter how fast he flew, he just could not keep up with the shikigami's massive strides. All he could do was follow the trail of broken forests and cracked earth the toad had left in its wake.

Would Kurara be all right fending off Tsukimi by herself? She was strong, but the princess was cunning. No one knew how to mess with your head better than the princess.

Then there was the matter of the toad. A wild shikigami complicated things. Who knew what it would do, or who it might attack?

"Why are we going down?" said Haru.

A curse escaped Himura's lips. He had not meant to descend. At some point, his thoughts had slipped, and the falcon had dipped close to the ground. Himura released a heavy breath and forced himself to concentrate.

The falcon surged forward with renewed strength, lifting higher into the sky, yet before it could reach the clouds, Mana suddenly shouted, *"Boy, watch your back!"*

Something hit the tail end of Himura's falcon. He whipped his head round as Haru and Mana both shouted in alarm.

The falcon was on fire.

"Someone shot us!" cried Haru.

There was no time to wonder who or why. Himura cursed as the fire spread across the paper falcon's back. Without a moment to lose, he lifted a foot and shunted Haru off the bird before the flames could reach him. Haru gave a yelp of surprise as he fell, but a few bruises and broken limbs were better than burning alive. Besides, he was a shikigami; he would survive the fall.

Himura had to save what little ofuda he had left. He brought the falcon low and then let it crumble beneath him. Mana shrieked, winding its coils around his arm and squeezing tight enough to numb his entire limb as they plunged through the air. Some of his ofuda was too burnt to save; Himura wrapped what little paper he had left around his body, forming a protective shell.

It was not enough to fully cushion their fall. He hit the ground with a sickening crunch, tumbling over protruding tree roots and rolling across the leaf-littered earth.

When he came to a stop, he lay there for a moment, winded, listening to the pounding rhythm of his heart. A line of paper lay strewn across the ground in his wake. He knew he should gather up his ofuda – a Crafter without paper might as well be stark naked – but he didn't think he could move right now.

Distantly, he heard Mana yell at him. *"Get up, boy! Get up!"*

The snake's voice was distorted, as if it was shouting at him from somewhere deep underwater.

"Himura!" Haru's voice joined in. Good, the boy was safe. *"For goodness' sake, open your eyes!"*

Himura had not realized he had closed his eyes until they snapped open. A loud, commanding voice sailed through the air. "Halt, Crafters! You're under arrest by order of His Imperial Highness the Lord Emperor!"

Himura looked up to see at least two dozen soldiers in black-and-gold military uniforms approaching them through the flattened forest of fallen trees.

"Rara and I passed those soldiers on our way to the mountain. They were looking for Princess Tsukimi," Haru whispered.

"Arrest? What for?" Himura forced himself to his feet. Mana circled around him, hissing at the soldiers.

"Do you think you can release a shikigami like that and not face consequences?" the officer in charge barked.

"What are you talking about? We have no control over what a wild shikigami does." Himura refused to be arrested over something so ridiculous.

"You say that it's a wild shikigami, but Princess Tsukimi was controlling it, wasn't she? We all saw her riding it."

"Then go and arrest Princess Tsukimi," said Himura. That was what the men had come for, wasn't it? Why were the soldiers bothering with a bunch of nobodies like them?

The officer drew his katana. "We have our orders to bring you in too."

Himura had met plenty of unreasonable soldiers before, but this was the first time he felt like punching someone. He didn't have time for this. With every second he wasted here, Kurara was being carried further and further away from him.

The sky was growing dark. As the sun dipped below the horizon, the gleaming light caught against the golden buttons on the soldiers' uniforms, making them glow like demons' eyes. Even in the darkness, Himura glimpsed a shifting shadow and his breath stopped short.

Yuurei. About three at a glance – but three were more than enough to completely destroy a small group of soldiers.

Before Himura could open his mouth to shout a warning, the yuurei attacked.

The first man was lucky, relatively; the yuurei touched his arm, leaving him alive but writhing on the ground in agony. Some were caught in the chest, but the yuurei missed their hearts. They screamed as they fell, curling into balls of pure pain and misery.

Others were not so fortunate. When the yuurei passed through them, they dropped to the ground, their mouths and eyes wide open as if they were surprised by their own deaths.

The soldiers were braver than most. Braver, and far better trained. Instead of panicking as Himura would have expected, the remaining men scattered so that the yuurei could not target them as a group. Some shot at the shadows with their hand cannons, but the bullets went straight through them and the flashes only served as a temporary distraction.

"*Why are you standing there like a lemon? Run!*" Mana shouted at Himura.

"But what about the yuurei?" cried Haru. "If we don't seal them…" He did not finish his sentence, but Himura knew what he wanted to say. If they did not seal the yuurei here, the shadows would drift through the land, wandering from place to place until they found someone or somewhere else to attack. They would hurt people. Kill people.

"If you do this, Kurara will kill you," Himura said. Who knew how many more yuurei Haru could seal inside his core before it cracked?

But … this was Haru's choice, and Himura would respect that. Even if it made him feel like he was stabbing himself with his own ofuda.

"It doesn't matter! I can't let the yuurei wander free!" Haru grabbed a fallen branch and began to carve the sealing circle into the earth. Then he stabbed the branch into the ground so that it stood upright in the middle of the circle and began to chant.

"All that lives shall die. As cicadas at the end of summer, as mayflies before the autumn moon, all that lives shall die. From this day forth, you will share my name. And I will welcome you inside." He used two stones to create a flame and set the branch alight.

At the sight of the fire, the yuurei turned their heads in unison and swooped towards it. The moment they entered the circle, Haru clapped his hands together. "May we be worthy of our name!"

A sharp wind lashed around the yuurei and a blinding light poured forth from the circle. A moment later, the yuurei were sucked into Haru's chest, into his core.

Seven hells, Kurara was going to kill them both.

"May you … be worthy…" Haru mumbled as he swayed back and forth. Himura darted forward, barely catching the boy as he fell.

"Freeze!"

A soldier held a katana to Himura's neck, pressing against his skin with just enough pressure to make a thin line of blood trickle down the edge of the blade.

Mana hissed at the officer, but the man did not back down. He lifted his weapon slowly, signalling to Himura that he should stand.

With Haru in his arms, Himura shakily rose to his feet. The other soldiers had their guns trained on him – a mixture of pistols and hand cannons that would no doubt blast him into oblivion should he try anything funny.

"We just saved you from the yuurei, and this is the thanks we get?" Himura eyed the soldiers coolly, though he doubted they even understood what had just happened. How dangerous the yuurei truly were. Or what Haru had done to protect them.

The officer bared his teeth at Himura. "If you don't want the boy to get hurt, you'll come quietly. We're taking you to Sola-Ea."

Interlude

You once said to me
Don't hurt yourself in wishing
For a better world
But then what shall I do with
These hands, these eyes, this bruised heart?

– from *A Prayer for a Blue Sky:*
Sorabito and Independence
(banned by the Patriots Office)

The deal with Shuichi was going well. In return for his silence, Tomoe and Sayo helped him with the engine room, feeding levistone into the boilers and keeping an eye on the pressure gauges, leaving him free to concentrate on making metal cylinders. So far, no one except Shuichi knew they had stowed away on the ship, and the *Kujiraza* was making excellent progress towards Sola-Ea. Tomoe tried her best to prise more information about the ship and the crew from the poor boy, but it quickly became clear

that he knew very little about what was actually going on around him.

"Has anyone told you what the cylinders are for?" Tomoe asked as Shuichi turned the hand-crank on the cylinder machine, which spat out another metal can.

"No, but I do know that they're important. After I make them, they go to someone else and get stuff added to them." Shuichi's voice was partially drowned out by the roar of the engines.

"What kind of stuff?"

The boy shrugged and turned the machine's crank again. Another cylinder hit the floor.

"Great, he doesn't know anything," Sayo muttered beneath her breath. "You know, when I imagined sneaking on board this ship, this is not what I thought we would be doing. Mindless busy-work."

"Don't think about that! Think about how every day brings us closer to Sola-Ea!" Tomoe happily piped levistone from a rusty old barrel into the boilers. There were more important things to worry about than what they were doing every day to buy Shuichi's silence. Things like the levistone cannon on Sola-Ea. Or the battle that would start the moment Sohma's ships reached the sky city.

Sayo muttered something beneath her breath.

"We should be grateful that we don't have to do anything worse than pumping levistone all day," said Tomoe. At least they no longer had to hide in a cramped storeroom. "Besides, are you saying my dazzling company isn't enough for you?"

Sayo gave Tomoe a playful shove, quickly looking away

to hide the jagged edge of her smile. Tomoe grinned back. It was usually so hard to get Sayo to smile, each one was an achievement.

Shuichi turned the crank. Another cylinder hit the floor.

"So you two know each other well?" he asked.

"Oh, we've known each other for *ages*! Right, Sayo? It's good to have someone you know watching your back. To, you know, help you kill the groundlings." Tomoe tried to recall the story she had given about wanting to fight for the Sohma cause and crush groundling worms.

Honestly, she was not sure Shuichi believed it. Or cared. It made Tomoe wonder what a boy who seemed to take no pleasure in the thought of killing groundlings was doing on a Sohma airship. He seemed so out of place among the burly numbskulls Tomoe usually pictured when she imagined Sohma rebels.

"So, why did you join Sohma?" she asked as the boy continued to turn the machine's crank.

"I mean, I guess I agree with some of the stuff Sohma says," said Shuichi, without looking at her. "But I don't care if you really want to kill as many groundling worms as you can, or if you're only here to hitch a ride to Sola-Ea. I just want to collect my pay and be done with things."

"We're flying into the middle of a war zone," said Sayo. This wasn't the kind of situation where one could, as Shuichi said, "be done with things".

"And people who pay the best during wartime are the ones with the armies!" cried Shuichi. "I don't know if you noticed, but levistone wasn't the only thing in short supply

on Sola-Re. There was hardly any food either. At least with Sohma, I get three square meals a day."

Tomoe had not noticed. For the brief time they were on Sola-Re, she had been so focused on finding levistone she had not paid much attention to anything else. No wonder Shuichi struck her as so odd – he didn't have the same passion as other Sohma rebels Tomoe had met during her lifetime. All the boy wanted was food and a wage, to keep his head down and work without having to think about right or wrong, or his place in the grand scheme of things.

She didn't know how she felt about that. Shuichi wasn't hurting anyone, but his lack of interest in anything outside of himself, his refusal to think about the war as something he was a part of, felt cowardly to her.

"Don't you believe in anything? Don't you want to take a stand?" At least when Sohma said that they were superior to groundlings, they truly believed it.

"I have parents to take care of. My family doesn't have much. I don't have the luxury of worrying about why we're at war, or who's right and who's wrong, or anything else," said Shuichi sourly.

Tomoe bristled. "Then the reason you don't know what the cylinders are for isn't because no one will tell you, but because you don't care to learn."

"It's not my place to know," said Shuichi.

"Spineless!" she snorted.

Shuichi shot her an offended look, but their argument was interrupted by the sound of echoing footsteps. Someone was approaching the engine room. Tomoe scrambled into

a dark corner with Sayo in tow, ducking behind a boiler just as the door swung open.

"Ah, Shuichi!"

Tomoe sucked in a sharp breath.

Kazeno Rei was a thin, unimpressive man with a sharp smile and a fondness for violence. An uncontrollable rush of anger flooded through Tomoe at the sight of her father. Her nails dug so deep into her palms she thought she might draw blood.

Her father was the last person she ever wanted to see. His presence brought nothing but bad memories and a sense of oncoming dread. Tomoe would never forget the first time her father had put a blade in her hand and told her to use it against any groundling who stood in her way. She had wanted to believe that he was just worried for her, that it was a measure of self-defence, but the glee in his eyes … the excitement he felt at the idea that his child would shed groundling blood had been impossible to ignore. He *wanted* her to hurt people – not to protect herself, but for the simple pleasure of hurting those he believed were inferior.

"How are you, my boy? I see you're hard at work." Her father sauntered past the boilers. He seemed friendly enough, but Tomoe knew just how quickly his mask of politeness could shatter into a cold rage.

It seemed Shuichi knew that too. The boy trembled like the last leaf in winter as Rei approached.

"S–sir! Am I in trouble?"

"Whatever for? You do good work down here. Important work. I thought that I should pay you a visit to make sure

things are going well." Rei smiled, but the look in his eyes was calculating.

As Tomoe watched him approach Shuichi with a viper's smile, her hand drifted towards the knife she kept tucked behind her obi. Her father did not *just* pay people visits out of curiosity or concern. People were nothing but pawns to him, and if he was down here, it could only be because he wanted something.

"Everything is fine, sir! Nothing is wrong! It's all fine!" Shuichi's eyes darted to the boiler where she and Sayo were hiding.

Tomoe bit back a curse. Could the boy act a little less suspicious? Or was he planning to sell them out because she had offended him? No, he would get in trouble too if he did.

"Good, because I need you to do something for me," said Rei. "The cylinders, boy. I need you to double the number you make each week."

"Double?"

"Don't disappoint me."

Tomoe finally let herself breathe a sigh of relief as her father turned to leave, but before he could even reach the door Shuichi suddenly spoke up.

"S—sir, if I – if I may ask… What do you need so many cylinders for? They're not soup cans, are they?"

"What in the seven hells is he doing?" Tomoe hissed.

"Well, you asked him about it," Sayo whispered back. "Maybe he's trying to find information for you? You did call him spineless."

"I didn't know he was going to take it personally!"

"Well, maybe you could have considered Shuichi's point of view a little more, instead of dismissing him like that," said Sayo.

Tomoe scowled.

"You want to know what the cylinders are for?" Rei considered Shuichi's question for a moment. His eyes gleamed with a fanaticism that, in the shadows of the engine room, warped his face into something demonic. "They're a vital piece of my plan to destroy the levistone cannon. As soon as we reach Sola-Ea, I will show everyone the might of the Sorabito. Prince Ugetsu, Princess Tsukimi, every rotten imperial soldier and groundling worm will be wiped from this land."

"P–Prince Ugetsu too?"

"Of course, boy. Why does that surprise you?"

"But we're allies … aren't we?"

"He's a groundling!" Rei snapped with such ferocity Shuichi whimpered. "We *Sorabito* are superior to the groundlings in every possible way. Why not kill every groundling worm that crawls before us? After everything we have endured, after everything that has been taken from us, why must we show our enemies mercy when they showed us none? Do you have any objections to that?"

"N–none at all, sir!"

Rei looked at Shuichi as though he was something unpleasant caught on the bottom of his shoe. His eyes flicked over the engine room, taking in the jungle of pipes and chutes along the walls, the sheets of metal yet to be made into cylinders, and the gleaming boilers churning with levistone.

His gaze landed on the spot where Tomoe and Sayo were currently hiding. Tomoe ducked further behind the boiler, pulling her knees up to her chest to make her body as small as possible.

Had he seen her? She pressed her back to the warm curve of the metal tank and held her breath. Gods, if her father found them now, what would he do? Would he have them thrown off the ship, or would he just stab them both and be done with it? Could she talk her way out of this?

"Just make sure you get things done," her father said to Shuichi before walking out of the door.

Shocked, Tomoe scrambled to peer around the edge of the boiler. That couldn't be right. Had her father really not seen her? But she had sworn that for just a second their eyes had met.

She stared at the door to the engine room.

Her father was gone.

Perhaps she got lucky. Maybe he had been distracted when he had looked her way.

Or maybe he was just pretending not to notice her in order to make her squirm.

"Tomoe?"

She jumped as Sayo's hand came to rest on her knee. Her friend looked at her, brows furrowed in concern. It was only then that she realized how fast her heart was pounding. Sayo's hand was an anchor, keeping her grounded when she wanted to launch into a flurry of panic.

With a sigh, Tomoe slumped against the girl's side. She hoped never to see her father again.

TWENTY-THREE

AFTER spending an entire day in this ancient dungeon of a prison, Kurara was itching to get out, but she forced herself to wait until the sun went down, knowing it would be easier to escape once the streets were empty and the military police were busy with night patrols.

It was difficult to keep track of the time down in the jail, but after what felt like an eternity of waiting, Ruki lifted its head and said, *"It is time to leave."*

Kurara rolled up her empty sleeve all the way to the stump of her elbow. Taking a deep breath, she concentrated and stretched the paper from her elbow into a short, stubby sledgehammer.

It wasn't the most elegant-looking thing, but it was as heavy and as hard as steel. Swinging her arm, she slammed the sledgehammer against the cell door with all the force she could muster. The hinges cracked. A moment later, the door fell to the ground with a thump.

She gestured for Ruki to follow her as she climbed up the stairs back to ground level. Outside, the soldiers had pitched a tent among the ruins of the building. Kurara checked to make sure no one was around then ducked inside. There, she found her ofuda stacked on top of a table next to some old military documents. Grabbing all the paper she could find, Kurara took a moment to remake her arm. Once she was done, she nodded to Ruki, and the two of them crept away.

Most of the city had been levelled; a wasteland of broken stone and burned wood. Lanterns shining from the remaining buildings burned so bright they made her squint. It was quiet; too quiet. A sense of terror still hung in the cold air. A city that did not dare to breathe.

It seemed to be a pattern – Kurara visiting places and bringing destruction with her. If she asked Haru and Himura, she wondered if they would tell her that it was worth it. At what point did the cost of destruction outweigh the righteousness of giving shikigami their freedom?

Could you even put a price on something like that?

A distant bang brought her back to the present. The light from the levistone cannon arched through the sky.

"Where do you think Entei went?" she asked as her gaze swept across the ruins of the city.

"Who knows? That toad was half mad already. I doubt it has a destination in mind. We should follow the path of destruction out of the city. Once we are far away from here, we will part ways." Ruki padded through the streets, following

the perfect line of broken roads and flattened buildings that divided the city into halves.

Kurara swallowed around the lump in her throat and crept after the shikigami. "Stay with me. It won't be long until the Star Seed blooms, and once it does you'll never have to worry about losing your mind again. You'll be truly free."

Ruki paused to think. *"Very well. I'll come with you."*

Kurara grinned. Ruki would be the first shikigami she would set free. The first of many. She could imagine herself travelling the world with Haru in search of shikigami to save. They would find some way to take the yuurei out of Haru's core, the war would end, Princess Tsukimi would disappear somewhere, if she wasn't already dead that is, and everything would be all right.

Yet despite her best efforts to remain positive, a choking feeling of unease began to creep over her, as dark and consuming as the shadows that painted the ruined city. Princess Tsukimi's awful, smug face swam to the front of her mind, taunting her, telling her that there was something she was missing.

"You don't *know how to make it bloom. You* think *you do, but you don't."*

No, that couldn't be right. Tsukimi was lying to her! Of course Kurara knew how to make the Star Seed bloom. The solution was the lullaby. A dying star fell from the heavens, and from that star grew a tree – the answer was right there! What else could it be?

"The fall doesn't matter. Only one thing does. Nothing is gained without sacrifice." Again, Tsukimi's voice needled at her.

Ruki padded quietly over the stone rubble. It wasn't easy to make their way through the city when the roads were so broken and uneven. As they turned the next corner, a circle of orange light spilled over the stones. A torch. A patrol officer was making his way towards them.

Kurara quickly backed away, but Ruki was not as fast. The light fell across Ruki's face, and the tiger froze. They had been spotted.

Opening his mouth, the officer took a deep breath and bellowed, "The prisoner! The prisoner is getting away!"

TWENTY-FOUR

"*GET on!*" Ruki lowered its body to the ground as the police officer reached for his sword. Swinging her leg over its flank, Kurara pressed her body flat against Ruki's back and clung tight to its paper fur. The tiger launched itself over the police officer's head. They soared through the air before crashing down on the other side of the road.

Angry shouts snapped at their heels, then came the low-pitched hum of vehicles. Glancing behind her, Kurara caught a glimpse of a few dozen qipaks flying low through the ravaged streets. On each of the brown, boat-like vehicles stood two soldiers – one to pilot the vehicle while the other took aim with a hand cannon and fired.

"After her! Don't let her get away!"

Bursts of fire whizzed past Kurara's head. Panic almost made her lose her grip on Ruki's fur, but she pulled herself together and held tight.

The soldiers were hot on their tail as Kurara and Ruki made their way out of the flattened city. Sparse bushes and tangles of knotweed lined the edges of the ponds and lakes that dotted the hills ahead.

"They're gaining on us!" she shouted as Ruki splashed through the mud, slowed down by the soggy terrain.

Another fiery bullet whizzed past them, then another, and another. A fourth bullet struck Ruki in the flank and the tiger crumpled with a scream, throwing Kurara across the wet earth as the flames spread over its body.

"Ruki!" Kurara picked herself up and sprinted towards the burning heap that was the shikigami's body.

The tiger lifted the remains of its head. *"No, leave me be!"*

"Ruki, you're going to die!" The flames would consume its core, and once the core was gone there was no coming back. She had to save it, though she didn't know how. If she touched Ruki, she might also catch fire.

"Leave! Before they burn you alive too!"

Kurara looked up to see the men heading towards her, weapons aloft. If she did not run, she would be a smouldering pile of ash as well.

There was no time for grief. Tearing herself away from Ruki's burning body, she ran. As she did, her left arm crumbled away and her ofuda swirled through the air, forming a paper wolf that galloped alongside her. She threw herself onto its back.

Don't look back, don't look back! Her head was pounding, and her body was screaming. Fear kept her moving, though her paper wolf was barely holding together in her panic.

A loud bang echoed through the air. Though the shot

sailed far over her head, it was enough to distract Kurara for a moment. Her wolf's front paw snagged against a large stone, tripping the beast and sending Kurara catapulting head-first into the nearby pond.

She spluttered as the water rushed into her mouth, but maybe this was the chance she needed to escape. Fighting the urge to resurface, Kurara held her breath, sank down to the bottom of the lake and waited, hoping that the soldiers would think she had drowned.

Eventually, the sound of engines faded into the distance. Kurara waited for just a second longer then broke through the water's surface with a gasp.

She hauled her body out of the pond and dragged herself onto dry land, where most of her ofuda wolf lay scattered in pieces.

The soldiers were gone. Kurara shivered and gathered the paper together until her strength gave out and she collapsed into the mud.

TWENTY-FIVE

KURARA was not sure how long she remained by the water's edge. Long enough that her clothes had started to dry and her body did not feel so limp and fragile. Long enough that every time the wind blew, the cold bit right through her.

Eventually, she managed to drag herself to her feet, swaying slightly as if she had forgotten how to stand. Mud covered the back of her legs, and her clothes stank.

She was aching and tired, but at least nothing was broken or on fire.

At least she wasn't a smouldering pile of ash.

Kurara looked back to where she had left Ruki. The tiger's last moments played again and again in her head. Everything kept going from bad to worse. She just wanted to lie down and become one with the mud.

No, she could not let this get to her, not when there were

so many other things she needed to deal with.

Kurara scanned her surroundings, checking for any signs of danger. The military police were long since gone, and the bogs and wetlands seemed devoid of all life.

She had never been alone before, not like this. Wherever she went, there had always been someone with her, whether that was a shikigami, Himura or Haru. She hugged her arms, shivering against the cold. The wind seemed to pierce right through her.

A sudden thought jolted her out of her stupor. The Star Seed! Did she still have it? Kurara ran a frantic hand over her stomach, only relaxing once she felt the familiar hard lump of the seed tucked tight behind her obi. Its weight was a comfort after everything that had happened.

"The Star Seed will bloom. I'll make sure it blooms," Kurara muttered to herself over and over like a prayer.

She had promised Ruki freedom, but Ruki was dead. A sudden anger seized her. She didn't want to delay things any more; she wanted the Star Seed to bloom right now, wanted *something* to go right, just for once.

Her left arm crumbled away and formed a pair of wings on her back. With a flap of feathers, Kurara launched herself into the air, higher, higher, until the land was a quilt of green and brown patches and the lakes were pinpricks of blue. Higher and higher still, past rainclouds and streams of sky fish, until the air was so thin it made her dizzy. Her back ached and her head throbbed, but she pushed herself on until she floated far above any mountain. Until she was almost as high as a sky city.

Kurara paused, chest heaving. She had never flown so far

or so high and the strain was taking its toll. She didn't think she could stay at this height for more than a few minutes.

Grabbing a few feathers from her paper wings, she rolled the ofuda together then stretched it out into a long piece of string. Tying the Star Seed to one end, she held it up to the sky.

"A dying star fell from the heavens, and from that star grew a tree."

She let the seed go.

It dropped like a stone clattering down a well. Kurara watched it tumble through the air, buffeted by the winds, until it was too small for her to track.

Nothing happened.

After a full minute of waiting, Kurara followed the string to the ground where she found the Star Seed lying in the grass, perfectly intact and completely unchanged.

Something snapped inside her. Kurara didn't know what it was, but it suddenly felt harder to breathe.

What had she done wrong? Was the fall not high enough? Had she missed something?

"A dying star fell from the heavens, and from that star grew a tree," she whispered, as if it were a password that would unlock the solution to the problem in front of her.

"*The fall doesn't matter. Only one thing does. Nothing is gained without sacrifice.*" Princess Tsukimi's smug face floated to the top of her thoughts once more. "*You* don't *know how to make it bloom. You* think *you do, but you don't.*"

Princess Tsukimi knew how to make the Star Seed bloom. Tsukimi always seemed to know things Kurara didn't. She understood Himura's frustration at the princess now. It wasn't fair. That knowledge should belong to the Crafters, to the shikigami, not some spoiled princess.

Now Tsukimi had been eaten by a giant toad, and who knew where she was or even if she was still alive?

As Kurara landed on the ground again, her gaze swept over the broken trees and craters in the earth caused by Entei's feet.

She had to go after the princess. She had to get answers, even if it meant beating them out of Tsukimi herself; but if she did, she might not find Haru and Himura again.

What should she do? What was more important to her: Haru or shikigami freedom?

No, the better question was which problem was more urgent.

"The Star Seed is more important," Haru had said. If he were here with her, Kurara knew what he would tell her to do.

Turning towards the trail of broken trees, Kurara headed after the toad.

TWENTY-SIX

AFTER surrendering to the soldiers, Himura was bundled into the hovercraft and taken to a much larger vessel hidden among the clouds.

The ship was a massive thing, silver and white, with one giant, bulky mast that seemed more like a shard of crystal piercing the sky. A glimpse of the ship's name flashed past too quickly for him to catch. The soldiers marched him across the deck, down the metal stairwell and through the ship's broad, well-lit corridors.

Mana hissed at the rough treatment, but Himura did not dare start a fight, not with Haru in his arms and half a dozen soldiers behind him, pointing weapons at his back.

"What's wrong with him?" The soldier in front frowned at Haru's still-unconscious body.

"Did you not see what he did?" Himura's arms strained

beneath Haru's weight. It was funny how paper could feel so heavy.

"I saw," the soldier replied through gritted teeth. "We've heard reports about deadly shadows. Yuurei, the people call them."

"Is that what all this is about then? What Haru did with the yuurei?"

"Play dumb all you like, Crafter, see how far that gets you." The officer scowled at him.

Himura stared at the man in furious bewilderment. "What are you talking about? I was minding my own business when your men shot down my falcon and tried to arrest me!"

Unless… Did the soldiers know that Kurara had released the yuurei from Suzaku's core? Was that it? Were they being blamed for the shadowy monsters that now haunted the land? Himura could not see how anyone could have found out about it, but it was the only explanation he could think of that made sense.

"If you have complaints, take it up with the Emperor! We're heading to Sola-Ea because he wants to speak with you," the soldier growled.

The Emperor? Now Himura was even more confused. A few hours ago, he would have gladly bet his right arm that the Emperor did not even know who he was, let alone have any reason to talk to him. What could this possibly be about?

They stopped in front of a large metal door at the end of the hallway. The soldier yanked the paper bracelet from his wrist and shoved him into the empty room. Himura stumbled inside without a struggle. Resisting would only put Haru in danger.

The room was small and bare; just big enough for two people to lie down side by side if they really squeezed in close. The moment Himura turned around, the door was slammed and bolted shut.

"*What a warm welcome.*" Mana slipped from Himura's sleeve and dropped to the ground, where it circled the room, inspecting every nook and cranny for a way to escape.

Setting Haru on the floor, Himura closed his eyes and searched for the presence of paper, but the room was empty and the walls and door were made of solid metal. There was nothing he could use.

Well, there was Mana – and Haru. He could take some of the paper that made up their bodies the way he had once yanked Akane's tail off, but even thinking of it made him wince.

Akane had deserved someone so much better than the man he had been.

"*Well, this is a fine mess.*" Mana gave up trying to find a way out and slithered back to Himura's side.

"Let's just wait and see what the soldiers have in store for us." Himura sat down next to Haru. Worry gnawed at the edges of his mind. That was another batch of yuurei absorbed straight into Haru's already delicate core. How bad was the damage this time? What was the point of sealing those shadowy monsters if Haru's core was going to crack?

Worse, what if absorbing too many yuurei had effects that went beyond just the cut on Haru's core? Having so many souls inside couldn't be good for you. It hadn't been good for Suzaku, and that shikigami had been purposefully made to hold several souls inside it.

Then there was the matter of the Emperor. Assuming this wasn't some elaborate prank, he had no idea what the ruler of an entire empire could possibly want with them. He sighed. At least they were heading to Sola-Ea. The *Orihime* would be there too, probably grounded inside one of the sky city's docking bays. He wondered if Sayo and Tomoe had made it back to the ship; if he would ever get the chance to see them or the crew while in the city.

He wondered if Kurara was having a better time than he was.

———o———

Himura did not remember falling asleep, but he woke to the sound of something inside the room with him. Something scratching and scraping against the floor.

His eyes snapped open. In the corner of the room, Mana was trying to climb the walls.

"What are you doing?"

Mana lunged at him, its fangs sinking into his arm. Himura threw himself backwards with a muffled shout. The sound seemed to knock some sense back into the shikigami. Mana released its grip and dropped to the ground, curling up into a tight ball of shame.

"I–I apologize. I did not mean to – I…"

Himura had never seen Mana so shaken. "It's fine." He pressed his fingers to the two bright spots of blood that bloomed on his arm. Honestly, he had suffered worse paper cuts than this. "It doesn't hurt."

His words did nothing to wipe the miserable look from Mana's face.

So you care about one measly bite, yet you don't care about me enough to consider bonding, Himura wanted to say, but he knew he would come across as bitter. If Mana was not going to ask, then Himura wouldn't offer again.

A soft groan broke the awkward silence between them. Haru stirred, his eyelids fluttering before suddenly snapping open.

"Awake at last, are you?" Mana seemed grateful for the distraction.

With a groan, Haru sat up, rubbing his head. "What happened?"

"You did something stupid is what happened!"

Haru opened his mouth to reply when a gasp of pain escaped his lips. He doubled over, clutching at his chest.

"Is it the yuurei? May I see your core?"

Reluctantly, Haru straightened, though he still looked woozy. "Just make it quick," he mumbled.

Himura was careful when he opened up Haru's chest. With a gentle swipe of his fingers, he parted the thread-like paper muscles until he could get a good glimpse of the core.

It was covered in thin cuts, none of them severe enough to go all the way through the core but they were deeper than before. It was a miracle his core had not cracked. If it had, Haru would be dead, setting loose a swarm of yuurei again.

"What? Is it bad?" Haru stared nervously at Himura's pinched expression.

"It's … concerning."

"That's just another word for bad!"

Himura readjusted the paper muscles and, with a flick of his hand, stitched up Haru's chest. He tried his best to describe what he had seen without causing alarm, but it was clear from the way Haru's expression morphed into a look of terror that he wasn't doing a very good job.

The boy closed his eyes and took a deep, steadying breath. Himura had seen Kurara do the same thing when she was on the verge of being overwhelmed – pulling everything back and pushing it down in a single breath. When Haru opened his eyes again, he seemed calmer.

We'll work things out. You're not alone. We'll find a way to handle this, Himura opened his mouth to say, but what came out instead was, "You shouldn't have absorbed those other yuurei. If you'd just let them attack the soldiers while we ran, we wouldn't be here and your core wouldn't be in such a terrible state."

"I just didn't want anyone to die." Haru pulled his knees up to his chest, making himself look smaller. It reminded Himura of how Akane would slink away with its tail between its legs whenever he snapped at it, and it made him feel like the worst person in the world.

"So you'll sacrifice yourself instead. What will Kurara think?" He tried to sound gentler, kinder, like the good master he was meant to be.

"I'm doing this for her too," said Haru. "She takes everything so personally. Everything is always her fault, it's always her responsibility to fix things. I fought Suzaku too. I wasn't able to stop Crafters from cutting down the Star

182

Trees either. And, unlike Kurara, I remember all the things that I did during the Crafter war. I *had* to seal those yuurei. They're my responsibility too."

Himura wondered if Haru and Kurara knew how alike they were at times. Both of them were all too willing to shoulder things alone for fear of being a burden to others. It made him want to tear his hair out in frustration.

He was about to suggest they try to get some more sleep when the ship suddenly rocked forward and the door to their room burst open.

A soldier stared down at them with barely disguised contempt.

"We've arrived at Sola-Ea. Get up and follow me!"

"The boy is sick. I'll go alone." Himura stood, but the soldier would not budge.

"The Emperor wants to see you both."

"Wait, the Emperor? As in *the* Emperor?" Haru hissed. Himura was glad that he too had no idea why they were being summoned.

"Get up!" the officer snarled.

Haru gripped the front of Himura's kimono and pulled himself to his feet. His face had an unhealthily pale sheen to it and he was breathing hard, but he managed to stay upright. The soldier shoved them both out of the room and into the ship's wide, open hallways.

More armed men were there to greet them. Himura glowered at them if they got too close and grabbed Haru by the elbow, using all his strength to help support the boy as they made their way down the corridor.

Instead of heading to the deck, as he thought they

would, they were escorted down into the depths of the ship, to a set of ornate double doors carved from ivory. Himura had never thought that he would be intimidated by a pair of doors, but their sheer size and bone-like sheen gave them an imposing air.

Outside, two guards stood to attention, armed with a pair of katana.

"Before you enter, I want you to give an order to your shikigami. Repeat these words after me," one of the soldiers ordered.

Himura glanced at Mana, who had hitched a ride on his shoulders, then at Haru, who was standing so close he could feel the boy's laboured breaths.

"You are about to stand in the presence of His Imperial Highness the Emperor. I order you not to hurt him at any point in time, now or in the future. And you are not to hurt anyone else in this room, no matter what happens."

Silently fuming, Himura repeated the order. Haru stiffened slightly, but the movement went unnoticed by the soldiers.

Satisfied, the soldier ordered the guards to open the doors and shoved Himura through.

Inside the mostly empty room, ornate glass windows loomed from floor to ceiling. Above, a sun-burst chandelier cast a constellation of small lights across the white stone floor. At one end of the room stood a raised dais with a bamboo screen hanging down in front of it.

A dark silhouette sat on a chair behind the screen, a sword at its waist.

The Emperor.

TWENTY-SEVEN

"YOU stand in the presence of His Imperial Highness, the most glorious Emperor of Mikoshima! Show some respect, Crafters!" A guard pushed Himura and Haru onto their hands and knees.

Haru yelped as he dropped to the floor, and Himura wanted to growl at the guard to back off, but he knew better than to cause a fuss. Not here. Not now. Not in the presence of the Emperor of Mikoshima.

His gaze slowly lifted to the figure behind the bamboo screen. Himura had never seen the Emperor before – not many people in Mikoshima had – and what few paintings there were of the ruler were more than thirty years old, depicting a slim but well-built man in the prime of life.

Behind the screen, the figure lifted a hand. A man standing next to the dais – a clerk of some kind – hurried behind the bamboo curtain and re-emerged with a pompous look on his face.

"Crafters!" the man screeched in a voice so high and piercing Himura was surprised the windows did not shatter at the sound.

There was that word again: "Crafters". Did he mean Haru as well? Did everyone here think that Haru was a Crafter too?

"His Imperial Highness, the Emperor of Mikoshima orders you to tell him where his daughter is!"

"You mean Princess Tsukimi? How would we know that?" cried Haru. .

The air bristled with tension. Himura glanced behind him. The guards inside the room were imperial Crafters, armed with tasselled spears and dressed in traditional armour. *No shikigami, though,* he noted. Still, he didn't think he could take them in a fight. Not without any ofuda on him.

"What rudeness!" the clerk screeched. "Why, I should have you—"

The Emperor raised his hand again, and the clerk snapped his mouth shut so fast he bit his bottom lip. With an alarmed look, he scuttled behind the screen once more.

All Himura could hear were the muffled whispers of "Yes, of course!", "No, Your Imperial Highness!", "Yes, Your Imperial Highness! I will!"

The clerk stepped out again, though looking far more flustered than before. Himura and Haru discreetly exchanged glances.

"Ahem!" The clerk cleared his throat. "You are Princess Tsukimi's imperial Crafters, are you not? No, do not try to lie – our soldiers spotted you with the princess," the clerk snapped when Haru opened his mouth to argue. "We know you have been travelling with her. His Imperial Highness demands to know what she's doing that is more important than obeying her honoured father and joining him here in Sola-Ea!"

Cold understanding dawned on Himura. So this was why the Emperor wanted to see him – he had not really wanted to speak to *him*, not to Himura, but to the person he believed was one of Princess Tsukimi's Crafters. The soldiers who had captured them had seen them with the princess as she had been whisked away and had assumed that they were working with her.

Each member of the imperial family was in charge of choosing their own bodyguards. Himura was not surprised that the Emperor didn't know who Tsukimi's Crafters were. Perhaps they could use this to their advantage.

"What? We're not— Augh!" Haru began when Himura elbowed him.

As random Crafters, they had no value; but as *Tsukimi's* imperial Crafters, there was a chance they could talk their way out of this. Especially if they offered up information about the princess.

"Your Imperial Majesty." Himura bowed as low as he could without pressing his head to the floor. "Tragically, Princess Tsukimi was taken away from us by a large shikigami—"

A distant bang echoed through the air, and Himura felt the ground shake. That had to be the levistone cannon they had built on Sola-Ea. The aftershock of its blast rippled through the ship, shaking the crystal chandelier above.

Mana squeezed Himura's arm tight as it retreated further

into his sleeve. The fastest way to wear down a shikigami's mind, Himura knew, was by overloading their senses with loud noises and gatherings of strangers.

Himura was so distracted by the blast and Mana's distress that he did not realize the Emperor was pointing at him until the clerk gasped. Holding up his thin arm, the Emperor curled a single finger, gesturing for Himura to approach the dais.

On unsteady feet, Himura stumbled forwards and paused a foot away from the bamboo screen.

The Emperor gestured again, bidding Himura to come to the other side.

"Y–Your Imperial Highness!" the clerk squeaked, but he did not dare protest as Himura side-stepped around the screen and fell to his knees, placing his hands and head against the floor in a respectful bow.

At first, he did not dare to look at the man sitting on the carved wooden throne. Himura held no great love for the Emperor, but even so *this* was the ruler of all of Mikoshima and its colonies. As much as he disliked the empire, Himura could not help but be affected by the importance of the man before him.

Taking a deep breath, he steadied himself and gazed upon the throne.

The Emperor was … an ordinary man. He was older than Himura had expected, his face wrinkled and his stomach slightly paunchy. There was a scar on his cheek that had not healed properly and a liver spot on his balding head. Himura had always known that the Emperor was a mere human just like everyone else, but after meeting Princess

Tsukimi he had expected him to be more like the wild beast his daughter was. Like a dragon that would devour the world. Not this. Not some regular old man dressed in expensive clothes.

With a wave of his hand, the Emperor gestured for Himura to stand and, in a voice that creaked like a rusty hinge, he whispered, "Did no one tell you during training that you're to report to me every month? A son declaring war against his own father. A daughter doing who knows what? None of you can keep those damn brats in line!"

Himura almost jerked back. He didn't know what the Emperor was talking about, but from the sounds of it, the Crafters who protected the prince and princess were also spies for the Emperor.

Did Princess Tsukimi know about this? Maybe she just didn't care.

The Emperor frowned at Himura's silence. "I have heard that Sohma have invented some kind of weapon made out of shikigami cores. Have you heard of it?"

Himura had not, but just hearing the words "shikigami cores" and "weapon" in the same sentence brought to mind memories of the yuurei. It was easy to forget that only a few people knew where the yuurei truly came from.

Noticing his hesitation, the Emperor's eyes narrowed. "You know something."

"I… Of course not. Forgive me for disappointing you, but—"

"You know something!"

The last thing Himura expected was for the Emperor to grab him by the wrist, but the moment he did Himura felt

Mana's coils squeeze his arm so tightly he feared it would snap his bones.

With a cry of pain, Himura flung his arm into the air, trying to shake the shikigami free. As he stumbled back, the bamboo curtain covering the dais came crashing to the ground, leaving the Emperor's face visible for all to see.

"Halt! No one move!" In a blink, the imperial Crafters flung their ofuda at Himura while Mana slipped free of his sleeve and lunged at the Emperor.

If only the guards had known the truth, perhaps they could have stopped the shikigami. If they had known that the order they made Himura repeat outside the room was useless, they certainly wouldn't have let the snake inside.

Mana did not have a bond with Himura.

Mana was free to do as it wished.

The snake coiled around the Emperor's neck and squeezed until there was an awful crack.

Interlude

Live in this moment
Live like the curve of a blade
And cut through your doubt

– Written by a Crafter of Unknown Origin
(from the library of the imperial princess)

Seeing her father again had Tomoe on edge. Although nothing had happened the day Kazeno Rei visited the engine room, she was certain that he had secretly spotted her and was going to return any day now with a horde of heavily armed men. In fact, the only reason he hadn't was because he wanted to make her sweat. It was mental warfare. She was sure of it.

Sayo did her best to comfort her, which for Sayo meant hovering over Tomoe's shoulder at all hours of the day and staring at her without saying anything. It was strangely touching and, on any other occasion, Tomoe would have laughed at how bad Sayo was at showing her support, but her mind was too frazzled.

Her father's looming presence was not her only problem. They needed to return to the storeroom every week or so for food, which meant leaving the engine room to crawl through the ship's vents in search of supplies they could take without anyone noticing. Tomoe had tried to get Shuichi to bring them what they needed, but the boy was too timid to steal for them.

Once again Tomoe and Sayo found themselves crawling through the narrow vents. Sayo had not wanted her to come, but Tomoe had insisted – between the two of them they could carry more food back to the engine room anyway. Though Sayo would never admit it, Tomoe knew her friend was worried about her, but that only made Tomoe all the more keen to prove that she was fine.

"Are you sure you need to come?" Sayo asked as she crawled behind her.

"I have two hands and a working pair of legs, don't I? I might as well help you bring back some food," Tomoe grumbled.

She moved slowly, careful not to make any sound. A light shone through the holes in the grate from the room below, and she could hear voices. Dragging herself closer to the grate, she noticed her father standing directly below, speaking to another member of his crew.

Tomoe drew back with a gasp, almost slamming into Sayo.

Her father looked up.

She froze. He had seen her, hadn't he? Yet if he had, he made no indication.

This was the second time this had happened. What was

her father playing at? He was toying with her; he just had to be. Thinking about him made her feel like a bird trapped in a tiny cage.

"What is it? Why did you suddenly stop?" asked Sayo.

Tomoe hissed at her to be quiet.

Holding her breath, she moved past the grate as quickly and quietly as she could, away from her father. Without paying attention to where she was heading, she came to a fork in the vent.

Without stopping to think, she took the path to the right.

"You're going the wrong way!" said Sayo, but Tomoe was too focused on putting as much distance between herself and her father to care.

The vents were a maze of long metal tunnels with no beginning or end. The occasional bottom grate let in the light from below, but they were few and far between, leaving her to struggle in the darkness for long stretches of time.

Her breath quickened and her body felt uncomfortably hot. Where was she? Tomoe had been so concerned with getting away from her father she had barely paid any attention to where she was going, or to Sayo, who had been quietly calling for her to stop. As she crawled forward, feeling increasingly panicked, the vent split into another fork.

"Left, go left." Sayo's voice was a comforting whisper in her ear. "Don't worry. I won't let you get stuck in here."

Taking a deep breath, Tomoe did as she was told. Knowing that Sayo was just behind her helped calm her down. No matter what happened, she could always rely on Sayo to have her back.

Soon enough, she noticed a grate on the bottom of the vent. Relief washed over her – she was sure this led to one of the storerooms. She pulled the grate aside.

"Wait," said Sayo. "That's not the—"

Before she could finish, Tomoe was already falling through the opening. The moment she dropped inside the room, a flurry of metal wings greeted her. She threw her arms over her head as a small flock of mechanical birds fluttered around her, stirred awake by her intrusion. This wasn't a storeroom, but the rookery – a room where the ship's crew kept the mechanical birds used to communicate with other ships.

Sayo dropped down next to her as the birds settled back on the edges of the shelves. "We won't find any food here," she said. "Let's go back."

"Wait!" Something had caught Tomoe's eye. She hurried to one of the many shelving units inside the rookery. "Take a look at this!"

She turned to show Sayo the small sphere in her hand. It was as smooth and white as polished bone, with dark red marks all over its surface.

A shikigami core.

Sayo stared at Tomoe for a full ten seconds before uttering a single, perfectly formed curse.

There were large metal trays below all the birds, each piled high with the same round spheres. This was the last place Tomoe would have expected to find a bunch of shikigami cores. They were valuable, sure – the empire paid good money for them – but beyond that they weren't much use to anyone who wasn't a Crafter.

194

So why did her father have so many? Was he selling them to the empire? With the war on, that seemed highly unlikely.

"Are those the cylinders that Shuichi makes in the engine room?"

Sayo's words drew Tomoe's attention to a wire rack at the very back of the room. Sure enough, Shuichi's metal cylinders stood lined up in neat rows.

Tomoe picked one up. The cylinder was heavier than she had expected. When she opened up the top, she could just about make out some kind of contraption inside – something with springs and metal jaws and enough space for a small, round item to fit inside.

"What is it?" Sayo peered over her shoulder.

Tomoe was the best engineer on the *Orihime*; just looking at the contraption told her everything she needed to know.

The mechanical birds stared at her, their glass eyes reflecting back her wide-eyed, pale face, as if they knew too.

"The cylinder is for breaking open shikigami cores. There's a spring-loaded trap inside that's meant to trigger upon impact." She hurled the cylinder to the floor, and a bolt of serrated steel sliced through the inside of the cylinder like a miniature guillotine.

Sayo drew an audible breath.

"Do you remember what Kurara told us? That every shikigami has a soul inside their core," said Tomoe.

"And that if those cores were cracked open, the soul would escape and turn into..." Sayo grimaced.

So this was what Rei was up to. He was not just going to destroy the levistone cannon; he was going to break open

the cores and release the souls, which would turn into those shadowy monsters, unleashing untold destruction upon the world.

If Rei released the shadows on Sola-Ea, the *Orihime* might be able to fly to safety, but Tomoe could not say the same of everyone else. How many people would die if her father succeeded in his plan? A hundred? A thousand? Tomoe imagined an entire sky city empty of life. A blank canvas for her father to do whatever he wanted.

"We need to burn all of the cores." Tomoe gripped Sayo's arm with sudden urgency.

"We can't," said Sayo.

"We have to! Rei has developed a new kind of weapon here! One that can be dropped onto towns and cities, releasing yuurei on innocent people!"

"I know!" Sayo hissed through clenched teeth. "I know what your father intends to do. But if we burn the cores now, we'll only draw attention to ourselves. Someone will come and check on them and realize they're all ashes!"

"So?"

"Your father will think there's a traitor on board and interrogate everyone. Shuichi might squeal, and even if he doesn't, your father will know that there must be someone else on board his ship. His men will hunt us down. And then what?"

"So we should just let Rei kill who knows how many people?"

"What's more important to you? Reaching the *Orihime* or this?"

"This! Saving lives! Doing the right thing!" Tomoe retorted. "You?"

"The *Orihime*!"

Silence rang in Sayo's wake.

With a pained look, Sayo tore her gaze away from Tomoe. "You want me to care about what happens to the people of Sola-Ea, but I can't," she whispered, as if she was ashamed to admit it. "I mean, I do care, but not if that puts me and the people I care about at risk. Not if it puts *you* at risk, Tomoe."

"But they're Sorabito too! They're our people!"

"They're strangers. I'm sorry, but I'm not like you or Kurara. I can't care about every little injustice in the world."

"But you care about me," said Tomoe.

Even in the darkness, Sayo's blush was clearly visible. She looked both embarrassed and affronted. "I already told you that I did."

"Then do this for me." Tomoe was used to wheedling small favours out of Sayo: an extra slice of castella cake, a spare flask of hot tea, star charts and books.

Yet this was so much more important than anything Tomoe had ever asked for. Her father had to be stopped. No matter what.

"Sayo…" Tomoe took the girl's hand in her own. Most of the time, all she had to do was lower her voice a little and Sayo would eventually cave like a house of cards.

Sayo seemed to know this too. When she looked at Tomoe, her expression was conflicted and betrayed, like she couldn't believe Tomoe would use such an underhanded tactic against her.

"This isn't fair. You can't do this to me," she replied stiffly.

Tomoe knew it was wrong to try to manipulate Sayo into giving in, but there were lives on the line. If they did not stop her father, everyone in Sola-Ea could die.

She was about to continue arguing when the door opened.

"Hello, daughter." A smooth voice sailed through the room.

Both Tomoe and Sayo whipped around.

The mechanical birds stirred but did not take flight, their glass eyes watching silent and unblinking as Rei stood in the doorway, his face drowned in shadow.

TWENTY-EIGHT

THE path Entei had taken across the country was unmistakable – a line of flattened trees and cratered earth. With something that big making its way across the land, Kurara was not the only one tracking its movements. As she made her way north, she crept past platoons of soldiers who were also following the path of destruction, and villagers who were fleeing from the toad's approach.

She did her best to avoid running into anyone as she followed Entei's trail, switching between walking and using her ofuda to travel. Every where she went, the land was battered and broken. Kurara found villages burned, forests flattened, and muddy battlefields littered with bodies and weapons. Sometimes, she would hear rumours of Sorabito who had been spotted stealing shikigami cores from combat zones.

As the days passed, a thousand little anxieties wormed their way to the forefront of her mind. How would she ever catch up with Entei? The toad could cover more ground in a single leap than she could in an entire day. Were Haru and Himura OK? What would she do if she ran into a platoon of soldiers or bandits or another wild shikigami?

Then there were all the other inconveniences of having a human-like body. As the weather turned even colder, finding a dry place to sleep became increasingly difficult, and she would often wake to sore limbs and an aching head. She had no supplies and had to rely on what little she could find by foraging and hunting.

It was an altogether miserable experience that made her miss Haru's ability to look on the bright side of every bad situation. Hells, she even missed Himura and Mana.

Now her only companions were her nightmares of Suzaku and the doubts that haunted her every step. Her last conversation with Princess Tsukimi plagued her thoughts, taunting her.

"*You* don't *know how to make it bloom. You* think *you do, but you don't. Is it because you don't have the guts for it? Are you afraid?*" Tsukimi had smirked at her.

Something didn't add up. Why would she be afraid?

"*The fall doesn't matter. Only one thing does. Nothing is gained without sacrifice.*"

Eventually the ground turned from soft wetland to wide fields peppered with the remains of rocky outcrops. Kurara had no idea how far she had travelled, only that Entei had definitely been this way – the land was split by long, spiderweb gashes as if something heavy had broken it apart.

Entei was heading west again, going further inland.

As far as Kurara knew, there was nothing that way except for one thing.

Sola-Ea – one of the seven Sorabito cities.

Kurara remembered Himura mentioning that the *Orihime* was docked there. And that the city was soon to become a war zone.

Did Entei know that? Was it purposefully heading towards the sky city? Or was it just hopping about blindly, heading wherever its fractured mind told it to go?

As Kurara picked her way through the trampled fields, she began to notice something odd. Bits of paper lay strewn over the land, blowing in the wind or else caught on the branches of broken trees. She picked up whatever she passed – there was no point in wasting good paper – but it made her uneasy.

Perhaps there had been another battle nearby; she had started to see more armies marching across the country. Maybe she would soon stumble across a field littered with corpses and dead shikigami. Another field picked clean by Sorabito.

It turned out, she was half-right.

There were no dead soldiers, but as the fields turned to flattened forests, she spied a large mound of paper in the distance. Small squares of paper lay scattered about the ground, but the rain had turned the rest into a sodden, muddy lump.

Rushing towards it, Kurara had to crane her neck up to stare at the top of the pile. The mountain of paper was at least ten feet high – it had likely been taller before the wind had blown some of it away.

Kurara froze.

Was this … Entei? She could think of no other shikigami that would leave such a huge mound behind when it died. The trail of destruction abruptly stopped here.

With trembling hands, she clicked her fingers and the sea of paper parted. Another twist of her wrist and the papers whirled through the air, lifting higher and higher. She shuffled through the sheets, searching for Entei's core, for Princess Tsukimi's body, lost beneath the avalanche of paper.

There was nothing. No core. No body. There was no sign of a fight either; nothing to indicate that hunters had come and destroyed the toad.

Princess Tsukimi must have killed Entei. She had been inside the toad and could have easily yanked Entei's core free, causing the toad to collapse from the inside. How could Kurara not have thought of that before?

Now the princess had disappeared. She could be anywhere, and Kurara had no way of finding her.

With a yell of pure, guttural rage, Kurara sent the remains of Entei's body exploding outwards, hurling paper across the ground. What was she supposed to do now? She would have to figure out how to make the Star Seed bloom on her own, without the easy answers Tsukimi might have provided. How long would that take? Could she be sure she would find the answer? And meanwhile how many more shikigami would suffer?

Kurara was about to leave when something caught her eye. On a large tree trunk nearby, there were words carved into the wood.

Going to Sola-Ea.
Bring the Star Seed.

The note reeked of Tsukimi's arrogance. It felt like a taunt. Like a trap. The fact that Tsukimi had – correctly – assumed that Kurara would come after her like a damn dog made her want to turn around and head in the opposite direction out of spite.

Yet she knew she wouldn't. Tsukimi had the answers she wanted. Even if it was a trap, Kurara would go to Sola-Ea.

The sound of boots squelching through the mud drew her attention away from the message. Kurara looked up just in time to see a young girl dart behind the mound of paper.

She was wearing a kimono that had been cut short at the hips, the bottom half replaced with a long, pleated skirt that fell to her ankles. Only Sorabito dressed like that. Kurara ran after her. The girl, noticing she was being followed, gave a squeak of fright and dashed off between the trees as fast as she could.

"Hey, stop!" Kurara gave chase. As she ran, she spotted something round and white in the Sorabito's hand.

Entei's core!

Was the girl one of the Sorabito going around stealing cores from battlefields?

"Stop!" Kurara reached out with her mind and gathered the pieces of paper that lay scattered on the ground. The sheets of paper merged together to form a rope that Kurara sent flying towards the Sorabito girl. It coiled around her ankles and pulled her legs from under her, bringing the girl crashing to the ground.

"No, stop! Please don't hurt me!" The girl rolled onto her back, waving her hands frantically in front of her face to shield herself.

Kurara began walking towards her when she heard someone else step out from behind the broken trees.

"Don't move!" A second Sorabito, much older than the first, pointed a pistol at her.

TWENTY-NINE

"LET her go, Crafter." The older Sorabito was tall and willowy, his long black hair pulled into a high ponytail at the top of his head.

Kurara did not let her captive go. With the remains of Entei's body close by, she had more paper at her fingertips than she had ever had before. With so much ofuda, she was confident she could take on both Sorabito without moving an inch.

"You're the Sorabito who have been stealing cores!" she shot back.

"What's it to you, Crafter?" the older Sorabito snapped.

"Did you kill the shikigami?"

"N—no, we don't kill any shikigami!" the girl squeaked. Though her arms were not bound, she was too terrified to move away from where she lay at Kurara's feet. "They're always destroyed when we find them. This one was already a mound of paper!"

So that confirmed Kurara's theory that Tsukimi had killed Entei by pulling its core free of the paper strings that connected the core to its body, causing the shikigami to collapse from the inside.

"Why are you stealing cores?"

"None of your business," the man growled.

The paper of Kurara's left arm sharpened like a knife. Her paper fingers twisted together and merged into a blade-like point which she pointed at the girl's neck.

"P–P–Prince Ugetsu wants them!" the girl stammered. "Sohma too! The prince and Kazeno Rei are heading to Sola-Ea to destroy the levistone cannon. I don't know why they want a bunch of cores, but they pay good money for them!"

Sola-Ea. Kurara thought of the note the princess had left.

Going to Sola-Ea.
Bring the Star Seed.

Did Tsukimi know that the sky city was soon to become a war zone? Perhaps she had gone there *because* there was going to be a battle soon.

Kurara had to get to Sola-Ea and fast, but it would take forever to walk. Even if she travelled by ofuda, she would have to stop and rest, and the longer she took to get to the sky city, the more time Princess Tsukimi had for whatever scheme she was cooking up.

What she needed was a faster way to reach Sola-Ea. Something like an airship. Prince Ugetsu's airship, to be exact.

"Take me to the prince," she said, her knife still poised at the girl's throat. If Ugetsu was going to Sola-Ea, he might as well take her along too.

The man snorted. "You think *sky rats* like us can just waltz onto the prince's ship and demand to see him just like that?"

"Holy skies, Genzo, just say yes!" the girl pleaded with him.

Kurara was starting to feel bad for the Sorabito girl. She often forgot that many people saw Crafters as little more than demons in human skin, their ability to control paper monstrous and dangerous. She pulled the blade away from the girl's neck and folded the paper back into a regular hand.

"The prince will see me." She pulled her paper arm off at the elbow and rolled her sleeve back so that the pair of Sorabito could see the inside of her hollow limb. "Tell him there's a shikigami who wants to talk to him."

———————o———————

The Sorabito kept a pair of qipaks hidden not far from the flattened forest. The boat-like aircraft creaked as Kurara stepped on behind the man.

"You sit up front," he barked at her, his face as stiff as a board.

Kurara could tell that the pair wanted to be rid of her as soon as possible. The girl's eyes kept darting towards Kurara, as if she were afraid Kurara might go mad and try to eat them at any moment, and the man kept leaning away from her like he thought she had some awful disease.

It did not take long to reach Prince Ugetsu's ship – it was sailing its way to Sola-Ea, heading in the same direction Entei had been before it died. It was a beautiful ship – all sleek white curves and silver embellishments in the shape of birds and flowers along the side. The name – *Hotei* – was carved into the side in elegant silver characters.

The qipaks circled the deck, signal lights flashing in a coded exchange of messages, before being allowed to land. The moment the aircraft came to a stop, the man jumped onto the deck, where he exchanged heated whispers with a pair of armed guards. They all looked back at Kurara for a second.

Kurara waved her paper hand.

The men turned away and the heated discussion continued.

One of the guards ran off below deck and emerged a moment later, gesturing for Kurara to step forward.

"The prince will see you now."

Without so much as a goodbye to the Sorabito pair, Kurara found herself escorted below the ship's deck and through its wide hallways. The inside of the *Hotei* was as luxurious as the outside suggested. Unlike the *Orihime*'s clean but unexceptional corridors, the *Hotei*'s floors were made of rich mahogany and the walls were decorated with carvings of curling vines and blooming flowers that swirled around the porthole windows.

Gods, what was she doing? Kurara had just wanted a quick way to Sola-Ea, but now she was having second thoughts. Who was she to demand an audience with the prince? What was she doing jumping into this lion's den of soldiers and rebels?

No, I need to be here! She tried to steel herself. All that mattered was that she reached Sola-Ea.

At the very back of the ship stood Prince Ugetsu's quarters. The guards gestured for her to go in, and soon she found herself inside a lavishly decorated room adorned with priceless china vases and portraits of the prince's smiling face hanging on every wall. A long table stood in the middle of the room, with chairs that had been designed to be as beautiful and as uncomfortable as possible.

Prince Ugetsu sat at the head of the table, wine glass in hand, admiring himself in the reflection.

"One moment." He smoothed a finger over his perfectly oiled moustache before finally turning his attention to Kurara, who stood awkwardly at the doorway.

There was something about Ugetsu's smile that seemed to cut right through her, as if he was only showing his teeth in order to sink them into her neck later.

"Well, well," he said. "If it isn't my sister's favourite shikigami."

THIRTY

PRINCE Ugetsu looked like he had stepped right out of one of those military propaganda posters. Kurara stood frozen before him. His handsomeness was almost intimidating.

"I'm told you insisted on speaking to me." Prince Ugetsu gestured for her to take a seat, eyes sparkling as if he knew the effect he was having on her.

Kurara shook herself out of her trance. This was not the time to let her nerves get the better of her. She was one of the first shikigami ever made, a Crafter who excelled at controlling paper – she was not going to be cowed by some spoiled prince.

"Why are you telling Sorabito to steal cores from battlefields?" she snapped. As far as she knew, Sohma didn't have any Crafters working for them – that would have gone against their ridiculous Sorabito blood-purity thing – and neither did Prince Ugetsu.

The prince did not look at her, but at the painting of himself fighting a giant shikigami, which hung above her head.

"Is this what you came all the way here to ask me? Why do you care what I tell those sky rats to do? I agreed to meet with you because I remember that my sister was obsessed with you. But if you're going to waste my time—"

"I want you to take me to Sola-Ea!"

A loud sigh escaped the prince's lips. "You have a funny way of asking for a favour. I'm sure my sister finds you fascinating, but I have no interest in shikigami. And I have no need for you."

Kurara bristled. "You sister is going to Sola-Ea! When I find her, I'm going to tear her apart!" Though first she would strangle information about the Star Seed out of Tsukimi's throat.

Every second wasted was a second a shikigami might lose its mind or die. Every minute squandered was a minute Tsukimi could use against her.

"Whatever squabble you have with my sister is of no interest to me either," the prince replied coolly.

"Really?" Kurara scowled. "I'm one of the first shikigami ever made and you have no interest in me? Are you not curious about why Tsukimi has gone to Sola-Ea, even though she doesn't care about the war? I didn't realize you were such a boring man."

Ugetsu placed his wine glass down. For the first time, he looked at her instead of at the furniture or his own reflection.

"What do you—?"

He was interrupted by the sound of the door flying open.

Kurara had to jump out of the way as a breathless, pale-faced soldier barrelled inside and gave a quick salute.

"Apologies for interrupting, Your Imperial Highness!"

"What is it?" said Ugetsu.

The man swallowed.

"Y–Your Imperial Highness, th–the Emperor is dead!"

It felt like a punch to the gut. Though Kurara didn't care two shakes for the Emperor, the news still left her shocked and confused. The Emperor? Dead? Surely that couldn't be right. This was *the Emperor* they were talking about. Important people like that didn't just die all of a sudden.

"Dead? How?" asked Ugetsu.

"He was killed by Princess Tsukimi's imperial Crafters. A pair of young men with a snake shikigami."

Kurara's breath caught in her throat. A pair of young men and a snake shikigami. That couldn't be… No, the soldier had said it was a pair of imperial Crafters… But that sounded just like…

She wondered where Haru and the others were. For the love of shikigami, she hoped they were staying *out* of trouble!

"What happened to them – the Crafters? Were they caught? Were they punished?" she asked.

The soldier jumped as if he had only just noticed her standing there. "The report doesn't mention what happened to the Crafters afterwards. I think they may have escaped. Or they were pardoned. Princess Tsukimi is now in charge of the empire. The reports say she arrived at Sola-Ea shortly after her father's death and took over. She will be crowned Empress in a few weeks."

Prince Ugetsu picked up his glass and hurled it at the soldier's head. It missed the soldier and shattered against the wall, staining the painting above the doorway and showering the soldier in glass shards.

That only seemed to anger the prince even more. Pushing himself to his feet, he snarled, "Tsukimi? Empress? She cares about nothing but her stupid shikigami! With her in charge of the empire, we'll lose our colonies one by one. The other empires will take the land that rightfully belongs to us! The glory of Mikoshima will be a thing of the past!"

The soldier did not know what to say. He could only tremble and nod in agreement.

"As the Emperor's only son, the throne is mine by right! All my life I have fought for the glory of Mikoshima! I would be the best Emperor this country has ever seen. Historians would write books about my brilliance! Artists would paint portraits and carve statues of my face! People would worship me for generations! Tsukimi would be a disaster!"

Kurara didn't know what to do in the face of Ugetsu's rant, but she still needed to reach Sola-Ea, and Ugetsu's ship was still the fastest way to the sky city.

She too was surprised that Tsukimi had taken over from the Emperor. Kurara had not thought Tsukimi was interested in ruling the empire, though perhaps the princess was doing it simply to spite her brother. Or maybe it was just easier for her to continue collecting books about Crafters and performing her experiments on shikigami if she had the power and resources of the empire behind her.

Kurara pictured the kind of experiments the princess would do to the Star Tree if it ever bloomed, and shuddered.

How quickly would Tsukimi's obsession turn to anger if – no, *when* – her experiments did not give her the results she wanted? How quickly would she chop down the Star Tree when it proved useless to her?

The sound of chair legs scraping against the wooden floor brought her back to the moment at hand. Ugetsu had calmed down. He smiled like a tiger barely restraining itself from biting at the bars of its cage. "Tell the crew to increase our speed. I want us at Sola-Ea by the end of the week."

While the soldier scrambled to do the prince's bidding, Ugetsu adjusted his hair in the reflection of the porthole windows. He tucked a few strands back in place, smoothed down his moustache, and strolled over to the oak drinks cabinet, where he took out another crystal goblet and bottle of wine.

"About Sola-Ea…" Kurara began as Ugetsu poured himself a new glass, but the prince silenced her with a look.

"You're in luck, shikigami girl." He tapped his fingers against the hilt of his katana, smiling like a cat who had just caught a very large mouse. "I think I have a use for you after all."

THIRTY-ONE

"OH Gods, oh Gods!"

Haru looked like he was about to be sick. His skin was clammy and pale, and his chest heaved like a pair of bellows. If he was going to throw up, Himura hoped he would do it somewhere else, preferably when they were not squeezed together between two teahouses, in the back of a narrow alleyway, hiding from the military police and the Emperor's imperial Crafters.

The dead Emperor's imperial Crafters.

"What do we do? What are we supposed to do now?" Haru whispered, frantic.

"We need to calm down. Then we should make sure that no one is following us, and after that…"

"After that…?"

Himura took a deep, steadying breath. Honestly, he was surprised that they were even still alive. Escaping had not been easy. Himura had taken advantage of the Crafters' shock to break out of his bindings and pull Haru free. While the clerk screamed at them, Himura had dashed for the windows and crashed through the glass, landing smack bang against the docking bay floor where the airship had come to land.

The drop had been a short one, no more than six feet, but still Himura's side throbbed where he had taken the brunt of the fall. The Emperor's Crafters had chased after them, but Himura had managed to drag himself and Haru out of the docks and into the tangled streets of Sola-Ea.

They were far enough into the heart of the city now that Himura reckoned they had lost their pursuers, but what were they meant to do now? Accident or not, one did not kill the ruler of a country and simply walk away.

Then there was Mana. The snake had darted away as soon as the Emperor's body had hit the floor, and Himura had no idea where the shikigami was now. It was not safe for Mana to be out here alone. He had to find the snake before anything else could happen, before Mana's unravelling mind compelled it to hurt someone else, before—

He slammed his fist against the wall. They just needed somewhere to lie low. Somewhere safe for Himura to collect his thoughts and decide on their next move.

"The *Orihime*," he said. "The *Orihime* is here. In Sola-Ea."

They could hide on board the ship. Sakurai would not turn them away. The captain of the *Orihime* was far too kind for his own good, with a terrible tendency to take in strays. Perhaps Tomoe and Sayo would be here too, if they had managed to make it to the city as well.

The thought of returning to the ship filled him with both relief and dread. The *Orihime* was a second home, a place of comfort and rest, but it was also the place he had lived with Akane, the place he had trained Kurara, where he had argued that shikigami were nothing but mindless tools. He was ashamed of the person he had been back then – he didn't want to be reminded of everything he had said and done.

"If you know where your ship is, lead the way." Haru nodded, though he still looked alarmingly pale. If not for the wall that he was leaning against, Himura reckoned Haru would have already collapsed.

"Do you think you can walk?"

Pain contorted the boy's expression. "I can feel them writhing about." He pressed a palm to his chest, as though he was afraid something might burst out of his core at any moment – for both their sakes Himura dearly hoped nothing would. "Do you think … could you order me not to pass out?"

"If you pass out, you pass out. I can't give you an impossible order," said Himura.

Haru sighed. Though the narrow alleyway where they had taken shelter was far from any main roads or populated streets, Himura could hear a commotion in the distance. He poked his head out, but had to quickly yank it back as a pair of soldiers tore past him.

"Princess Tsukimi! The princess has arrived at the city!" one of the men shouted at another pair of soldiers somewhere up ahead. "Hurry up, everyone is assembling at the plaza to greet her!"

An officer cursed. "Damn convenient of her to turn up now! Where in the seven hells has she been?"

"Mind your tongue, she's going to be Empress now!" a third, sullen, voice grumbled as the soldiers moved further and further away.

"But wasn't it her Crafters who killed the Emperor? Are we crowning murderers now?"

"I said watch it! From now on, she's going to be the one giving orders around here."

Himura waited until he could no longer hear the sound of the soldiers' footsteps before poking his head out of the alleyway again. For the first time since this whole blasted mess had started, Himura's spirits lifted. If Princess Tsukimi had finally arrived at Sola-Ea, perhaps she might call off the search. After all, she had hated her father – what did she care that someone had killed him? Especially if everyone thought her father's killers were her own Crafters.

"Himura." Haru's voice jolted him from his thoughts. "Did you hear that? Princess Tsukimi is here. Do you think Rara is with her?"

"I don't know. It didn't sound like it." Himura was concerned about Kurara as well, but there were only so many things he could worry about at once.

"We should look for Rara," said Haru.

"We *should* find the *Orihime*," Himura countered. Looking for Kurara could come later, once they had somewhere safe to stay.

Haru frowned but did not object. Was it because of the bond? Had they been together long enough now that Haru was less likely to argue with him?

"*I want something honest,*" Mana had said to him once. Himura finally thought he understood what the shikigami had meant by it. Relationships could not be genuine when one side was forced to feel a certain way about you; they could not be honest. As long as they were bonded, he would never really know how Haru thought or felt about him.

"I'm sorry."

Haru blinked at him. "What for?"

"Nothing," said Himura. "Let's go find the ship."

THIRTY-TWO

THE best thing about cities was that they were full of paper – lanterns hanging from rooftops, books displayed outside shops, paintings on canvas, discarded newspapers, forgotten memos, love notes and the scraps of a receipt that had fallen from someone's pocket. Himura had no trouble pulling more than a dozen pieces of paper towards him until he once more had a bracelet's worth of ofuda around his wrist.

Armed with paper, he felt a lot less anxious. Now it was simply a matter of sneaking into the docking bay where the *Orihime* was held.

Dock Seven was a large metal building with a curved tortoiseshell dome. Himura and Haru clambered up onto the roof using Himura's ofuda as a rope and peered down through the skylight.

Docking guards in brilliant, bright blue uniforms

patrolled across the ceiling beams like eagle-eyed birds, staring down at the ships below. Past the rafters, illuminated by the low amber lights, Himura spotted the *Orihime* standing in the middle of a row of other airships. It was in better condition than when he had last seen it – the holes in the hull were patched up and the guard rails were fixed – but there were still scorch marks on the side and a sharp dent where something had hit the prow hard.

Himura had never thought he would miss anything about the *Orihime*'s noisy crew or its captain, yet his pace quickened with every step he took up the gangway. As he got closer, his unease melted away, replaced by a longing he wasn't quite prepared for. He wanted to eat the head cook's soba noodles and listen to the crew argue about the latest gossip from the sky cities. Hells, he even wanted to share a cup of Captain Sakurai's awful, watered-down sake.

Pulling a handful of ofuda from his bracelet, he made a small knife out of paper and used it to prise open the skylight.

"We need to do this quietly," Himura whispered to Haru as he gestured for the boy to follow him.

The docking guards were so focused on watching the ground below that they didn't notice when Himura slipped through the skylight and onto the wooden beams holding up the ceiling. Silently, he grabbed Haru and sailed to the ground using a long paper rope.

They landed in the shadow of a large airship. The dim lights helped to hide them from the guards as they ducked from ship to ship, sticking to the shadows, until they reached the foot of the *Orihime*.

The airship was dwarfed by two much larger vessels. Pressing himself flat against the metal hull, Himura pulled his bracelet off and twisted his ofuda together into a thick rope.

"Can you hold on to me?" He offered his hand to Haru.

The moment Haru grabbed hold of him, he sent one end of the rope curling around the ship's railing. With a flick of his fingers, the rope pulled them both towards the top of the ship, where they landed on the deck with a thump.

There was only one other person outside: a single deckhand currently swabbing the patchwork deck. He whirled around so quickly Himura had to duck the swing of his mop.

"Who goes there—? Wait … Mr Himura?"

Pressing a finger to his lips, Himura whispered, "Let me inside!"

The deckhand gave a terrified nod and opened the deck hatch, allowing both Himura and Haru to slip into the ship unnoticed.

"I – I'll call for Captain Sakurai!" The deckhand all but raced away.

They did not have to wait long for Captain Sakurai to come sauntering through the ship's hallways, as if he was not the least bit surprised that Himura had shown up out of nowhere with some boy in tow. Sakurai looked much the same as ever, armed with two silver pistols and dressed in a breezy silver kimono that slowly turned to blue at the hems, but there were dark circles beneath his eyes that Himura did not remember being there, and his hair looked thinner and messier.

Still, his smile was the same.

"Mr Himura," he said. "Welcome home."

━━━━━━━━━━━━○━━━━━━━━━━━━

Himura stared at his room. Aside from the fine coat of dust over everything, it was exactly the same as he had left it: the books, the patch in the ceiling where Kurara had once smashed through the wood, the small ink stain in the corner of the tatami.

It didn't feel like his room any more; this belonged to the person he had once been. He was different now.

Different, but not better. No, a better man would have been able to save Mana. A better man would be able to help Haru through the problems with his core. Standing inside his old room only reminded him of all his shortcomings.

"The two of you can rest here." Captain Sakurai leaned against the doorway.

"Oh, thank God!" Haru wasted no time in rifling through Himura's closet and pulling out an old futon.

Himura didn't protest. After everything, the boy deserved rest and some time to himself. He rubbed his hands over his face. As much as he would like some sleep as well, he didn't think he could rest yet. Captain Sakurai's questioning gaze burned against the back of his neck.

"You're wondering what we're doing here, aren't you? It's a long story."

"Why don't you tell it to me in the mess hall, Mr Himura? I bet you've missed our cooking," said Sakurai.

He had. By the Gods, Himura would have killed for

a plate of anything that wasn't mushrooms, shoots or millet.

The mess hall looked the same as ever: the long, sleek tables lined with chairs that had been screwed to the floor; the chrome counters where food was served; the tray dispenser that had been polished until it gleamed. But though the hall looked the same, it was as silent and empty as an open grave.

"All Sorabito ships are in lockdown," Sakurai explained as he slipped behind the food counter to scoop them each a bowl of rice steeped in green tea, heaping a side of pickled radish onto a smaller plate. "No one can leave or enter Sola-Ea."

Himura stirred his chopsticks through the bowl. The crew must have had a rough time. He was sorry that he had not been there to help them through it. Maybe if he had been on board the ship, they would not be stuck here in Sola-Ea in the first place.

"But enough about me and the *Orihime*," said Sakurai. "Tell me what happened after you left."

Himura took a deep breath. "First, there are some things I need you to know."

What came next was not easy. There were thorns in his throat; each time he tried to speak, he felt something drag at his voice, trying to hold him back. With a wince, he explained as quickly as he could everything that had really happened on Sola-Il: how he had betrayed Kurara and sold Haru's core; the real reason Akane had died.

It felt like a confession – by recalling his mistakes, he was taking responsibility for them. He spoke about what had happened after he had left the *Orihime*, about meeting Mana, and discovering the truth about shikigami. About travelling with Kurara until they were forced apart, and their encounter with the Emperor.

It was difficult to tell how well Sakurai took everything. The crew used to say that you could tell what Sakurai was feeling by the length and angle of his smile, but Himura had been gone far too long. He could no longer read any difference in the curve of the captain's mouth.

"The Emperor is dead," Sakurai repeated Himura's words. "I heard some kind of commotion outside earlier, but I didn't think... Well, good riddance, I say. If I'm to be honest, I don't like the idea of Princess Tsukimi becoming Empress, but it's not like the Emperor was a saint either. I certainly won't mourn his passing."

"But now Haru and I are wanted men."

"Are you? We're at war. Things change as quick as a tiger blinks. One day you're a criminal, the next you're a hero."

Himura's grip tightened around his chopsticks. A hero? That sounded unlikely.

"So shikigami have souls. They were once human." Sakurai nursed his cup of water. Himura had been waiting for him to bring up Akane, to tell him that he was a murderer and a terrible person besides, to at the very least tell him how disappointed he was.

"Does that change anything?"

"Of course it does! Wild shikigami still have to be stopped. We can't let them hurt people, but if I had known, I would have been more ... gentle about things." Sakurai tipped his head back and downed his cup before dropping his head into his hands. His gaze wandered to the kitchen door. "And

Miss Kurara and that boy. You say they're shikigami too?"

Himura sat up a little straighter. "You don't mind that Kurara isn't human?"

"You just said that shikigami are people, didn't you? Why would I mind? Miss Kurara is still the same person she's always been."

It was just like the captain to make things sound so simple. Himura doubted many others would see things that way. Or maybe he had just assumed that other people were all equally as bad as him – after all, when he had found out the truth, he had treated Kurara terribly.

He tilted his cup so that the tea caught the light. He wondered if Kurara would forgive him for Haru. The state of Haru's core might not be directly his fault, but he was supposed to keep Haru safe – and in that he had failed spectacularly. Akane, Mana and now Haru. Perhaps that was just what he did: let shikigami down.

"So, what do you plan on doing now?" asked Sakurai. "You're not returning to the *Orihime* for good, are you?"

Himura couldn't meet the captain's eye. "I'm sorry." He had missed the *Orihime* certainly. To his surprise, he had even missed the crew. But the ship belonged to a chapter of his life that he was ready to say goodbye to. He wanted a clean break from his past self, a chance to be a better man and not just a different one. Even if Kurara still hated him, he knew he would continue to aid her in her goal to save the shikigami.

"Don't be." The captain waved away his apologies. "For us Sorabito, our crew is our second family. As family, the only thing I want is for my crew to find happiness, even if it means leaving the ship – you know that, right?"

"Of course, Captain."

Sakurai's lips split into a grin. "Ha! *Now* you show me some respect! I can count on one hand the number of times you've called me Captain!" He slapped him on the back so hard Himura's face almost ended up in his bowl of rice.

Spluttering, Himura recovered just enough to smile.

"Thank you, Captain."

Interlude

Moth, how easily
You flutter towards the flames,
Charmed by your own doom

– Written by a Crafter of Unknown Origin
(from the library of the imperial princess)

As Rei stepped forward, the click of his boots echoed through the rookery. "Tomoe, did you think I wouldn't notice you sneaking around my ship like a rat?" He smiled, arms behind his back like a patient teacher waiting for his misbehaving student to see reason.

While Tomoe backed away, Sayo stepped between them, baring her teeth in an almost feral snarl.

"Such ill-mannered company you keep, my dear daughter." Rei sighed.

"Don't look at her!" The moment Tomoe snapped, she knew she had made a mistake.

"*Find the vein and stab deep,*" her father always said.

His every word was a test, searching for the right place to insert the blade, and he had found it. He had managed to get a rise out of her.

Rei's eyes flickered over Sayo, as if seeing her in a new light. The smallest of smirks tugged at his mouth and Tomoe bristled.

"You disappoint me, daughter. And here I was thinking you came to aid me in our glorious fight for independence."

Tomoe puffed out her chest. "A glorious fight? Is that what you call murdering innocent people?" She gestured to the shikigami cores piled high on the shelves. "How can you even *think* about doing this? You've seen those things that emerge from a shikigami's core. Once they've killed everyone in the city, then what? How will you get the shadows to leave once you've unleashed them?"

Rei considered Tomoe's questions with the same scorn of someone regarding the horse manure at his feet. "Must you be so emotional all the time? I am only doing what needs to be done."

Tomoe seethed. They could talk all day, trading snide barbs and cutting insults, but ultimately getting nowhere. Her father didn't care about the Sorabito, only his desire to be the hero who won them their independence, and nothing Tomoe could say would change that.

"Tomoe." Sayo's voice held a note of warning. "Be careful."

"Yes, listen to your *friend*, Tomoe." Rei chuckled. "Before you do something the both of you will regret."

Pushing Sayo out of the way, Tomoe drew her tanto. She lunged at Rei, but her father was quicker, blocking her first swing with his own katana and pushing her back towards the wall.

"Tomoe!" Sayo shouted.

"Stay back!" Tomoe rolled out of the way of her father's sword.

She ducked beneath Rei's katana and closed the space between them, but her father blocked her attempt to slit his throat, and the force of their clashing blades sent her tanto flying out of her hand.

Before she could react, Rei landed a kick to her gut, sending her staggering backwards into the wire rack. Metal cylinders crashed to the ground around her.

Her vision blurred. She spluttered, winded, as pain lanced through her body. When she finally managed to look up, Rei was already lifting his katana above his head, ready to strike again.

"Tomoe!"

Sayo shoved her out of the way. Her father's katana came down in a vicious arc, slicing Sayo from shoulder to waist.

Blood erupted across Sayo's chest. She fell as if in slow motion, hitting the ground with an awful thud.

"SAYO!" Tomoe screamed.

The tanto slipped from her grip.

Sayo! No, no, no, no!

A searing pain exploded through Tomoe's body. She gasped, not quite able to comprehend what had happened, despite the blood seeping through her clothes. Despite her father's katana sticking into her side.

Her father stared at her down the length of his sword. She screamed as he pulled the blade free.

"A pity," she heard him mutter as she fell.

THIRTY-THREE

THE news of the Emperor's death still had not fully sunk in when Prince Ugetsu ordered his servants to prepare dinner for the both of them. Kurara remained standing near the doorway while a line of men entered Ugetsu's room and set the table.

Once the servants bustled out of the door, she turned her attention to the spread of food laid out before her. There was enough here to constitute a mini-feast: vegetables finely sliced and simmered in soy, slices of beef marbled with fat, hearty turtle broth, thin buckwheat noodles, and rice so white and fluffy it looked like powdered snow. To one side of the table stood thin slices of cantaloupe and pink, chewy mochi filled with red bean paste for dessert.

On a silver and white trolley next to the table stood a decanter of wine, a jug of fresh water, and a pot of green tea with the appropriate glasses and cups for all three types of refreshment. It had been so long since Kurara had eaten anything more than mushrooms and millet and shoots, her mouth watered.

"Don't be shy now. Help yourself." Ugetsu sat down at one end of the table and filled his glass with more wine. "Can you eat? I'm not sure what a shikigami like you is capable of. If not, you can just watch while I eat."

"I can eat," said Kurara tightly, and picked up a pair of chopsticks.

"The broth is a local recipe taken from one of our southern colonies, though we improved the ingredients and the flavour." Ugetsu gestured for her to try the soup inside a large clay pot.

"So it's not a local recipe." Kurara sat down.

Prince Ugetsu regarded her with a strange twinkle in his eye. The change in his attitude set her nerves on edge. She could hardly enjoy the marbled beef with him looking at her like that.

"So, I've decided to take you to Sola-Ea after all." Ugetsu ran a hand through his perfectly oiled hair. "Tell me about my sister. What has she been up to? What is she after?"

Kurara chewed her rice slowly, giving herself time to think. She told Prince Ugetsu about Tsukimi's obsession with shikigami and her desire to control them herself, leaving out all mention of the Star Seed and Star Trees. She recounted her meeting with Tsukimi at the Mountain of the Falling Star and how they had accidentally awoken a giant shikigami that had grabbed Tsukimi and whisked her away, until the princess had broken free and killed the toad.

That Sorabito pair took Entei's core. Kurara wished she

had been able to speak with the toad some more, to ask it about her past. She wanted to ask what they had done with it. Where did the cores go after they were delivered to Prince Ugetsu or Sohma? She wasn't sure she could ask; or if Prince Ugetsu would even tell her the truth if she did.

"So my sister went to Sola-Ea. Why?" asked Ugetsu.

"I don't know," she admitted. Perhaps the key to making the Star Seed bloom lay somewhere on the sky city.

"The fall doesn't matter. Only one thing does. Nothing is gained without sacrifice." Kurara still didn't know what Tsukimi meant by that. All she knew was that she could not let the princess have the Star Seed, no matter how tempting the offer. Even if Tsukimi made the Star Seed bloom, the princess would hoard the Star Tree for herself – and eventually cut it down when her experiments failed to give her what she wanted.

While she stewed in her thoughts, Ugetsu took her bowl and replaced it with another filled with soba noodles in a thin soup.

"I wasn't done with my rice."

Ugetsu ignored her. "Have the noodles; you'll like them more."

Kurara ate a grudging mouthful. The noodles were divine. That irritated her even more.

While she ate, Prince Ugetsu swirled his wine against the rim of his glass, staring at the angles of his reflection.

"My sister isn't the type to concern herself with battles or wars. With anything except shikigami and Crafters really. My father would never give up the throne without a fight, but Tsukimi knows what she wants – and it's not the throne.

As you say, what she really wants is to have a shikigami of her own. I believe I can negotiate with her. And you, my dear shikigami, will be my bargaining chip."

"You want to sell me out to Tsukimi in exchange for an empire?" Kurara wasn't sure whether to be flattered or offended. Surely, she wasn't worth that much.

But Ugetsu was right; Tsukimi's true desire was a shikigami of her own – one that she could bond with and control like a puppet. Tsukimi knew Kurara had the Star Seed too. It was possible the princess would give up the throne in exchange for the two of them.

Tsukimi is proud, though. Would she step aside for her brother? Or did she hate him so much she would cling to the throne out of spite?

Kurara stirred a spoon through her soup with all the caution of someone stirring a barrel of liquid levistone. It was worth a shot. She wasn't going to hand over the Star Seed to Princess Tsukimi, but she was also confident that she could fight her way out of most situations. She could play along until they reached Sola-Ea.

"If you object, you're free to leave my ship." Prince Ugetsu regarded her with a calculating smile.

Kurara schooled her face into a blank expression. "Who said I objected?"

Ugetsu's smile turned into a grin. "Then I'll have someone show you to your room."

THIRTY-FOUR

WITH each day that passed, the *Hotei* came closer and closer to Sola-Ea, closer to the levistone cannon and to Princess Tsukimi. Kurara's quarters were more lavish than anywhere she had ever slept before. Her bed was a bulky wooden thing with clawed feet that raised it off the ground and strangely squishy pillows. There was a fireplace in the corner to keep her warm on chilly autumn nights and a writing desk stocked with paper and ink brushes.

Yet, despite all these luxuries, she still suffered from nightmares. As soon as she fell asleep, Suzaku was waiting for her as usual. The phoenix shikigami spread its wings and screeched at her. Sometimes, Entei would make an appearance too, screaming about wasting time. Sometimes, it was Princess Tsukimi who showed up, the echo of her smug voice following Kurara through her dreams.

"The fall doesn't matter. Only one thing does. Nothing is gained without sacrifice."

Whenever she jolted awake, gasping for breath, she reached for the Star Seed and squeezed it tight. Its weight was a comfort: a reminder of why she was here and what she was fighting for.

———————◦———————

During the day, Kurara tried to piece together everything she knew about the Star Seed. She had thought that the lullaby was the answer, but, according to Princess Tsukimi, falling from the sky – or "from the heavens" as the lullaby stated – would not make the Star Seed bloom. Kurara had tested it herself. Yet if the fall didn't matter, then why had Tsukimi gone to a sky city?

Maybe it was the impact of the fall that would make the Star Seed bloom? Or the heat as the seed burned through the air and crashed to the ground.

There were not many experiments she could do – or dared to do – while on the ship, but she tested whether heat would do something to the Star Seed by flinging it into the fireplace, and waited several torturous hours for the flames to die out before she could retrieve it.

The Star Seed was warmer than before, but otherwise unchanged.

It did not prove anything for certain. Perhaps the fire was not hot enough. When she had thrown the Star Seed to the ground, perhaps she had not been high enough. Maybe what she needed was a combination of several things. Kurara could spend the rest of eternity experimenting and never getting anywhere. That was why she needed Tsukimi – or rather, she needed the answers Tsukimi had about the Star Seed.

While she was lost in her thoughts, she heard people coming and going from Ugetsu's quarters. His room was right next to her own, and she often overheard his dampened voice through the walls, humming to himself or ordering his servants to adjust his uniform.

"No, no, the gold buttons look better, don't you think?" His muffled voice drifted in and out of hearing. "Yes, the tassels do look silly, don't they?"

The sky outside her window was surprisingly clear despite the awful weather they had been having lately – a blazing strip of blue that reminded her of summer on board the *Orihime*. A moment later, the ship's bells began to ring. Kurara had just tucked away the Star Seed when a great shadow blocked the sunlight from outside.

She rushed to the porthole window just in time to see a whole fleet of Sorabito ships approaching. The flagship was as large as a sky whale, though it looked more like the kind of whale one might find in the ocean. About half a dozen smaller ships trailed behind it, all of them Sorabito in design. Some were sleek and silver, trailing white sails that looked like fish tails; others were painted the deepest midnight blue, with thin, sharp prows made for ramming straight into the enemy. Their arrival meant one thing: they had almost reached Sola-Ea.

Footsteps echoed through the corridor. A soldier knocked at Prince Ugetsu's door.

"Sir, Kazeno Rei is here to see you."

Kazeno Rei? That was the name of Sohma's leader. Tomoe's father. The man who had, according to his daughter, spent his life provoking both groundlings and Sorabito to fight each other. Kurara clenched her teeth together. She did not know Rei well, but from what she had heard of him and his group of rebels, they were dangerous and fanatical.

"Everything is ready…" Rei's voice was slightly muffled.

The men exchanged several words Kurara couldn't quite make out. She rushed to the wall separating their two rooms and pressed her ear against the wood.

"I have already sent Tsukimi a message. She knows my terms," Ugetsu was saying as she listened closely.

"And you think this will work? That your sister will just roll over and give you the throne?"

"I believe that she … after all, she…" Prince Ugetsu's voice drifted in and out of earshot. He was moving around the room.

"I thought you wanted her dead." There was a sharp edge to Rei's voice that was noticeable even through the wall.

"I do, but… She *will* die, just not right now… I can see an unfortunate accident in my dear sister's future," said Ugetsu.

"What about the cores? My men worked hard to make those weapons."

Kurara jerked her head away from the wall. Cores? Was Rei talking about using shikigami cores?

"That's for if talks break down," said Ugetsu. "I want you to be ready for… Wait for my signal…"

The conversation turned to other things, but Kurara was still stuck on the mention of cores. She had thought it odd

238

that there were Sorabito scavenging shikigami cores from battlefields. If they wanted money, surely there were easier ways to get it. Now she understood.

Jumping to her feet, Kurara barged out of her room and into Ugetsu's quarters before the guards could stop her.

"You're using shikigami cores as weapons." She threw the doors open.

Kazeno Rei was a thin, bald man with a sharp gaze and a sharper smile. As Kurara burst into the room, he turned to look at her the way one might look at a poisonous sea creature.

Prince Ugetsu, who had been standing near a marble bust of himself, turned to her with a grim smile. "You were listening, were you?"

"Are you planning on breaking them open and using the yuurei inside to attack Sola-Ea?" said Kurara.

"So what if we are?" Rei growled.

Kurara felt the floor disappear from under her feet. She was falling down a deep, dark chasm of her own fear. Prince Ugetsu and Sohma were going to use shikigami cores – the yuurei – as weapons.

"That's completely insane!" she cried. "Once the yuurei are out of their cores, you have no way of controlling them! No way of stopping them!"

It was not just a dangerous idea, it was stupid too. The yuurei would not only wipe out Rei and Prince Ugetsu's enemies but attack their own forces as well.

"We wouldn't unleash them anywhere near our soldiers," said Ugetsu, as if reading her mind. "If we were to use them – and note that I said *if* – we would drop them into the sky city. Yes, the yuurei would eventually scatter and attack other places, but wild shikigami do much the same thing and yet we live still with the death and destruction they cause. The people of Mikoshima are made of stronger stuff than your average person. Besides, it's a last resort. If you're so opposed to it, then you had better hope that our talks with Tsukimi go smoothly."

Kurara was about to protest when a loud chime came through the ship's voice-pipes.

"Sir, Sola-Ea is in our sight!"

The floor trembled beneath Kurara's feet. She could feel the engines working hard as the ship raced forward.

"Come with me," said Ugetsu.

Outside, on deck, Kurara could see the fleet of Sorabito ships properly. Each ship was armed to the teeth with cannons, ready for battle. A foghorn echoed through the air, like a rallying cry calling the troops to war.

Ugetsu strode forward, the golden buttons of his jacket gleaming. In the light of the sun, he looked every bit the dashing hero about to wage war against a pack of evil monsters. With every step he took, Kurara's nerves grew. At last they were at Sola-Ea, and if things went badly there would be a fight.

If things went badly, Ugetsu would unleash a pack of yuurei into the world. No matter what, she could not let that happen. She could not stand to watch more people suffer, to bear witness to yet more destruction.

"Sir, your sister awaits your arrival. She's … she has … well, it may be best to see for yourself." A soldier handed him a bronze spy glass.

Prince Ugetsu lifted it in the direction of the sky city.

"Ridiculous!" he spat. To Kurara's surprise, he thrust the spy glass against her chest. "Take a look at my sister's stupidity."

When Kurara placed the glass to her eye, she could see the sky city in the distance. It was surrounded by only a few ships – a sign perhaps that Tsukimi did not intend to fight.

Sola-Ea was a single dome sitting atop several large metal gates that led into the city. The Emperor's levistone cannon poked out from the glass dome, its long barrel raised in a salute to the sky. Around the bottom of the dome, someone had wrapped a banner, miles long, like a ribbon around a cake.

WELCOME, MY DEAR SHIKIGAMI!

Kurara could almost hear Princess Tsukimi's mocking laughter. Far from a welcome, it felt more like a taunt.

THIRTY-FIVE

"LET'S go." Ugetsu clicked his fingers.

At his command, a pair of soldiers pushed a qipak across the deck towards him. The small brown aircraft was the same size and shape as a rowing boat, with wings. Kurara stared at it. She had expected the prince to sail towards Sola-Ea with the full might of all his forces, his katana raised to the sky and the wind billowing through his hair. This little qipak was not fancy enough for Ugetsu's usual style.

"My sister has insisted you and I come alone. The other ships will remain here, but they'll be ready to open fire should something go wrong," the prince explained.

He turned to Rei, and placed a hand on the man's shoulder.

"Return to your ship and await my signal."

With a pleasant smile, Kazeno Rei bowed, but Kurara

caught the way he clenched his teeth together so tightly they looked as though they might shatter. When Ugetsu's back was turned, Rei wiped his shoulder as though the man had smeared dirt all over it.

A sense of deep unease grew as Kurara was ushered towards the qipak. She noticed that Ugetsu had replaced his pistol for a flare gun.

"Ah, this brings me back! I flew one of these qipaks during the war against Estia back when the empire was fighting against the Western kingdoms. I flew right over the heads of the foreign devils, and each time I swung my sword, our enemies fell before me! Why, the poets wrote a thousand haiku in celebration of my achievements!" Ugetsu grabbed the vehicle's controls, forcing Kurara to take the backseat.

It was cramped inside the qipak, but Kurara did her best to hold on to the sides. In a burst of blue jet-fire, the qipak's engines roared to life. A moment later, it raced across the length of the deck and lifted off into the bright blue sky. On the other side of the clouds, Kurara could just about make out a line of silver battleships hovering close to the city.

"What do you plan to say to Tsukimi when you see her?" she asked as the wind whipped through her hair.

"I'll tell her that she can have you if she just steps aside. She can remain princess, she can have her library and continue her experiments in peace. Just as long as she stays out of my way and lets me rule," said Ugetsu, though Kurara remembered him wanting his sister to meet an unfortunate accident. She doubted he intended to let Tsukimi live for long.

"And what will you do as ruler?" she asked.

"I'm thinking of expanding further west. The other empires don't know how to run a colony like we do."

Kurara was glad she was standing behind Ugetsu so he couldn't see her flinch. *"Run a colony,"* he had said. As if a whole country of people was just a factory made to squeeze out wealth and resources.

"And you'll give the Sorabito their independence," she said.

Ugetsu shrugged. "Sure. I'll gladly give the sky rats a little piece of paper that says *Independence* with my signature below."

Sky rats, Kurara thought. It wasn't just what Ugetsu said but the *way* he said it. *Sky rats.* Like they weren't even people. He had started this fight because he said he wanted the Sorabito to be free, but really all he had wanted was an excuse for a war.

The Sorabito deserved better than some tyrant who was only using their suffering for his own ends. Kurara's hands itched to push him off the qipak and watch him tumble through the sky, but she was afraid it would cause Princess Tsukimi and Sohma's airships to open fire on one another.

As they came closer to the city, and closer to the silver battleships standing guard in front of Sola-Ea, a loud bang grabbed her attention. Ugetsu pulled out his flare gun, ready to fire, but the explosion was not a gunshot or cannon fire.

Though it was only early afternoon, fireworks shot from the decks of Princess Tsukimi's battleships. From the tall watchtowers, each ship broadcasted what sounded like a gramophone recording of an old children's song.

"Welcome home, welcome home. We all hold hands in a big circle and sing! Welcome home, welcome home!"

The disturbingly shrill song blasted through the air. The battleships were all playing the same song slightly out of sync, resulting in a jumbled, noisy mess.

"She's making fun of us!" Prince Ugetsu swore.

They endured the questionable parade of daylight fireworks and screechy gramophone recordings until they reached Sola-Ea.

WELCOME, MY DEAR SHIKIGAMI!

Up close, the banner hanging from the bottom of the dome seemed even more insulting. Guiding lights blinked and a pair of metal gates at the bottom of the city opened up, leading them through a tunnel into an empty dock.

If Tsukimi wanted to ambush them, this would be the perfect place for an attack. Kurara stiffened, on high alert as Ugetsu landed the qipak and the gates leading into the city opened before them.

Whoever had designed Sola-Ea must have been very drunk. The entire city was orange. It was a small mercy that not every building was the same blinding neon tone, but various shades of burnt umber, ginger and bright pumpkin, some of the colours verging on yellow or red. In another life, she could see herself wandering through the streets, caught in some kind of autumnal wonderland. Instead, she was as tense as a coiled spring, just waiting for something to go terribly wrong.

The words

WELCOME, SHIKIGAMI!

were painted onto the ground in front of the docks. When Kurara looked up, she noticed more messages on some of the building stacks, written in ten-feet-tall characters.

THIS WAY! THIS WAY!

they cried, with large red arrows pointing to somewhere in the city, almost offensive in their cheeriness. Kurara wondered which poor servant had been forced to climb up those building stacks to write those messages.

"Prince Ugetsu, I presume." A woman was waiting outside the docks.

Kurara felt a jolt of electricity lance up her spine – the telltale sign that the person in front of her was a Crafter.

"Princess Tsukimi is waiting for you beneath the autumn palace." The woman wore paper rings on every finger. She bowed and gestured in the same direction that the large arrows were pointing.

"Beneath?" said Ugetsu.

"There is a whole network of tunnels that run underneath the city. Tunnels full of cables that fuel the levistone cannon."

Kurara understood Ugetsu's hesitation. It sounded like a trap. It was already a huge risk coming to Sola-Ea alone, and now Tsukimi wanted to meet somewhere underneath the city?

They had no time to discuss their options though. Before

246

Kurara could so much as open her mouth, there was a loud bang and the ground beneath them shook.

Spinning around, Kurara looked up to find both imperial and Sohma ships moving towards each other, trading cannon fire and bullets. The larger battleships sent out a swarm of smaller crafts – fiery red kohanes built like mechanical wasps; star-streamers that looked like bullets with a cockpit and an engine. They shot towards the ships, riddling the decks with gunfire.

"What's going on?" cried Kurara.

The Crafter woman pulled a paper ring from her finger. In a blink, it transformed into a giant scythe, the blade of which she pointed squarely at Ugetsu.

"Did you give the order to attack?"

"No, of course not! Why would I?" the prince growled.

"Then why are your ships moving towards the city?"

"I don't know. Those are Rei's ships! What on earth does he think he's doing?"

Kurara thought back to the dark look Rei had given Ugetsu when the prince wasn't looking. If Ugetsu was just using Sohma, then Sohma was just using Ugetsu. Perhaps this was what Rei wanted all along – a chance to kill both Prince Ugetsu and Princess Tsukimi by bringing down the entire city.

Sohma's ships charged onwards, crashing right into one another in a shriek of splintered wood and screeching metal. Kurara watched as the Sorabito ships began to fan out around the city, releasing smoke canisters to blind the enemy.

An awful, shattering sound caught Kurara's attention. When she looked up, she noticed that the dome above them was broken. A cannonball had struck the glass, leaving a giant hole in its wake. It was a small mercy that the city was low enough that the air was still breathable, though the people of Sola-Ea might find it uncomfortably thin.

Rei's ship hovered above the dome, casting its shadow on the city.

"Rei! What do you think you're doing!" Ugetsu screamed up at the whale-like ship, as if Rei could possibly hear him from so far away.

The bottom of the ship opened up like a gaping maw and something fell out.

Silver metal gleamed in the light. A metal cylinder hit the ground next to Kurara's foot. There was a snapping sound and a stream of smoke escaped from the top of the cylinder.

No, not smoke. Shadow. A yuurei.

Kurara held her breath. This couldn't be happening. She didn't want to believe it. She had known that Rei and Ugetsu had been planning to use the yuurei as weapons, but Ugetsu had said it would be a last resort.

More cylinders fell around her. A deadly silver rain. Each one hit the ground with a snap like the sound of a life breaking apart.

THIRTY-SIX

HIMURA'S eyes snapped open the moment the *Orihime*'s bells rang.

"Attention, all crew. Attention, all crew. Sola-Ea is under attack. Please stand by at your stations and await further instructions."

"An attack?" Haru's eyes widened just as an earth-shattering blast rocked the ship, flinging them both, and Himura's books, against the walls of his quarters.

By the time Himura had picked himself up, the alarm bells had stopped ringing, and only the sound of Sakurai's voice remained, echoing down the brass voice-pipes as he barked orders for the crew to gather on the deck. Himura didn't know what the captain intended to do. Even though Sohma was firing on the city, all of Sola-Ea was in lockdown and the ships in the docking bay were not allowed to go anywhere.

"Let's go!" said Haru, though his face was pale and his breathing strained.

"You don't look so good," said Himura.

"It's fine. I can manage," Haru insisted. "Let's go to the deck like the captain ordered."

Himura frowned. Kurara would have said something soothing like, "You don't need to force yourself to be all right." Mana would have been firm yet reassuring, but Himura only knew how to be blunt and awkward.

"Are you sure? You could stay here. You could…" What could Haru do? Just sit and twiddle his thumbs while dozens of souls squirmed inside his core and explosions rocked the city?

Haru shook his head, his expression set with determination. "Wherever you're going, I'm coming with you."

Himura wasn't going to waste time arguing. Besides, a part of him felt better when he was able to keep an eye on Haru. With a nod, he headed to the deck. Some of the crew were already standing by the sails, ready to furl or unfurl them depending on the situation. Another was placed at the lookout, and another stood on the prow, staring out at the situation below.

Across the wide expanse of the docking bay floor, a small crowd had gathered near the exit gate where a docking guard was trying to bar the way. Angry shouts echoed through the air as the crowd yelled at the man to let them out.

"Open the gates! We won't be detained here any longer."

"No one is to leave or enter Sola-Ea. Those are our orders!" The officer held his ground. On the ceiling beams above, more guards patrolled the top of the docking bay, looking down upon the commotion with steely eyes and weapons at the ready. It was only the threat of their presence that kept the crowd in line.

Another blast shook the very foundations of the dock. Himura could understand the crowd's panic; most of the ships here were merchant vessels or pleasure cruisers – even those that had cannons were not experienced in battle. The continuing tremors were a reminder that at any moment they could all be blown to bits by a stray explosion. The whole docking bay could cave in, crushing them all like ants. Or the city might crash to the ground, dragging them with it. Most of the crews had been here since the declaration of war and had been caught in the city-wide lockdown. They just wanted to leave.

"I'll deal with this," Himura said to Haru, before vaulting over the edge of the guard rail and landing on the floor in a cushion of ofuda.

The guard was yelling back at the crowd, ordering them to return to their ships and wait, but the Sorabito were not budging. They pushed back, yelling and screaming their demands to be let out. If things continued like this, the men on the rafters might start firing on the crowd.

Himura's pace quickened. In the middle of a battle, the last thing anyone needed was more chaos. Besides, he would not let the *Orihime* be destroyed by a random bomb, or crushed beneath rubble without a fighting chance at survival.

"Open the gates out of the city!" He shoved his way to the front of the crowd. He made sure to let his ofuda flutter around him as he spoke. Being a Crafter gave him some semblance of authority – though at times like this he was not sure how far that authority would stretch.

"But—"

Himura's ofuda formed jagged rings in the air that spun around him. They cut through the air with a soft whine, as sharp as knives. If an order did not get the guard to move, perhaps the threat of violence would. "I was asking nicely. You can move, or I will *make* you move."

"And what will happen if I let all these ships out? These are all Sorabito ships! Can you say for certain that they won't just turn around and join Sohma in the attack on the city the moment I let them out of this docking bay?"

"Most of these ships here are merchant vessels; they barely have a cannon between them. They're not going to throw themselves into the heat of battle the moment you let them leave. All they want is to get away from here!"

The guard hesitated. Then, with a frustrated yell, he shouted, "Open the bloody gates!"

The docking bay shook as a dozen cogs creaked into motion. Levers and pulleys rattled to life, groaning as the massive doors that led in and out of Sola-Ea were pulled open to reveal the bright blue sky.

The Sorabito scrambled back to their ships, each one wishing to be the first to escape. Himura returned to the *Orihime* to find Captain Sakurai waiting for him on the deck.

"The ships are leaving. I suggest the *Orihime* does so too. Fly away as far as you can."

"What are you going to do?" asked Sakurai.

"The levistone cannon was built to fight against Sohma, but the military might mistake any ships trying to get away for Sohma vessels and open fire. Or maybe they won't care and will just shoot at anything that looks like a Sorabito ship. I'm going to stop it. I'll make sure the cannon doesn't shoot at you while you're trying to get away."

Perhaps this was Himura's way of paying Captain Sakurai back for everything he had done for him, for taking him in and giving him a home all those years ago. As long as Haru and everyone else on the *Orihime* could escape in one piece, he would be satisfied.

Captain Sakurai nodded. He had a whole crew to look after; it was not as if he could spend his time chasing after one former member. Turning to his men, he barked out an order to prepare for take-off.

"Wait, I'm coming too!" Haru pushed his way forward as Himura climbed down the gangway.

Himura stopped and shoved his palm against Haru's chest, sending the boy staggering back. "You should stay on the *Orihime*; Captain Sakurai will look after you!"

"What? Why? I can help! I'm not leaving without you!"

"You only say that because of our bond!" He was tired of this. No wonder Mana had hated it so much. He did not want Haru risking his life because of some imagined connection between them. For a bunch of feelings that weren't even real.

"So I wouldn't be brave if not for the bond – is that what you're saying?"

"That's not what I meant!" Himura's head was beginning to throb. Seven hells, the boy was as stubborn as Kurara. He wondered who had got it from whom, or if they had always been two equally stubborn stars in the night sky, refusing to do anything but shine on their own terms.

"If you want me to stay, order me to do so. Otherwise, I'm coming along!" Haru retorted.

Himura clicked his tongue in annoyance. Haru only dared him to give an order because he knew full well that Himura would never do it.

Turning on his heel, Himura marched out of the docking bay and into the city. No one stopped him as he left, and Haru followed soon after.

Bell towers tolled a warning, but there was nowhere for the residents of the city to run. Outside, the streets were already awash with chaos. Cannon fire and bombs had blown up parts of the building stacks, and fighting on the street had left shops broken and belongings strewn about the roads. There was a great hole in the glass, destroying the city's temperature-controlled air system. No wonder the atmosphere felt so thin; it was still breathable, but Himura's lungs had to work a little harder for air.

Suddenly, Haru grabbed at his sleeve.

"Himura, look up there!"

A large Sorabito ship hovered in the air just above the hole in the dome. The bottom of the airship was open, and from the hatch a dozen or so silver cylinders spilled out of the ship and onto the streets of Sola-Ea. As they hit the ground, there was a metallic snapping sound and something seeped out. Himura drew a sharp breath as he realized exactly what was emerging from those cylinders.

Yuurei.

Interlude

Oh crimson lotus,
Devour this impure world
And blossom with pride

– from *Conversations with Yōkai*
(banned by the Patriots Office)

The most surprising thing to happen to her all day was waking up. Tomoe groaned and rolled over, her eyes flying open as a sharp jolt of pain skewered her side. Rei's katana had missed everything vital, but that did not mean it did not hurt like the seven hells.

She sat up, hands flying to the puncture wound near her gut. Someone had wrapped bandages around her middle and cushioned the wound with a wad of cotton. Judging from the metallic tang of blood mixed with the herbal smell of medicine, her injury had been cleaned before being sewn shut. As Tomoe inspected her stitches, everything came flooding back. The rookery, the cores, her father, the fight, Sayo…

"Sayo?" Tomoe didn't know where she was, though she could tell from the vibrations running through the floor that she was still on an airship. And that she wasn't dead yet.

It was so dark she couldn't even see her own hands in front of her face. What had happened after the fight? Who had bandaged her up? She could not imagine someone like Kazeno Rei taking the time to carry her out of the rookery and tend to her wounds. Perhaps he had ordered one of his men to do it – yes, that made more sense, though that did not answer her question of why she was still alive in the first place.

"Sayo?" Tomoe said again.

The silence was deafening.

Tomoe drew a deep, shuddering breath. When she thought about the fight with her father, she could only see Sayo falling to the ground. Blood. There had been so much blood. Surely no one could survive that…

Panic snatched the air from her lungs. Sayo, oh Gods, Sayo. The thought of her was a chasm in Tomoe's heart. Never again would she be able to coax Sayo into a smile. She would never get to steal slices of fish from Sayo's breakfast. Never watch Sayo spar with the deckhands or read her weather charts. They would never sit together on the *Orihime*'s deck at night and point at the stars.

This was all her fault. She should have just stayed behind in the engine room instead of insisting on crawling through the vents. She should have just listened to Sayo when she said to leave the cores alone instead of wasting time arguing. Was this her punishment for not listening? For always thinking that she was right?

Her chest was a hollow, cavernous ruin and her shoulders shook with grief. Was this why her father had kept her alive? To torture her with the consequences of her actions? The only reason Sayo had been cut down was because she had placed herself in the way of a blow meant for Tomoe.

Maybe it would be better to stay here, in this dark abyss where she did not have to look at herself. It would be so easy to simply float away on the sea of her pain and never emerge again.

But what about the cores her father planned to unleash on Sola-Ea? What about the innocent people who would die? Sayo would not want her to just give up and flop over like a limp soba noodle. Not when there were people she could save.

Her palms swept over the ground, trying to work out the size of the room by touch alone. The floor was made of tatami and the walls were metal, as was the locked door. Tomoe brushed her hands over the hinges, trying to find some way she could prise the door open.

"Hey! Can anyone hear me? Hey, let me out!" Tomoe pounded her fists against the door. Her throat was so dry that when she yelled, her voice cracked, but she kept shouting: "Hey, let me out! Someone, let me out of here!"

How long had she been unconscious? She couldn't tell. If only she were like Kurara or Himura – she bet that Crafters like them never had to deal with the helpless feeling of being locked up. They were strong. Talented. Compared to them, what could she do?

You useless Sorabito. Tomoe shoved her shoulder into the

door. It did not budge, but the burning ache in her shoulder was a welcome relief. She felt like she deserved it.

The ground shook beneath her feet. The walls echoed with gunfire and the world around her tilted to one side, sending her sliding backwards. Something scraped against the outside of the ship, and exploded nearby.

Gods, had they already reached Sola-Ea? Was this the final battle? Had her father unleashed the shadows yet?

She shoved her shoulder into the door again. Pain rang through her bones, but she didn't care. Again, she charged at the door.

It swung open.

She went flying into the hallway and toppled over a warm, soft body. A lance of white-hot pain shot up her side, leaving her hissing in agony while the person beneath her groaned.

The bright lights of the hallway blinded her, but she recognized that voice.

"S–Sayo?" As her eyes adjusted to the light, she found herself staring at her friend's pinched face.

Sayo's eyes were squeezed shut, one hand clutching at her stomach. Like Tomoe, someone had treated her wound – the smell of medicine herbs was so strong Tomoe almost choked on the scent – but the front of her clothes remained a blood-soaked, grisly sight.

Tomoe scrambled to her feet, not caring about how her stitches tugged and bit at her skin. Was this a dream? Was she seeing ghosts? Or maybe Tomoe was the one who was dead.

"Sayo!" she cried. "Sayo, please, I…"

With a groan, Sayo lifted her head and cracked open one eye. "Tomoe?" Her voice sounded as raw as Tomoe's, as parched and painful as a month in the desert without water.

"You absolute idiot! I'd hit you if it wasn't against my morals to hit an injured person!" There were tears in her eyes, and she didn't care. She probably looked a mess, but she had never been so relieved in her life. It made her want to say something dramatic and cheesy like "I can't do this without you" or "Please don't ever leave me" or "I think you're as lovely as starlight".

"You have morals now?" Sayo joked.

Bloody skies, the world had to be ending if Sayo was the one trying to be funny.

Tomoe's hands shook. Finding Sayo alive did not ease her terror. In fact, she was even more afraid than when she had first woken up. What was happening? How was Sayo alive? Somehow, it felt too good to be true. Like there was some terrible price she would have to pay for all this. What if she lost Sayo again? What if it was forever this time? How could she live with herself?

"Sayo," she said despondently. "I'm so, so sorry. You were right. I should have just left the cores alone. I should have—"

"Just let people die?"

Tomoe stared at her.

"You were right," Sayo huffed, though Tomoe knew how much she hated to admit it. "What Sohma wants to do is disgraceful. Wiping out a sky city? And they dare to call themselves Sorabito? I'm glad that you care about other

people, Tomoe. I just wish you hadn't spoken to me like that. I wish you hadn't tried to *use* me."

Misery clawed at Tomoe's chest. Her father used people. He found whatever they cared about and turned those things against them. She never wanted to be like him.

"I know. I'm *so sorry*," she said. "I don't want you to feel like you're the one giving and giving everything, and I always have to have my way. I don't want you to feel like I don't care about you."

The tears she had tried so hard to hold back came spilling over her cheeks. Tomoe sobbed into her hands.

"H–hey!" Sayo's eyes widened in alarm. "I, er, oh Gods… There, there. It's OK?" She gave Tomoe's head an awkward pat, but that just made Tomoe bawl even louder.

Gods, Tomoe wanted to hug her so badly. Her fingers trembled with the urge to press them against Sayo's cheek. She only held back because she knew it would hurt both of them. The last thing either of them needed was to rip open their wounds.

Sayo looked like she wanted to disappear into a hole in the floor. "Can we talk about this later? Please?"

Wiping away her tears, Tomoe forced herself to calm down. They were still on her father's ship in the middle of a battle. Later, she swore she would make it up to Sayo one thousand times over, but for now they had to decide their next move.

As if to remind them of the situation outside, a blast shook the walls. The hallway rang with orders to open fire, shouted through the voice-pipes and delivered throughout the ship.

"Sounds like the fight has already started," said Sayo grimly as Tomoe helped her to her feet. "I woke up in the room next to yours. Something hit the ship and the tremors caused cracks to run up the wall and around the door. It broke the hinges right off. When I stepped out, I heard you yelling so I unbolted your door and…"

She looked seconds away from keeling over. The wound on her stomach was not fully closed, and Tomoe was afraid she had made it worse by falling on her.

"Listen, Tomoe. I don't know what's going on outside, but you can still stop your father."

Tomoe shook her head. She didn't want to do anything that might take her away from Sayo's side. "What if it's too late? What if the cores have been released?"

"You won't know until you find him. I can barely move, but you can go. Leave me."

"Bloody skies, Sayo! Don't be so dramatic! I can haul you over my shoulder, no problem. Or would you prefer to be carried like a princess?"

"Tomoe."

"*Sayo.*" She took Sayo's hand and squeezed it tight, as if afraid that Sayo might disappear if she didn't hold on.

"Go on. I'll be fine here," said Sayo. "I know you. And I know that if you don't do something to try and stop your father, you'll hate yourself for it afterwards."

She was right. For all their differences, Sayo could read her better than one of her star charts.

"I'll come back for you," Tomoe promised.

From the porthole window, she could see Sorabito ships

flocking towards Sola-Ea while more were flooding out from the city's docks – merchant ships and luxury cruisers fleeing while the battle raged. The clouds were awash with groundling ships too, though it was hard to tell which ones were on their side and which belonged to the empire. The skies were a confusion of cannon fire and bullets.

More voices screamed through the pipes to return fire. Taking a deep breath, Tomoe began to move. Her side throbbed with pain, but she kept going.

She knew exactly where her father would be.

THIRTY-SEVEN

THE last of the yuurei rose from the metal cylinders and swarmed together, a writhing mass of shadows. Kurara narrowly avoided them as they lurched towards her, their mouths open wide in an attempt to swallow her whole.

Prince Ugetsu drew the flare gun from its holster.

"What do you plan on doing with that?" asked Kurara as the yuurei began to surround them.

"Just watch." Ugetsu fired the gun above his head. A bright light burst from the nozzle and shot into the air.

The yuurei chased after the light. While they were distracted, Ugetsu made a break for the docking bay where he had left their aircraft.

"Not so fast!" The Crafter who had come to meet them swung her paper scythe at Ugetsu's head.

The prince threw the flare gun away and drew his katana to block the blow. The woman pulled two more paper rings from her fingers and turned them into a pair of spinning blades.

"You planned this, didn't you? You meant to kill everyone in this city!" she yelled as she threw the blades at Ugetsu. They missed the top of his head by an inch and curved through the air towards Kurara instead.

Kurara had not expected the attack. She lifted her left arm, hardening the paper, and used her limb as a shield. The blades hit her wrist and bounced off, circling above her head before flying towards her once more.

"The yuurei are returning!" Kurara cried as she knocked the spinning blades away from her again. This was no time to be fighting.

Neither Prince Ugetsu nor the Crafter seemed to hear her. The yuurei moved with surprising speed, scuttling over the ground like crabs. They spread across the street then swirled together like water in a river and rushed towards the three of them.

Kurara and Prince Ugetsu ran into the docking bay, but the Crafter was not as fast. The yuurei's arms passed through her shoulders. The scythe and the spinning blades immediately fell apart and fluttered to the ground as the woman shrieked in pain, but the yuurei did not stop trying to grab at her. Their smoke-like hands and arms clawed at her face, her neck, as they pushed their heads through her chest.

The Crafter's body hit the ground.

Kurara stared at the dead woman in horror. What should she do? If she used the ashes in her own core, she could try to seal the yuurei away, but she had nothing to draw a sealing circle with and no fire to distract them.

It did not take long for the yuurei to move on. Prince

Ugetsu swung his sword at the swarm, as if that would help keep them back. His flare gun was outside the docking bay, lying on the side of the road.

Kurara made a run for it. Jumping over the yuurei lunging for her, she ran outside and dived for the gun.

It was empty. There was no flare for her to shoot at the shadows.

"Get back, you fiends!" Prince Ugetsu yelled. Inside the docking bay, the yuurei surrounded him. He backed away then burst into a run, heading for the qipak, but the yuurei were faster and his body was lost beneath the swarm.

Before they could turn on her, Kurara dropped the flare gun and ran. She did not try to enter the docking bay, but headed further into the city, following the large arrows painted on the buildings.

Outside the dome, a battle raged between Sohma's ships and Princess Tsukimi's, the airships trading cannon fire across the sky. Blasts shook the city. Sohma's ships bombed the streets of Sola-Ea, setting the city on fire. The sight took Kurara's breath away. So much chaos, so much death, and for what? Did it really have to come to this?

The yuurei scattered among the flames, drawn to the different fires burning across the city. Kurara made it past the crumbling teahouses and sagging building stacks that looked ready to snap in half. As she reached the town square, she saw yet more yuurei swooping over the ruined roads like buzzards circling a kill.

Then she heard the screams.

Kurara could not believe that the city was still occupied. Men and women ran for their lives, tugging their children along and carrying the elderly on their backs. Kurara stared at them in confusion. Why had they not evacuated already?

The yuurei spread themselves among the crowds, picking out their prey with ease.

"No! Wait!" she called, fruitlessly, after them. She never thought she would want to be chased by yuurei, but it was a damn sight better than letting them kill innocent people.

Something struck the dome and smashed through the glass, slamming into a building stack. It toppled over, crashing into the streets below. A man fell, his legs trapped by a falling beam. A yuurei swooped, caught the man through the chest and left his body lying there beneath the wood.

"Rara!" A qipak pulled up in front of her with Haru and Himura on it.

Kurara froze. She couldn't believe it. Haru? Her horror at finding him here, in the middle of a war zone, could not overcome the sheer relief she felt at seeing him again. Seven hells, she was even glad to see Himura.

"You two!" She rushed towards them, almost barrelling Haru over as she wrapped her arms around him in a crushing hug. "What are you doing here? Are you all right?"

She pulled away to look Haru over, checking for injuries. He looked perfectly healthy, but who knew how well he was holding together with the yuurei sealed inside his core.

"I'm fine, Rara. What about you? Are *you* OK?" Haru ran his hand down her arms.

"That can wait! We need to leave!" said Himura. Kurara could not help but notice that Mana was not with him, though she could not bring herself to ask why.

She shook her head. "Princess Tsukimi is here,

somewhere beneath the city. I need to talk to her."

"About what?" Himura looked like he was biting back a curse.

"The Star Seed. I thought that all we needed to do to make it bloom was to let it fall from somewhere really high, but I was wrong. It's not the fall that matters," she said, repeating the words the princess had told her. "Tsukimi knows how to make the Star Seed bloom. I'm going to beat the answers out of her!"

Haru and Himura exchanged silent glances.

Kurara scowled at them. She had only been separated from Haru and Himura for a while and they were already having wordless conversations with each other.

"But does Tsukimi really know the answers? Or is she just tricking you into coming to her?" asked Haru.

"Whatever it is she knows, we can figure it out without her. We should leave the city first!" said Himura.

Kurara's eyes narrowed. Between the three of them, perhaps they could work out how to make the Star Seed bloom, but how long would that take?

"YOU WASTED ALL OF OUR TIME!" Kurara remembered how Entei had roared at her. The pain in the toad's voice as its mind fell apart.

There was no time to waste. Besides, there had to be a reason Tsukimi had come to Sola-Ea of all places. Why lure Kurara here unless the location was important?

"Tsukimi came here for a reason. It must have something to do with making the Star Seed bloom."

"...All right." Haru caved. "Do you know where she is?"

Kurara nodded. "Beneath the autumn palace there's

a way down into the city's foundations. She's underground."

"And what about the yuurei?" asked Haru.

Kurara looked up at the swirling clouds of smoke. Now that they were free and swarming about the city, it was going to be a massacre.

"Tsukimi first," said Himura. "The yuurei will be here, no matter what happens; I cannot say the same for the princess. We should find her before someone – or something – else does."

"Leave me here. I'll deal with the yuurei. You two go ahead and find the princess," said Haru.

"No! You're coming with us!" Kurara grabbed Haru by the wrist. She bet if she let Haru run off, he would find some way to seal the yuurei inside his core or do something else equally stupid and self-sacrificing.

"Come on, let's get going!" Himura gestured for them to pile up onto the qipak.

Kurara hopped on the back, behind Haru, and wrapped her arms around his waist. It reminded her of the first time the three of them had met, when they had escaped from the crumbling *Midori* together on a qipak. That had been the day it all began – the day she had discovered that Haru was a shikigami. The day soldiers had burned him alive and she had teamed up with Himura to save Haru.

As the qipak raced through the city, Kurara squeezed Haru tighter. Perhaps, after the Star Seed bloomed and the shikigami had their freedom, they could go back to their home and rebuild it. Maybe Haru could try growing radishes again. She'd even let Himura visit if he was good. After everything they had been through, they could have a simple, peaceful life, free of guilt.

THIRTY-EIGHT

YANKING at the levers, Himura drove them onwards to the heart of the city. As they made their way through the streets, Kurara recounted the broad strokes of what had happened after they had been separated – from the moment Entei had flattened a city, to her imprisonment and escape with Ruki, to meeting Prince Ugetsu.

"I'm sorry I wasn't there for you, Rara." Haru reached down and covered her hand with his own.

She shook her head. What mattered was that they were together again, and now that they had found each other, Kurara was not going to let Haru out of her sight.

"What about you? How did you end up on Sola-Ea?"

"Rara…" Instead of answering, Haru's grip on her hand tightened. "I need to tell you something."

Whatever he was about to say was interrupted by the

loud rattle of the engine as Himura brought the qipak to a stop.

"This is it!" He hopped to the ground.

"Where are we?" Kurara took in her new surroundings. Following the arrows marked around the city had led them to a sprawling estate full of extensive sand gardens and buildings made of the finest mahogany. The main building was rather small compared to the towering building stacks that populated the rest of the city, but there were so many annexes and smaller buildings dotted here and there that the whole estate looked impressive nevertheless.

"This is the autumn palace. One of the imperial family's many residences," said Himura.

Some of the walls were broken. A stray cannonball had struck the dome, crashed through the glass, and hit the west side of the grounds, leaving a smouldering crater behind. "H–halt!" A startled soldier drew his katana in quivering hands.

Kurara jumped off the qipak and grabbed the man by the collar of his uniform. Using her ofuda to bind his arms to his sides and wrap his legs together so that he could not run, she snarled, "How do I get below the city?"

With a squeak, the soldier pointed to one of the buildings attached to the main palace. "Through – through there! There's a ladder leading down to the city's maintenance tunnels. The pipes that connect the city's power to the levistone cannon are down there!"

Kurara glanced at the small wooden building then up at the shipyards in the distance. The levistone cannon towered over everything. Its enormous barrel poked out of the dome like a crooked flagpole.

Throwing the man to the ground, Kurara released him from the paper ropes and headed into the building.

The only thing inside was a single hatch leading down into the city. When Kurara threw it aside, the stench of levistone was so overpowering Kurara could taste it on her tongue. The ground seemed to vibrate with a hum that filled her ears like a mosquito whine.

This felt like a trap.

Haru reached for her hand. It was only then that Kurara realized she was shaking, though whether from anticipation or fear, she did not know. Something about facing Tsukimi felt like facing down an avalanche. The thought made her breath quicken and her stomach churn. She pulled her hand away.

"I'm fine." She had to be, or Princess Tsukimi would bury her alive.

"I'll go first." Himura's tone left no room for argument.

A rusty metal ladder plunged into the bottomless darkness below. In single file, they slowly climbed down into the bowels of the city until they hit Sola-Ea's foundations.

"Whoa, this is amazing!" Haru whistled.

"Amazing" wasn't the word Kurara would have used to describe it. The air stank of levistone. Dim amber lights embedded in the ceiling illuminated the narrow tunnel that lay before them. The walls were made of wood and covered with wires and cables that tangled together like the roots of some massive tree. Metal pipes ran along the floors, gurgling and rattling so loudly they were giving Kurara a headache.

There were only two directions: forward or back. Carefully, they crept through the tunnels, ready for an attack.

Eventually, the tunnel opened into a cavernous room filled with all sorts of equipment that Kurara didn't understand – weird pumps and bellows and mechanisms made of cogs and steel chains. The walls crawled with yet more pipes and wires.

Just ahead, Kurara spied a figure slowly walking further into the darkness.

"Tsukimi!" she roared.

At the sound of her voice, Princess Tsukimi turned around.

"So you found me."

THIRTY-NINE

THE princess was dressed plainly in a simple kimono and hakama, with a katana and a pistol at her waist. Her hair was tied back into a ponytail, but otherwise she looked just as she had the first time they had met: cold and beautiful and eager to eat Kurara alive.

"My little shikigami, I'm so glad you've come to see me. You brought the Star Seed, I hope," Tsukimi said, grinning from ear to ear.

Kurara brushed a hand against her obi, where the Star Seed bulged slightly against the sash. Tsukimi noticed and smiled.

"Good. I see my brother isn't with you. I thought he wanted to talk."

"Your brother is dead," Kurara spat.

Tsukimi's face lit up. "Even better! Now, give me the Star Seed. Let's make it bloom. Together!"

Kurara eyed the princess as though Tsukimi was a tiger about to pounce. "Why don't you tell me how to make it bloom, and *I'll* do it."

"Don't you already know?"

Kurara winced. She desperately hoped the princess wouldn't notice, but the smile slowly spreading across Tsukimi's face said she had.

"You still don't know!" Tsukimi shrieked with laughter, as if Kurara's ignorance was the most hilarious thing in the world.

The temptation to punch Princess Tsukimi in her smug face was almost too difficult to resist. Taking a deep breath, Kurara did her best to shut out the sound of annoying laughter and solve the puzzle the princess had presented her with.

"Here. Maybe this will help." Tsukimi threw a book at Kurara.

With a snap of Kurara's fingers, the book froze before it could hit her in the face and gently glided through the air towards her.

"Hey, that's my journal!" Haru's offended tone was coupled with a look of embarrassed outrage. "Did you – did you read all of it?"

Tsukimi's lips curved into a delighted smile. "It was *most* entertaining."

Haru made a sound that was half mortified wail, half indignant yell.

"Read the first few entries. The answers are right there," said Tsukimi.

Kurara's hands brushed the cover of Haru's journal.

"What does it say? Read it aloud," said Himura.

Kurara pulled a face at him, but did as he said.

"*We decided to take shelter at the Mountain of the Falling Star. Long ago it was from the peak of this mountain that Crafters witnessed a once-in-a-millennium meteor shower. Stars fell and left large scars across the land. They fell and killed many people. Seems like a bad omen to make a home near a place named after a tragedy.*"

Her eyes drifted up to Tsukimi's smug face, keeping the princess in her line of sight.

"Do you understand now?"

Kurara glared at the princess. No, she didn't. That was why she had come here – to get the answers straight from Tsukimi's mouth instead of wasting time puzzling it out by herself. The harder she wracked her brains in search of an answer, the more her head began to throb. She thought of everything she'd learned about the Star Seed from their journey to the Mountain of the Falling Star – the lullaby and her own experiments with the Star Seed; the cryptic things Tsukimi had said and the first entry in Haru's journal.

What was the answer? What did she not understand?

"There's a war waging out there," said Haru, his expression wary. "People are fighting for their lives. There are yuurei outside. This isn't the time for this! Can you really hole yourself away in here with your little obsessions while the world burns outside?"

"But of course I can!" Tsukimi laughed. "Do you pay attention when insects kill each other outside your window?"

Haru tried to take a step forward, but Himura and

Kurara both flung their arms out to stop him. Tsukimi was a shark in the water. It was never a good idea to get too close.

"Here's another hint," said the princess, obviously disappointed that Kurara still didn't understand. "I came here to Sola-Ea for a reason. The Star Seed can only bloom here. Why do you think that is?"

Kurara's hands shook.

"A dying star fell from the heavens, and from that star grew a tree."

"The fall doesn't matter," Tsukimi had told her.

She thought of Haru's journal: *Stars fell and left large scars across the land.*

Those were the stars that became Star Trees. The dying stars that fell from the heavens and became trees.

They fell and killed many people.

Why had Tsukimi come to Sola-Ea of all places? Hadn't she known that it was due to become a war zone?

A sudden chill fell across her shoulders. She glanced at Haru and Himura, as if they might suddenly be able to read her thoughts and tell her that she was wrong.

She wanted to be wrong.

"Then why haven't you done anything yet? Is it because you don't have the guts for it? Are you afraid?" Tsukimi had taunted her. At the time, Kurara had not understood why the princess would think she would be afraid.

She understood now.

"Death." The word dropped from her lips like a stone falling down a well. "A long time ago, there was a meteor shower. Those meteors – those dying stars – fell across the land, killing many and blooming into Star Trees. But it wasn't the fall that made them bloom. They bloomed because when they fell they killed so many people."

She hoped she was wrong. She waited for Tsukimi to ridicule her and tell her how stupid she was, but instead the princess gave her an approving nod.

"Close enough! It's souls, actually. Do you know the old folktale about how to make a cherry tree bloom with flowers that are pinker than usual, flowers that are almost red? You bury a corpse beneath it! The tree absorbs the blood of the dead, which dyes the cherry blossom a vibrant hue. It's the same with Star Trees. They absorb souls in order to bloom."

Nothing is gained without sacrifice.

If she wanted the Star Seed to bloom, lives needed to be sacrificed.

Haru gave a choked-off gasp. He was pale and trembling. Kurara had never seen him so shaken, or so furious.

"So that's why you're here," said Himura grimly. "You came because it's a war zone. There will be lots of dead soon enough. Lots of souls."

Kurara wished that she could be as calm as Himura. Her thoughts were a mess of tangled vines, each one covered in thorns. She could not unpick them without hurting herself.

"That's why you didn't want to fight Ugetsu straight away, why you agreed to these talks. You didn't want people to start dying until you had the Star Seed."

"Well, people are dying right now," said Haru angrily. "There are yuurei all over the city, killing innocent people!"

"Which is why you should give me the Star Seed. I must hurry and harvest as many souls as possible!" Tsukimi's eyes were hooded in the darkness. There was something in the princess's voice that made the hair on the back of Kurara's neck stand on end. Like lightning before a storm; like the first glimpse of a hungry predator slinking through the bushes. "You can't do it, can you? You can't kill a bunch of innocent people. Well, I can. Up ahead is the levistone cannon. My father built it especially for fighting the Sorabito. If I trigger the machine to overheat while it's full of levistone, it will implode and bring this entire city crashing down to the earth. The souls of all those who live on Sola-Ea will be used to make the Star Seed bloom!"

Himura stiffened. His paper bracelet crumbled into a dozen squares of ofuda that swirled around him, fluttering nervously. The princess stared at the ofuda orbiting through the air with hunger in her gaze. A hunger and an anger. As if that fluttering paper was something that was purposely being kept from her.

"We don't have to fight," said Tsukimi. "Leave this place and let me do what has to be done. You can blame it all on me – the evil princess who doesn't care who dies in order to get what she wants."

"You're going to bring the city down? I assume you have a way to escape yourself?" Himura glared at Tsukimi, his grey eyes like a storm.

"As do you, Crafter. You have enough paper to fly away, don't you?"

Tsukimi made it sound like she was doing them a favour, but the smug look on her face said that she had them exactly where she wanted.

Kurara had never hated anyone more than she hated

the princess. Tsukimi might like to think of herself as some generous and compassionate saviour shouldering a great burden on their behalf, but in the end she only wanted the Star Seed for herself. For her own experiments.

But Tsukimi was also right. If the Star Seed needed souls to bloom, then bringing the city crashing down was their best option.

"You know, when I was inside Entei's belly, I got to have a good conversation with the thing. Well, as good a conversation as you can have when speaking to a half-mad beast while you're trapped inside its stomach," the princess said airily.

"Is that why it headed to Sola-Ea? Because you were talking to it?" asked Haru.

"I don't know if the beast really understood anything I said. Although I understood everything *it* said to *me*. Apparently, during the great Crafter war, you told a bunch of shikigami that you would set them free. But then after all the Star Trees were cut down, both you and the Star Seed disappeared. Do you know what happened to the shikigami you left hanging on your empty promises? They all died. Or they went insane and then died."

Kurara flinched. She didn't dare look the princess in the eye.

"What about the shikigami that exist today? Will you run away and disappear again? Will you leave them to go mad and die?" Tsukimi's words circled her like sharks smelling blood in the water.

Kurara sucked in a sharp, panicked breath. Could she let everyone in this city die? What were a few hundred – or even a thousand – lives compared to the freedom of the shikigami?

"*It's all your fault!*" Suzaku's screech pierced through her. The things she had done to Suzaku; the people who had been killed by the yuurei; Entei and the city the toad had crushed – all those tragedies had, in some way or other, been caused by the things Kurara had done. The things she had done for the Star Seed.

If the Star Seed didn't bloom, what was the point of everything? How else could she excuse all the suffering she had caused?

She had to let everyone die, didn't she?

Without warning, Himura's ofuda swirled together and shot at Tsukimi like a sudden cannonball to the face. The princess drew her katana in an instant, deflecting the blow.

Himura's ofuda retreated and whirled around him like a miniature hurricane. "I don't care what the two of you decide; I won't let you bring this city to the ground," he growled. "And if Kurara won't stop you, I will!"

FORTY

HIMURA'S ofuda formed a large spear, which he swung at Tsukimi. Again, the princess blocked with her katana. She swung her blade at his head in retaliation, forcing Himura to jump backwards to avoid the blow.

"Haru, what am I supposed to do?" Kurara grabbed hold of his sleeve as Himura and Tsukimi continued to exchange blows.

"I don't know. Stop the princess from killing Himura, maybe?" Haru cried.

Kurara tried to gather her ofuda together to form a weapon, but her resolve wavered. Nothing was gained without sacrifice, and if this was the sacrifice the Star Seed demanded, then maybe…

Maybe she should let Tsukimi do as she wished.

"Rara…" Haru took her hand. "We'll find another way."

"And what if there is no other way? What will we do then?" Panic seized her chest. She was going to be sick. Should she agree with Tsukimi's plan? What if she made the wrong decision?

What if she looked back at this moment as the one and only time she could have made the Star Seed bloom and did nothing?

But what if she let all these people die and then drowned in the guilt?

How could she do anything when she didn't know what the consequences of her actions would be or how she would feel about them tomorrow?

Haru squeezed her hand. "We *will* find another way, Rara. I promise!"

A sharp cry of pain broke through her fog of terror. Himura was pinned against the wall, the tip of Tsukimi's blade buried in his shoulder.

Kurara snatched a handful of ofuda from her arm and tossed the pieces of paper into the air. They hardened and folded into arrows, shooting towards Tsukimi and forcing the princess to retreat.

"Is that your final answer?" She turned to Kurara with an icy expression.

Was it? Even now, Kurara wasn't sure, yet she did know one thing – she could not let the princess have the Star Seed.

Tsukimi sighed. "How unfortunate. All I ever do is try to help others and this is how I'm repaid." She pointed her katana at Kurara's chest. "Well, then, we'll settle this the only way you beasts know how."

The princess closed the distance between them at an

alarming speed. Kurara barely had time to form a matching sword from her ofuda as the blow slid across the edge of her hardened paper.

Grinding her teeth together, Kurara pushed Tsukimi away. Himura moved to help, but the princess was careful not to let him get behind her. Each time they tried to corner her, she ducked out of the way, never allowing them to pin her down.

"I grew up around Crafters and shikigami all my life. I know how you lot fight." Tsukimi drew her gun.

Kurara dodged the shot, but the princess had not been aiming for her. The bullet hit a pipe next to Kurara and a small trickle of levistone splashed onto the ground. Tsukimi's next shot severed an electric cable on the wall. As the sparks touched the ground, the puddle of levistone exploded.

Kurara wrapped herself in a hardened cocoon of paper as the blast sent her flying across the room.

"Rara!" she heard Haru call.

"Stay back!" Kurara shed her cocoon, shaking off the burning paper before the flames could claim the rest of her ofuda.

"You look worried." Tsukimi smirked. "Oh, you're so powerful when you fight, but introduce a little fire and you become as timid as a cornered mouse."

Kurara glowered at her. There was no reasoning with her, no running away. Tsukimi would have to die just like the rest of her rotten family.

"Why are you looking at me like that?" The princess's eyes narrowed. "Like I'm the bad one. You're far worse than

I am. After all, I've killed, what, maybe a handful of maids and orphans in my experiments? Some soldiers here and there. But you – you set those shadows free and let them roam across the land. You're responsible for far more deaths than me, so aren't you the real villain here?"

Kurara's ofuda faltered.

"This is all your fault!" Suzaku had screeched at her.

"Don't let her get in your head!" Himura snapped. "You're fighting for freedom. What is Tsukimi doing but chasing her own selfish goals?"

The princess laughed. "You're deluded if you think that what she's doing isn't for herself!"

"Shut up!" Kurara launched herself at Tsukimi with her paper sword. She swiped at the princess, catching Tsukimi's shoulder and drawing a trickle of blood.

As she jumped back to prepare for another attack, Himura sent a rain of paper knives towards the princess. Tsukimi leapt out of the way, but they curved through the air and followed her as she moved. Even though she deflected some of the blades with her katana, a few managed to pierce her legs and arms. Tsukimi grunted with pain, but not a single scream escaped her lips.

While the two battled, Kurara cloaked herself in ofuda. Pieces of paper crawled up her body, wrapping around her arms and legs. Using the additional speed and strength her ofuda afforded her, she was fast enough to get behind Tsukimi's back.

She jumped, her ofuda unravelling and wrapping around her fist in the form of a dragon's claw. Kurara would have crushed Tsukimi's head with it, but the princess flung herself to one side, even as Himura's weapon sliced into her arm.

"Marvellous! What wonders you can perform! You're so much more than any of the run-of-the-mill Crafters I've known." Tsukimi backed away with a grin on her face.

They traded blows back and forth. Whenever Kurara needed to retreat, Himura was there, ready to shield her with a blade of sharpened paper in his hands. They fought in perfect tandem, covering for each other's blind spots as they swiped and slashed at the princess. When Kurara saw an opening, she lunged forward and buried her paper fist into Tsukimi's stomach with such force it sent the princess staggering back.

Tsukimi snarled and charged at them both, katana raised above her head. Himura blocked Tsukimi's furious swing with his sword. While he kept the princess busy, Kurara dropped to the floor and swept the legs from under her.

The princess hit the ground with a grunt and drew her pistol, aiming it point-blank at Kurara's face.

The bullet tore along Kurara's cheek and hit the wall behind her, severing another cable. Hot, blistering pain seared across Kurara's face. She didn't scream, but she clutched her cheek in agony.

"Rara! Watch out!" Haru shouted as the broken cable came loose.

Himura threw himself at her, sending them both flying across the ground. The cable swung through the air, missing Tsukimi, who was still lying flat on her back, and colliding with one of the humming generators.

There was an awful crack and the generator exploded,

sending chunks of flaming metal flying through the air. Tsukimi finally screamed as bits of shrapnel hit her. Kurara tried to squirm free, but Himura held her tight, using his body as a shield.

"Himura! What are you doing? Get off!" she cried, but Himura's arms only tightened around her even more.

"Rara! Himura! The princess!" screamed Haru.

That made Himura move. They both looked up to see Tsukimi's bleeding and battered body moving towards them. Despite the shards of metal piercing her legs, her steps were steady. Laughter spilled from her lips as she dragged the tip of her katana across the floor in one bleeding hand. With her back to the spreading flames, she looked like she had when they had met at the mountain. She looked like she could devour the entire world.

"My little shikigami, I've had enough—" Tsukimi's body suddenly jerked, cutting off whatever she was about to say next. Blood trickled from her mouth, the sight of which seemed to surprise her just as much as it did Kurara.

Without warning, Tsukimi collapsed to the ground, to reveal Haru standing behind her, holding a long shard of metal now red with blood.

"Is it over?" Haru asked, eyes wide with fright.

Kurara stared at Tsukimi lying there in a pool of her own blood.

As if in answer, the ground shook and dust fell from the ceiling. Outside, the airships were still bombing the city and the yuurei were roaming the streets.

Kurara shook her head.

"No, not yet."

FORTY-ONE

KURARA stumbled to her feet as the ground shook once more. She clutched the Star Seed so tightly it left an imprint in her palm.

Her fingers brushed the side of her face. There was a long gash running from her cheek to one corner of her mouth where Princess Tsukimi's bullet had grazed her. The paper around the injury felt flaky and charred.

"Here, take my ofuda." Himura handed her a handful of paper. They had both lost a lot of ofuda in the fight with Tsukimi, most of it burning up in the flames caused by the electric cables. There was not enough for the both of them. At least, not enough for them to create anything useful unless they pooled their resources.

Kurara reluctantly accepted Himura's ofuda, though she barely had time to fold the handful of paper back into her left arm when the walls shook. Small fires burned all around them, and chunks of the ceiling fell to the floor.

"We need to get out of here," said Haru.

"Agreed." Himura limped towards them.

"Y–you're injured!"

"It's nothing."

It was definitely not "nothing". The blood seeping down his limbs was soaking into his clothes, turning them dark red. He had only been hurt because he had protected her when the generator exploded. Why had he tried to shield her? Was it just out of guilt for his past betrayal?

"Do you really want me to forgive you that badly that you're prepared to die for me?" Kurara looked at him in disbelief.

"Oh, please. I didn't do it for you. I did it because it was the right thing to do." Himura snorted.

Another explosion sent more rubble falling into the room. Something hit a pipe, and a small stream of levistone burst forth and exploded into flames.

Kurara ducked behind the rubble as fire carved a path across the ground, cutting the room in half and separating Kurara and Haru from Himura.

"Himura, are you all right?" She rushed as close to the fire as she dared, trying to catch a glimpse of Himura from behind the curtain of fire.

"I'm fine!" he called, though he sounded slightly more anxious than before, which in Himura-terms meant that he would panic the moment he thought they were not paying attention.

The ground shook, bringing several small gears and bits of wood crashing over their heads.

"I think this whole place might collapse in on itself," he said. "You two get out of here!"

"Without you?" Haru sounded appalled.

Kurara glanced over her shoulder. The door behind her led back to the tunnel from which they had come, to the ladder that would take them up into the city, but there was no way Himura could cross the flames. The only way for him to go was through the door on his side of the room that led to the levistone cannon.

"Listen," said Himura. "The *Orihime* is out there. If you're quick, you might be able to find it. Get on board and leave this place. The way to the levistone cannon is behind me. If the fire reaches the cannon while it's still connected to the levistone pipes, it will blow up and Tsukimi will get her wish – this whole city will come crumbling down. I need to switch it off before that happens."

"And what if the fire spreads before you can escape? What if you just end up trapped down here with the cannon?" Kurara flinched as the ground shook again and the flames jumped higher. She had taken all of Himura's ofuda and she could not give it back to him now, not through the wall of flames. If there was no exit, how would he get out on his own?

"There has to be another way out. Don't worry; we'll meet again," Himura said, but the only thing Kurara focused on was: *"There has to be another way."*

Yes, no matter what problem they faced, there was always another way. Another way out. Another way to make the Star Seed bloom. Another way for shikigami to be free.

"No, we can't leave him here!" Haru yelled.

Kurara clutched the Star Seed to her chest. As much as she wanted to help, there was nothing they could do for Himura. Going through those flames was a death sentence for both of them.

"I'll be fine!" Himura shouted over the roar of the flames.

"I'm not leaving you!" Haru cried.

"That's just the bond talking!"

That wasn't true and Kurara knew it. Though she hated to admit it, she was sure that Haru would have liked Himura even without a bond.

"Let me do this," said Himura, his voice softer, gentler. "I can protect you both. Like I should have back when we first met."

The memory of their initial meeting blindsided Kurara. Bloody skies, it felt like a lifetime ago. The *Midori*, the attack, their attempted getaway on an aircraft far too small for the three of them.

She swallowed past the lump in her throat. "Are you sure?"

Their eyes met across the flames. Himura did not need her forgiveness; he would do what he thought was right.

Kurara nodded.

"Haru!" Himura called through the fires. "It's fine. I'll see you again."

Something in Haru relented, and Kurara seized the moment to pull him away.

"Come on, Haru!"

The ground shook as they turned and ran back the way they had come.

FORTY-TWO

IT didn't matter if he was going to die. It didn't even matter if it would be a painful death. The only thing Himura cared about in that moment was making sure his death counted for something. If he could just switch off the levistone cannon, he could protect the *Orihime*; he could protect Kurara and Haru. *That* would be worth dying for.

Urging his battered body through the narrow passages beneath Sola-Ea, Himura pulled himself towards the only place he could go: the levistone cannon. He felt naked without any ofuda. Fire licked at his back and smoke curled through his lungs. With every limping step he took, he could feel the heat snapping at his heels. There was just one way to go, and that was forward. Behind was only the choice between a fiery death or a slow, suffocating one.

He was sure that he was getting close to the cannon,

judging from the smell of levistone and the tremors that rocked through the ground. Sure enough, an imposing metal door came into view, covered in warning signs and threats to keep out. Gritting his teeth against the pain, he bashed his shoulder against the door and was surprised when it gave way with a hefty groan.

Himura all but fell into the cannon's control centre. The room was monstrously large in order to accommodate the size of the cannon's base, which was as big as a shed and stood surrounded by cooling fans and generators, humming with energy and glowing a faint blue from the levistone being pumped into it by the pipes on the ground. The barrel of the cannon disappeared somewhere above ground. At the front of the room stood a panel with dials and buttons and all sorts of gauges he did not understand.

It was also empty. The chairs were tucked beneath the control panels as if they had never been touched. If anyone had once been here, they had left long ago – likely before the battle had even begun.

Himura hurried to the generators. He was no engineer, but the power switches were clearly marked. Flicking them off one by one, Himura watched as the lights around the base of the cannon faded and the humming dwindled to an uncomfortable silence.

There. Even if the fire reached it, without levistone pumping through the base of the cannon it should not explode. The city would not come crashing down.

Next, Himura turned his attention towards searching for an exit. He slowly made his way around the room, checking the walls and floor for a door, a hatch, a ladder – anything that might lead out into the city again. With each step, his hopes sank and panic rose.

Was there really no exit? Maybe he had passed one on his way to the cannon room without noticing. Limping back towards the door he had come through, he stopped short. Fire blocked the way out of the room, the flames slowly crawling towards him.

There was no way back. He was trapped.

A calm acceptance washed over him. Despite everything he had told Kurara and Haru, Himura had a feeling that this would happen. Retreating to the furthest corner of the room, he slumped down and waited for the end. Was this how Akane had felt when he had ordered his shikigami across the burning library? Had it faced the flames and leapt through them knowing that it would die?

"I love you, Master." Akane's voice echoed through his head. How fitting that he should meet the same fate as his shikigami. This was karma all right. This was exactly what he deserved.

Outside, somewhere beyond the city, the battle was probably raging on. An explosion shook the walls, causing part of the ceiling to crumble.

There was a hole in the roof, far above Himura's head. The light that shone through the broken ceiling seemed to taunt him rather than offer any hope. There was no way he could reach a hole so high up, not without ofuda, and he had none left.

Flames crawled up the walls of the room and along the floor. The city shook again. It would be just his luck if he stopped the cannon from exploding only for the ships outside to bring the whole city down anyway.

Another tremor sent more chunks of the ceiling falling to the floor. Himura flung his arms up to shield himself even as a burning lump of metal struck his leg.

With a howl of anguish, he brushed the debris away, but the metal had burned through his clothes to his skin. His leg throbbed with agony, the skin purple and angry. He didn't think he could move it, it hurt too much.

This really was the end, wasn't it? Himura let his head drop back. Sweat and dirt clung to his clothes as the heat of the flames licked at his skin. Himura didn't know if it was fatigue or just the smoke that was making him so sleepy. He lifted his head and stared at the hole in the ceiling, wondering if he would get to see the sky one last time, when something caught his eye.

Small squares of paper fell through the hole and burned upon the flames below. Himura's breath stopped short. He could barely believe his eyes. Was this divine intervention? A sign from the heavens?

More paper rained from above. In the shaft of sunlight that broke through the room, they seemed almost golden. Stretching out his hand, Himura called them towards him. At his command, the bits of paper shot through the air and gathered in front of him.

Summoning all the strength he had left, he fashioned the paper into a thin but strong rope, imagining a steel cable capable of holding his weight. He shot it carefully towards the hole above him. The end of the rope sharpened and buried itself in the concrete above. Himura gave it a tug and the rope remained stuck in the ceiling.

Angling his body so that he did not swing straight into the fire, he shortened the rope and let it pull him up, past the flames, through the air, towards the hole. Once he was close enough, he jumped and grabbed the edge of the opening, his fingers digging into the concrete as he did his best not to breathe in the smoke.

Flames snapped at his feet. Gritting his teeth, he hauled himself through the hole, up into the street above.

For a moment, all Himura could do was lie there panting, drinking down the delicious clean air. He was alive. Gods, he was still alive.

But where had that paper come from? Himura had thought it was an act of the Gods, but now that his head was clearing from all the smoke he was beginning to doubt that.

"*Fool.*" A familiar voice echoed through his head.

Himura cast his gaze around the abandoned street until his eyes came to rest upon the trembling shikigami in front of him.

Mana lifted its feeble head just enough to pin him in its gaze. Half of its body was gone, and the rest seemed much thinner and weaker than before. Paper scales lay scattered around it.

"Mana? Holy skies, Mana, what have you done?" Himura crawled towards the shikigami.

It was a pointless question; he knew what it had done. Mana had ripped the very scales from its body and tossed them down to him so that he could escape. The image stabbed at his heart. He had not wanted this sacrifice. He would have rather died.

As if sensing his thoughts, Mana laughed. *"I told you,*

I was always fond of fools." The snake slumped against the ground. *"Please, take my core. I cannot— I feel my mind slipping away. It is too much for me to bear. Take my core. I know you will look after it until the day comes when my body can be made anew and my heart freed."*

With half its body gone, Mana's core was already exposed to the elements. *"I want something honest,"* Mana had once said to him. Himura had been a fool for believing that Mana did not want a bond because it did not trust him. Without a blood bond, their connection was something they had to choose every day. They chose to care about each other, chose to worry about each other, chose to think about each other.

And now Mana had *chosen* to sacrifice itself for Himura.

"Thank you." Himura owed Mana his life ten times over. No, he owed it more than just his life. Companionship, loyalty, protection – Mana had given him everything and more.

Leaning over the shikigami, he reached inside, wrapped his fingers around the smooth, bone-like surface of the paper core and pulled. The snake gave one last shudder, and then its body collapsed around Himura's hand like a house of cards.

The skies were awash with yuurei, and the city was burning, but Himura held the core close to his chest, as if Mana might still be able to feel his beating heart.

Interlude

I looked to the stars
But the night sky is so vast
And yet so empty

– from *Life in the Skies: 100 Sorabito Poems*
(banned by the Patriots Office)

The airship shook. Occasionally, something big would hit the hull and Tomoe had to grab hold of the walls as the floor tilted beneath her feet. Footsteps echoed somewhere on the floors above her. Crewmen shouted at each other to fire the cannons. Hissing through clenched teeth, Tomoe struggled onwards despite the pain in her side.

Her tanto was missing, but Tomoe grabbed a knife from the ship's kitchen and continued downwards through the hallways. The engine room was filled with boilers keeping the *Kujiraza* in the air. They hummed as they burned, their egg-shaped furnaces rattling from the demand the ship was putting on them. Tomoe used to love the sound of churning

 297

engines, but now what had once been a familiar lullaby sounded like an ominous groaning.

Clutching her side, she limped through the forest of boilers and past the tables set aside for making those awful cylinders. Barrels of levistone sat nearby, the smell of wet earth and blood leaking from beneath their lids. Near the end of the engine room, a ten-foot-wide hatch in the floor was open, letting in a cold rush of air that whipped through the room.

Kazeno Rei stood at the edge of the open hatch, his sleeves fluttering like the wings of a moth as the wind blew through them.

Tomoe's hands shook. When she looked at him, she remembered their last encounter – her father swinging his katana at her, cutting down Sayo. The terror. The fear. The bone-crushing grief when she thought that Sayo had died to protect her.

She took a deep, steadying breath. No matter what, she would not let Rei see how rattled she was. He did not deserve her fear.

"You shouldn't leave that hatch open," Tomoe said. "It interferes with the temperature of the boilers."

When he turned to face her, there was no surprise in his expression, only a cruel smirk.

"Who let you out of your cage?"

"That's not important." Tomoe marched forward, her eyes darting to the crate beside him. It was filled with metal cylinders that glinted in the engine room's amber lights. No doubt they were filled with cores.

Rei's eyes followed her gaze and his smile widened.

"Do you want to do the honours, dear daughter?"

"Stop, this is madness!"

"Stop? But look how beautifully they fall."

With a shove of his foot, Rei pushed the crate out of the bottom of the ship.

"No!" Tomoe watched in horror as the cylinders poured through the open hatch and through a large hole in Sola-Ea's dome. They cracked open as they hit the ground, and the shadows spread through the city, blanketing the streets in more darkness.

"What have you done?" she screeched as the last of the cylinders plummeted through the sky. "Our people are down there. At least let the Sorabito evacuate first!"

"And risk the groundlings sneaking out of the city?" Rei's lips curled in disgust.

"You'd rather let all those people die than save a single groundling?"

"Why are you asking me such stupid questions? You already know the answer."

Yes, Tomoe supposed he was right. She knew exactly what kind of man her father was – petty and mean and spiteful. A man made of nothing more than ego and hatred, who cared more about personal glory than the independence he supposedly championed. Why was she still disappointed each time he reached a new low?

Her father moved to the corner of the engine room, where a small voice-pipe hung down from the ceiling.

"Relay this order to all our ships! It's time to move into Formation B!" he ordered.

Tomoe braced herself as the ship began to move.

Through the open hatch, she watched the *Kujiraza* and the other Sohma airships gather around one another and open fire on a groundling vessel.

"That was Prince Ugetsu's ship," said Rei. "Don't worry; the prince is probably lying dead on the streets of Sola-Ea. We're just cleaning up the rabble."

"What? I thought you were allies. Why would you do that?" Tomoe stared at him in horror as she watched Prince Ugetsu's ship explode.

"Why? Because I am not Ugetsu's servant! Because we Sorabito won't be handed our independence like a dog accepting a bone from its master; we will win our freedom with our own hands! Because the glory of freeing the sky cities belongs to me – and me alone!" her father roared. The grin that spread across his face was nothing short of terrifying. He seemed caught in some kind of blissful glee at the destruction and death he had caused.

"You're a pathetic man." Tomoe raised her knife level with her chest and braced herself for an attack.

"I'm creating a better future for you, my daughter. Isn't that what any loving father would do?"

"I suppose loving fathers stab their children and leave them for dead."

"You're alive, are you not? As is that friend you hold so dear. Do you know why? Why I did not kill you both, even though you're stupid and ungrateful and never listen to a thing I say?"

Tomoe ground her teeth together. She always listened to

the things Rei said – it was just that everything that came out of his mouth was awful.

"It's because I love you, Tomoe." Rei held his hand out to her. "You are my daughter. Stupid and over-emotional though you are, I am trying to make a better world for you."

Tomoe's eyes narrowed. Rei had never once thought about her beyond how he could use her. He was no father. How could he stand there and appeal to her sense of family now? Captain Sakurai, the crew of the *Orihime*, Sayo – *they* were her family.

"If you want to be a good father, I have a suggestion for you."

"Oh?" Rei stared at her, a butcher sizing up a pig at a market fair.

"Let me have Sohma. You can leave your little group to me in my inheritance after you die."

Rei laughed. "What nonsense is this? What would you do with Sohma? The people who follow me do so because they can't forget the injustices they have suffered. Do you think their hatred will disappear when the war is over? Do you think any strides towards peace and understanding could possibly soothe their suffering? Are you going to tell them their hatred is wrong? Do you have the gall to ask them to forgive the groundlings?"

"I'm not going to ask them to forgive anyone. I only ask that they don't get in the way of people who are trying to make things better!" Tomoe gripped the hilt of her blade tighter so that her father would not notice the slight tremble in her hands.

She would do it this time. She would kill her father. Perhaps it would be satisfying to cut him down the way he had cut Sayo. She wasn't strong enough to fight him though, not without a little help. Adjusting her grip on the handle of the knife so that the blade was pointed backwards, Tomoe stabbed the boiler behind her and jumped out of the way.

A jet of scorching hot steam spurted out, hitting her father head on. Rei screamed and dropped to the ground, rolling out of the way, but the brief exposure was enough to leave his skin bubbling, red and blistered across his face and arms.

"You brainless girl! I'll kill you!" Despite his injuries, Rei drew his katana. His arms shook with pain but his gaze was steady, and in his eyes there burned only one, single-minded desire to make her suffer.

Now, with both of them injured, they might finally have a fair fight.

She stabbed another boiler, then another, using the jets of steam to cut off parts of the engine room.

Warning lights blinked an angry red, alerting the ship's crew to the damaged boilers. Tomoe could sense that they were losing altitude.

As if to confirm it, the voice-pipes screamed: "Engineers, to the boilers! What in the seven hells is going on?"

"Is this how you repay my mercy? I kept you alive when I could have gutted you like the snake you are! I kept your friend alive! I did it for *you*, Tomoe!"

Tomoe's steps faltered. Noting her hesitation, her father charged at her, katana swinging. Tomoe ducked, wincing in

pain as her wound protested at the sudden movement. She was an idiot for hesitating.

The katana clattered against the edge of another boiler, though not hard enough to slice it open. Tomoe used the moment to push a barrel of levistone towards him. Rei jumped out of the way and it rolled through the hatch behind him.

Get it together! she hissed at herself. Staring at the manic gleam in her father's eyes, she understood now why she and Sayo had been spared. Mercy was simply another tool he could use to unsettle her, to catch her off guard while he stabbed her in the back.

"I'll bury you! I'll bury you so far beneath the disgusting earth that even the worms will have trouble finding you!" The blisters on Rei's hands and arms had begun to weep with blood and fluid.

Tomoe ignored him and braced herself as he charged at her. Their blades clashed, but he had the advantage of height and weight, and managed to topple her to the ground. Tomoe bit off a scream as she landed on her bad side. Her father pinned her down and slammed his knee into the wound.

She screamed. The pain was so agonizing she almost blacked out. Her side was bleeding again. A warm wetness fused her kimono to her skin. Rei lifted his sword to stab her through the neck.

Desperate, Tomoe plunged her knife into the meat of his thigh. As Rei howled, she used the opportunity to wriggle out from beneath him. Panting hard, her body drenched with

sweat, she staggered to her feet and kicked him squarely in the jaw.

The force of the blow sent her father teetering towards the open hatch. She only had time to catch his widening eyes, the look of terror on his face, as he stepped back and realized the floor was no longer there. With barely a gasp, he fell through the hatch, through the sky, plummeting towards the ground far, far below.

Tomoe thought she would feel something over the death of her father, but there was nothing except a numb kind of hollowness. Perhaps the complicated feelings would come later, when she was not in agony and drained of everything. Hauling her aching body towards the edge of the hatch, Tomoe collapsed to her knees.

There, between all the clouds and smoke, she caught a glimmer of the *Orihime* slipping out of Sola-Ea's docks and into the air like a fish through water. Grabbing the edge of the hatch, she lifted her aching arm towards it as if she might be able to hold the ship within the palm of her hand.

Gods, she just wanted to go home.

FORTY-THREE

COUGHING, Kurara hauled herself back to the surface. The smoke from the fires had filled the tunnels quickly, turning their journey into a race against the flames. She only hoped that Himura had found another exit.

She and Haru crawled out of the hatch and back into the city, where they both lay for a moment, in the shadow of the autumn palace, panting for breath. Himura's qipak was still there, miraculously undamaged by the bombing.

Screams echoed in the distance. Yuurei swirled through the air, darkening the sky. Kurara watched them for a moment, swooping down and disappearing behind the building stacks. Gunshots and explosions shattered the air, almost drowning out the wail of frightened children while, outside the broken city dome, the sound of cannon blasts continued to thunder through the sky.

As soon as she surfaced, anxiety hit her like a sledgehammer. What was she meant to do now? Maybe she should have let Princess Tsukimi have her way. Everyone was going to die at the hands of the yuurei anyway. At least she could have used their lives to—

No. Kurara stamped out the thought. Using people as tools was exactly what Aki would have done. Kurara was not Aki. There would be another way. *She* would find another way.

But … what if this was her only chance? Nothing was gained without sacrifice. What if that sacrifice was the lives of everyone in the city?

"We need to…" She glanced up at the sky again. Need to … what? Seal the yuurei? Stop the fighting? Save the lives of the people in this city? Let them die to make the Star Seed bloom?

Why did it feel like she was always running everywhere, trying to put out a million different fires? She felt as though she had given so much of herself – dashing from emergency to emergency, concentrating on just keeping her head above water – that she could not think properly any more.

"Rara, I know a way to make the Star Seed bloom. One that doesn't sacrifice the lives of an entire city." Haru pointed to the sky. "We'll use the yuurei."

"But…" Kurara hesitated. Corrupted and twisted though the yuurei were, was it right to use them like that?

"The dead aren't meant to dwell in the world of the living. That's why they want to burn away or return to the safety of a core." Haru's expression twisted into a look of pity. "They're suffering. We can help them. We can put an end to their misery *and* make the Star Seed bloom."

Kurara bit her lip. It sounded risky, but what other choice did they have? "All right, how do we do this?"

"We'll use my core to absorb them and then sacrifice them all to the Star Seed."

Kurara jerked back as if he had slapped her. "What? No!" How could he even think that she would allow him to do that?

Something in Haru's expression shifted, and an awful, cavernous fear carved its way through her chest.

"Rara, open up my chest and look at my core."

With mounting dread, Kurara did as she was told. She gingerly swiped a finger down the middle of Haru's bared chest and made an incision through the paper. Though it was a bloodless procedure, she couldn't help but feel squeamish. No one wanted to see the inside of their friend's chest.

The moment she looked, Kurara wished she hadn't.

Haru's core was a horror. The paper was tattered and covered in long gashes. Fear seized her throat. It was so much worse than when she had last seen it.

"We're not like Suzaku," Haru said. "Our cores weren't created to hold multiple souls, and this is the result. It's getting worse."

"I can fix it. I—I can try, at least!" she said, as a war drum of terror beat inside her.

"I doubt even an expert like Princess Tsukimi would know how to fix this." Haru pressed a hand to his chest.

Hastily, Kurara closed the cut she had made and let Haru bundle himself up again like his core was a dirty secret they were both too ashamed to face.

"Is this my fault?"

Haru's eyes widened in horror. "No!" he cried. "No, of course it isn't! Listen, I can handle one more batch of yuurei."

"And then you'll sacrifice yourself?" she snapped.

"Nothing is gained without sacrifice," Tsukimi had said. It felt like, even in death, the princess was still mocking her.

"And the souls inside me. With as many as I've absorbed, it should be enough to make the seed bloom. My core will probably crack open sooner or later. At least this way I won't become one of those *things* up there."

There was a note of both pity and disgust in his voice as he said the word "things". The yuurei were mindless creatures, motivated only by their desire to either die or return to a core. Kurara had no wish to see Haru reduced to something like that either.

"No! How can you even suggest this?" Her panic was running away with her now. She couldn't think straight. Couldn't breathe. How could Haru expect her to agree to this?

"You wanted another way. This is the only other way!" said Haru.

"Then I should have let Tsukimi bring the city crashing down!"

They stared at each other: Kurara's chest heaving and her throat sore from shouting; Haru's jaw stubbornly clenched and his eyes dark.

"You don't mean that."

Kurara punched him.

Her fist collided with his cheek, sending him staggering back. She had never hit Haru before, not even when she was at her most furious. Not even when she found out that he had been keeping the secrets of her past from her. Not even when he went and formed a blood bond with Himura behind her back.

When she screamed "I hate you!" what she really meant was *I love you and I'm terrified*.

Her tears stung her face. She could not breathe without shaking; her body rattled under the strain of holding back each violent, ugly sob.

"Why are you suggesting this now? Why didn't you just tell me to let Tsukimi kill everyone when I had the chance?"

If she had known this was how things would end, she would have helped Tsukimi crash the entire city into the ground. Nothing was gained without sacrifice, but what sacrifice was worth Haru's life? She couldn't live without Haru. She didn't want to.

"I like it," Haru said quietly. "The idea of becoming a tree. It'll certainly be more peaceful for a change," he joked. "Please, let me do this, Kurara. I don't want to end up like Suzaku."

Her eyes burned. How she hated the way he so casually talked about dying. How she despised him and this entire world that might take Haru from her.

But she had seen Haru's core. Even if it didn't break today, or tomorrow, or even the day after, it would one day. This was Haru choosing his fate, and wasn't that what Kurara had always wanted for them, for their kind? The nobility of choice.

"Give me the seed, Rara."

Kurara swallowed. She hated this. She hated this so

much. Carefully, she handed him the Star Seed. He was the only one she would trust with something so precious.

"Just one thing," she said. "In order to absorb the yuurei, you need to draw the sealing circle. Let me help."

At least then she could be with him a little longer.

At least then they did not have to say goodbye yet.

Haru pocketed the Star Seed.

"Let's go."

FORTY-FOUR

KURARA did not climb onto the vehicle immediately. With shaking hands, she pulled a square of paper from her left arm and transformed it into a long thin blade as hard as steel and as sharp as the point of a carving knife.

With all the strength she could muster, she thrust the tip of the knife through the qipak's fuel tank.

"If we don't want to miss any yuurei, the sealing circle needs to cover the entire city. That way, we can ensure we get them all. We can use this fuel to draw the sealing circle," she said as a steady stream of liquid levistone flowed from the punctured metal. She picked up a hand cannon lying abandoned by the side of the road and looked back at the fuel pooling on the ground.

Haru nodded and hopped onto the craft. They would have to be quick if they didn't want to run out of levistone.

As soon as Kurara was perched upon the back of the vehicle, he took off.

She wrapped her arms around Haru's middle and held on tight, too tight, as if she could keep him from leaving her. Her head ached. Her body was numb. There was nothing inside her but a persistent thrum of misery deep in the hollow of her chest.

Part of her hoped they ran out of fuel. She hoped that this ride would never end. It was a selfish wish. If they did not succeed, everyone in the city would die. But if they did, Haru would...

She wiped the tears from her eyes.

The qipak skimmed just above the ground, leaving a greasy trail of fuel behind as it swerved over the rubble, beneath the shadows of broken building stacks and past the charred, crooked remains of street lamps. Twisting around, Kurara took aim at the trail of fuel and pulled the hand cannon's trigger. Fire roared to life, licking at the qipak's tail.

She hoped the blaze devoured her.

They stuck to the outskirts, close to where the glass dome met the ground. From there, Kurara could see the ships outside, locked in fierce battle.

The ground shifted beneath them as if something had rammed the entire city.

"What was that?" Haru yanked the qipak's levers and increased their speed as a flaming aircraft came spiralling through the remains of the dome, shattering glass and crashing into a building stack several feet away. A domino effect brought building stack after building stack down in its wake.

312

Cannonballs hit Sola-Ea one after another. Kurara couldn't tell whether any of the ships were purposefully aiming for Sola-Ea or if the city was being bombarded by stray cannonballs that had gone off target. Either way, the next shot hit something key to the city and the foundations tilted to one side. Kurara cursed as the world lurched beneath her.

"Hold on, I've got the circle down. I just need to draw the star!" cried Haru. "Just a little more and we're done!"

He pulled a lever and the qipak veered away from the outskirts and through the heart of the city. As the cannons continued to pelt them, they passed people buried beneath the rubble, people hiding behind ruined statues. Kurara bit her lip and tried to shut out their pleas for help. They couldn't afford to stop now.

Yuurei circled the air like vultures then dived at them, a mass of writhing limbs and wailing mouths that reached towards the ends of Kurara's hair and snatched at her face.

She screamed as she noticed flashes of teeth from somewhere in the shadowy mass. The qipak snapped forward, flying so fast Kurara's sleeves whipped into her face and her hair felt like it was being torn away from her scalp. Haru's hands shook as he gripped the vehicle's levers.

"Haru, your core – is it—?"

"It's fine!" He yanked at the controls and the qipak took a hard right, creating another line in the eight-pointed star they needed in order to seal the yuurei.

The qipak rolled to a stop in the middle of a deserted road. Now the sealing circle covered the entire city. Yuurei dived towards it like ravenous moths flitting around a flame.

Kurara was careful not to stray too close to the lines of

burning levistone. The high-pitched whistle of cannonballs falling through the air made her ears ring. It felt like the end of the world.

"This is it," said Haru.

She didn't want this to be it. Kurara didn't want anything that brought her closer to the point where they would have to part.

"Wait." She grabbed Haru's hand before he could turn away from her. "Let me stay with you. I'll absorb some yuurei into my core too. We'll go together!"

What scared her was not death, but the thought of being without Haru, of living in a world where she could not hear his laughter or bask in his smile. They had always been together, twin stars in a shining constellation. They had entered the world side by side. Didn't it make sense that they should depart it that way as well?

Haru shook his head. "You can't leave the Star Seed to blossom alone. Who will protect it? Who will make sure the shikigami gain their freedom? What if people try to cut the tree down once it has grown?"

"Himura can take care of all that!" And she knew he would. He was a different person from the man she had first met; she was finally willing to admit that.

"Rara, we don't even know if Himura is still alive."

"I'm sure he is. He's very capable!"

"And so are you. Rara, I was perfectly happy being a servant forever, perfectly happy to just let the world be the same as always. It was you who wanted to change things. You who thought that we could. Not many people have your heart, or your strength."

No, Kurara refused to give in.

"Let's go together! We've always been together!" She clung to the front of his kimono. Perhaps if she screamed loud enough or begged hard enough, Haru would take pity on her. Maybe if she just held on to him, he wouldn't be able to leave her.

The screams from the city sounded distant and unreal, like they were coming from somewhere far below a vast ocean. Even the sound of cannon fire was somehow muted.

Haru pulled her into a fierce, bone-crushing hug.

Kurara wished that the moment could last forever – a moment in which nothing and no one else existed but Haru and herself. If only they could just run away and leave their responsibilities behind as Aki had done.

"Rara, will you let this all be for nothing?" Haru whispered in her ear.

"It's all your fault! You wasted all of our time!" Suzaku's and Entei's voices merged together in her mind, screaming at her. The Star Seed had to bloom. To give meaning to everything she had done. When she thought about Suzaku, about Entei, about all the shikigami that had died or gone mad, she knew that she could not abandon those out there who were still suffering.

Haru was right. Once the Star Seed bloomed, the Tree would need to be protected. It would need to be managed, and someone had to make sure the shikigami were given their freedom. She could not run away from this. Running had only ever led to misery. As tempting as it was, she would not repeat the same mistakes as her former self.

"Don't blame yourself, Rara," Haru said, as if reading her

mind. "Dwelling in guilt forever is like rolling in the mud. You rise above it and do better. Just like a lotus flower."

Pulling away from Haru, Kurara scrubbed her arm over her eyes. "I'll take care of everything."

He nodded, and she stepped back. Taking a deep breath, her left arm crumbled away and the pieces of ofuda whirled around her, slowly fashioning a pair of wings with large feathers that trailed against the ground and towered over her head.

"Haru, I…" Her words died in her throat. There was so much she wanted to say, yet none of it felt right. In the end, she said nothing. With a large flap of her wings, she flew into the sky.

"Rara!" Haru called to her. "You're my star. You know that, right?"

Kurara turned. From above, he looked so very small, yet his smile had always been able to rival the sun.

"Of course. You're mine too."

Her shooting star.

FORTY-FIVE

WITH Mana's core tucked safely against his obi and the remains of Mana's body wrapped around his wrist, Himura limped towards the nearest dock. His bad leg burned with every motion, but he clenched his teeth against the pain and forced himself to keep moving. He had to get out of here. Mana had given him its body, its core. He could not let himself die here.

The city was doomed. All around him, buildings toppled to the ground and yuurei swooped through the sky. He was not fast enough to run if the shadows came after him. All he could do was keep dragging himself forward and pray.

As he reached the nearest docking bay, his heart sank.

The gates to the sky were open, and the ships that had once filled the bay were all gone. There was a crowd of people inside the battered shell-like building, all, like him, looking for a way off Sola-Ea. Some people were screaming and wailing at the clouds for help, others slumped over in the corners, staring silently at nothing.

That meant the only way off the city was to jump – a bad idea when you lived so high up you could no longer see the ground below. Himura gazed up at the battle still playing out in the distance, across the swathes of blue sky. If he really concentrated and stretched his ofuda thin, he might have just enough paper to fly away on his own, but could he leave all these people trapped here? Leave them to die? Even if the yuurei did not get them, the city was falling apart beneath their very feet.

But what else could he do?

"Get out of the way!" someone bellowed.

Himura looked behind him just in time to catch sight of a man on a qipak hurtling towards him. People lunged at the man and were dragged along as they grabbed hold of the sides of the vehicle.

"Get off!" The driver kicked them off. "Get away! This qipak is mine, you hear me? Mine!"

As the qipak hurtled towards the exit, Himura threw himself in front of the vehicle and flung his arms out.

He only half expected the qipak to stop. As it screeched to a halt mere inches from his feet, he realized how easily the pilot could have run him down.

"What in the seven hells do you think you're doing? Get out of my way!" the man cursed.

Himura did not budge. "Give me your qipak! I'm a Crafter. If you let me borrow your vehicle I can gather more paper and come back. I'll return your craft to you, I promise."

The man sneered at him. "No way! You'll just steal it for yourself and flee! This is mine; why should I give it to you?"

"I can save everyone! I just need more paper. I can get it if you lend me your qipak!" Even as he spoke, Himura knew how foolish he sounded. He should just use his ofuda to leave. This kind of selfish heroism was something Kurara or Haru would do, not him.

The man growled at him. Not that Himura could blame him. If their positions had been reversed, he wouldn't surrender his only means of saving himself just because some idiot asked him to.

He should just give up and leave, but … but Mana had sacrificed its body for him. Mana had helped him when it could have just slithered away, and Himura felt the foolish need to pay that kindness forward somehow.

"Would you let all these people die just to save yourself?" he asked.

A hushed silence fell over the crowd. The man's eyes darted around him, jumping from face to face.

"I'm trusting you." He stepped aside.

"Thank you," said Himura, surprised by how much he meant it.

Taking care not to strain his injured leg, he clambered onto the qipak. A few people tried to climb on too, but they quickly gave up as soon as they realized he was steering the craft back into the city, back towards the fires and the yuurei and the bombs. He had a plan, but it would only work if he was quick.

Outside the docking bay, yuurei swooped towards him. Himura turned sharply and flew the qipak faster and further than the shadows could reach.

As he made his way through the ruined streets, he grabbed whatever paper he could find; whatever had not already burned to cinders: books and letters, lanterns, paper screens from shoji doors. The essence of people's lives deconstructed and combined together. After fifteen minutes of flying, he had more paper than he had ever held before. Himura only hoped he was strong enough for this. Strong enough to support the weight of all the people waiting for him in the docking bay.

"I told you I'd be back," he said as he returned.

"So you are." The man clearly had not believed that he would return, which made Himura wonder why he had surrendered his craft in the first place.

The crowd parted for him. After limping to the open gate, Himura spread all the paper out in front of his feet like the world's largest flying carpet. Taking a deep breath, he smothered the flicker of doubt that crossed his mind. He knew that it would take all his strength to keep the ofuda together, and he wasn't exactly in prime condition. But it was either this or leave all these people to die.

"Jump!" he shouted back at the crowd. A murmur of confusion ran through the people around him.

Well, if no one was going to be the first, he would just have to lead by example. Swinging his leg over the edge of the city, he tipped forward and fell out of the gate onto the carpet of ofuda below.

The blanket of paper held together, but then Himura had plenty of experience carrying his own weight. As one brave soul and then another jumped and was caught by his ofuda, he could feel the strain mount. It was too much. There were too many people. He couldn't keep the blanket together. It was going to crumble and fall.

"Hey, give me control over some of your ofuda!"

When Himura turned, he found a Crafter in military uniform swooping towards him on the back of a large snowy owl shikigami.

"Why?" He tensed, expecting a fight.

"This battle has descended into chaos. Prince Ugetsu is dead, and no one knows where Princess Tsukimi or the leader of Sohma is. Everyone's just shooting at each other because no one has ordered them to stop. We imperial Crafters are meant to take our orders directly from the princess, but we've lost contact with her. At least *you* look like you know what you're doing," the woman said.

I really don't, Himura wanted to argue. The only thing he knew was that he couldn't let innocent people die.

"So, are you going to let me help or not?" the Crafter asked.

Passing control of your ofuda to someone else was much like trying to pass water from one hand to another without spilling a drop, but slowly they managed it, and Himura felt the immense relief of no longer having to hold up so much weight on his own.

As they worked to slowly lower the carpet of ofuda closer to the ground, he was surprised to find other Crafters joining in, using their own ofuda to add to the growing paper carpet. When questioned, each said the same thing: the pipeline of orders had dried up and they didn't know what else to do.

Himura definitely sensed a change in the air. The battle was winding down — not with a bang but with a confused whimper.

Interlude

Glittering electric stars;
When I close my eyes
I sleep among the heavens
And dream of falling upwards

— *Sorabito folk song*

Tomoe did not know how long she remained in the engine room slumped dangerously close to the open hatch while the wind bit through her body. At some point, she must have closed her eyes because the next thing she knew someone was shaking her awake.

"Tomoe! Tomoe, open your eyes, damn it!"

Tomoe looked up to find Sayo crouched next to her.

"I … killed him, Sayo. I couldn't stop him, so I killed him. My father," she said.

Oh no, here came the conflicting feelings. Tomoe had hoped they would not rear their ugly heads until at least a few months down the line – hopefully when she was

322

not bleeding and exhausted and caught in the middle of a war. Her father had been an awful man, but he had been her father.

"Gods, Tomoe, I'm not going to judge you for that. Good riddance, I say. Now, let's get out of here." Sayo carefully eased her to her feet.

Her side screamed at her in protest.

"You opened your wound," said Sayo, a note of disapproval in her voice.

"Technically, Rei opened my wound."

Sayo clicked her tongue. There was a loud ripping sound as she tore the sleeve from her kimono and used it to bind Tomoe's side, staunching the sluggish bleeding. Perhaps it was due to the blood loss, but Tomoe had never witnessed anything quite as heroic.

"Did you see the *Orihime*?" said Sayo. "It's here! We can take a qipak from the hangar and leave. Let's go. Let's go home."

Home. Yes, that sounded like an excellent idea.

"Come on, Tomoe. You need to see a healer."

"We *both* do." Tomoe limped towards the ship's hangar.

Inside were a handful of mismatched crafts. Among them, Tomoe found a qipak that looked to be in sky-worthy condition and helped Sayo wheel it back to the engine room.

It was not a craft made for battle – a qipak was nothing more than a rowing boat with a levistone engine and a pair of wings. The top was completely open, vulnerable to any stray bullet that might whizz through the air – but it was better than nothing. Outside, the battle seemed to be fizzling out,

though Sohma and the imperial ships were still taking pot shots at one another.

Tomoe checked that there was enough fuel in the tank and Sayo started the engine. As the vehicle came to life, they eased it towards the open hatch and jumped on. Tomoe only had time to hold on to Sayo's waist as the qipak trundled forward then dropped into the sky.

With a lurch, the wings sprang out from beneath the body of the craft and the engine propelled them forward. Cannons boomed and bullets zipped through the air. Smoke streaked across the sky, making it impossible to tell where they were going. As Tomoe scanned the clouds for a glimpse of the *Orihime*, a loud bang erupted behind them, and the engine began spewing smoke.

Someone had shot them. Tomoe wasn't sure if it had been on purpose or if they had just caught a stray bullet, but the effect was the same: they were going down.

As they fell, Tomoe noticed a perfect ring of fire encompassing the entire dome of Sola-Ea. There were small fires everywhere, but this one did not look as though it had happened by accident.

Before she could dwell on it, the qipak bucked. Biting back a curse, Tomoe resisted the urge to throw up and gripped the edges of the craft even tighter.

"I can see the *Orihime*!" shouted Sayo, and Tomoe's head whipped forwards, like a bloodhound catching a scent.

The *Orihime* soared through the sky, weaving past both Sorabito and groundling ships as cannon blasts glanced off

its side. A cannonball barrelled into its front, blasting a hole beneath the prow.

All of a sudden, a burst of light erupted from within Sola-Ea. A fierce wind whipped through the air, sending their ailing craft careening through the sky towards the *Orihime*.

"Holy skies!" Tomoe held on for dear life.

Sayo cursed as battleships thundered past. The qipak rattled so much Tomoe felt as though her brain was being tossed about inside her skull.

As they neared the ship, the craft gave a stomach-lurching drop. They screamed as the vehicle landed at a terrible angle, skidding over the deck of the *Orihime* until it hit the guard rails and came to a hard stop.

Tomoe clambered out, sure that something had shaken loose inside her stomach. Her legs were jelly. They gave out the moment her feet touched the deck, and she collapsed flat on her back, staring up at the smoke-tinted clouds and the blinding blue sky.

"Sayo? Tomoe? Bloody skies!" Captain Sakurai appeared in her frame of vision.

The *Orihime*'s deck thrummed beneath her, the vibrations from the engines purring against her skin like a cat rubbing against her in greeting. Her vision misted with tears. How she had missed this. The red sails, the metal guard rails, the ridiculous wonky yellow star painted on the hull next to the ship's name.

"We're home!" she cried.

Sakurai smiled down at them both with a gentleness Tomoe had not felt since joining her father's ship.

"Welcome back."

"Tomoe…" Sayo wheezed as she tumbled onto the deck next to her and lay there, staring up at the blue sky. "We're really back, aren't we? We're on the *Orihime*?"

"Yeah." She could hardly believe it herself.

Laughter spilled from Tomoe's throat, simple and unending. The kind of laughter that was so joyful it bordered on hysteria. She turned to Sayo, who was staring back at her with a dazed expression that slowly slipped into a soft smile.

Tomoe took Sayo's hand.

They were home.

FORTY-SIX

ON paper wings, Kurara headed towards the sky.

Outside the city's glass dome, the air felt fresher, free of the flames and the yuurei. As she turned to face the city again, a blast of light shot up from the very centre of Sola-Ea and disappeared almost as quickly as it came.

The yuurei were gone, the shadows safely sealed away inside Haru.

"Haru!" She screamed his name into the sky. Her core felt as though it would burst from her chest.

She hovered close enough to Sola-Ea that she could still see the broken building stacks and shattered stone roads. Through tears, smoke and flames, Kurara caught a glimpse of a single figure striding towards the edge of the city.

"Haru!" It was him, she was sure of it. How could it be anyone else? Embers smouldered across his body as he swayed, unsteady on his feet. Kurara wanted to scream at him to stop, that it wasn't too late if he wanted to change his mind, but her voice would not reach him.

Tipping over the edge of the city, Haru fell.

Kurara felt the world screech to a halt. She knew that this was meant to happen, that they had agreed to this, but that did not stop her screaming out in terror.

She wanted it to be a bad dream; wanted to dive towards Haru and wrap him up in her arms; wanted to cry until she had drowned the entire world in her tears. Instead, she hovered in the air and watched Haru's body leave a trail of burning paper and ash through the sky.

Her wings were heavy against her back. They strained at her shoulders, where they were wrapped tight around her body. *Don't look away,* she told herself. Haru had wanted this. The least she could do was pay witness to his final moment. Even as her vision blurred from unshed tears, she looked on.

The city was so damaged that parts of it broke away and fell to the ground, though the rest of the dome miraculously remained in the air. The ships beneath it began to flee. Shikigami and their Crafters dodged out of the way as chunks of concrete and stone fell like comets towards the earth, but Kurara's eyes were only for Haru, his body a tiny glimmer among the hail of flaming debris.

A dying star fell from the heavens, and from that star grew a tree. The seed was a star, but so was Haru. He had always been her star, her guiding light, always watching over her, always with her, as constant as the sun and as bright as the Summer Triangle.

As the flames crept over him, a golden light glimmered

from Haru's front. It was a little lower than where his core would be, closer to his obi. It took a moment for Kurara to realize that it was the Star Seed. The Star Seed was glowing.

Nothing is gained without sacrifice.

The light from the Star Seed grew brighter and brighter. The embers spread along Haru's arms and across his face, engulfing him in fire.

"Haru!" Kurara's scream tore at her throat.

Though she was too far away for him to possibly hear her, for a second she swore that he turned to look at her.

The Star Seed, like the heart of the flames, was growing brighter and larger, expanding beyond Haru, pulsing outwards as if it would consume the world.

It was so bright Kurara had to squeeze her eyes shut. The moment she did so, a sudden gust of wind knocked her back, sending her tumbling through the air. The blast was followed by a sound like that of the world being ripped apart.

"Haru!" When Kurara opened her eyes and steadied herself, the world had shifted. The skies were clear; the rubble had been blown away.

There, far below her feet, a golden tree sprouted from the earth, its branches spreading like a spiderweb towards the sky.

The battleships' cannons had fallen silent. She imagined everyone had stopped to gawk at the tree. It was unlike any they had seen before; its trunk was so wide it would take several men standing with their arms outspread to form a ring around it. The roots dug deep into the ground as if reaching for the core of the earth.

A dying star fell from the heavens, and from that star grew a tree.

FORTY-SEVEN

WHEN Kurara landed in front of the tree, her knees almost gave out. She managed to run all the way to the protruding roots before her legs collapsed beneath her.

The Star Tree was as beautiful as she had imagined: golden bark glimmering like the sun, its velvety leaves as dark as midnight and speckled with flecks of silver that shone like the light of stars. If she stabbed its trunk, she knew the sap would run blood-red. The blood of the stars. The key to saving shikigami from their bonds with Crafters.

She had done it. Haru had done it.

"Haru!" Her nails raked through the earth, gouging at the ground as if she could dig Haru out from wherever he had disappeared to.

No, he was gone, and nothing she could do would change that. She had seen him fall, seen him burn. The Star

Tree stood silent, towering over her like an uncaring God. She had sacrificed so much for this, for it to bloom, and it had taken Haru from her. Or at least that was what it felt like. In that moment, there was nothing in the world she hated more than this damn tree.

The thought was so sudden and violent it almost took her breath away. She heard airships land around her, heard the breathless whispers of awe and wonder as people spilled out of their ships to stare up at the tree. Sorabito, groundlings and Crafters alike wandered across the ground in a daze, their battle forgotten. The appearance of the tree had erased any notion that they were still enemies, that they were still technically at war and should be killing each other. They had witnessed what seemed like a miracle, after all – to continue fighting after this seemed improper.

High in the sky, Sola-Ea hung limp like a broken moon knocked askew.

"Gently now! Don't let them fall!" someone shouted.

In the corner of her eye, Kurara noticed a bunch of Crafters manoeuvre a huge paper carpet to the ground. As the ofuda drifted closer, the Sorabito clinging to the carpet tumbled off the edge and stumbled over the ground like newborn foals learning to walk.

Kurara watched them bury their hands in the dirt and grass. Those nearest flinched when they saw her face. Gingerly, she reached up and touched her cheek. She had completely forgotten that Tsukimi had shot her, and that the bullet had left an ugly gash. She could feel the torn paper edge of her wound beneath her fingers. Neither Haru nor Himura had mentioned it, and she had been so preoccupied that she had barely noticed the throbbing pain until now.

What did she look like to others? she wondered. This strange girl with paper wings and a bloodless gash on the side of her cheek. No wonder no one dared to take a step towards her. No one knew what she was – as far as they were concerned she had appeared with the sudden blooming of the Star Tree. She clearly was not a human, but she did not look like any kind of shikigami they knew of either.

Maybe she could use it to her advantage.

"This tree is the sacred Star Tree!" she bellowed, surprised by the strength of her own voice. "If you touch it without permission, you shall be cursed for a thousand years!"

Those around her backed away.

What was she doing? Only a moment ago she had wanted to burn the damn thing down.

"Kurara!" a familiar voice shouted, though it wasn't Haru's voice – the voice she wanted to hear. Kurara watched as Tomoe and Sayo pushed their way through the crowd towards her.

Tomoe wrapped her arms around Kurara's neck and pulled her into a tight hug.

"Kurara! Holy skies, are you all right? What happened to your face? No, sorry, that was an insensitive question, wasn't it. Are you OK?"

OK? Of course she wasn't. How could Tomoe even think of asking her that?

"Gods, Kurara! Everything's in chaos!" cried Tomoe. "I heard that the entire imperial family is dead!"

"The empire is going to collapse," said Sayo, with considerably more restraint. "If we're not careful, there may be another war over who gets to control Mikoshima now. Things are an absolute mess!"

That was the perfect word to sum up how Kurara felt too. She was a mess. What was going to happen now? What about the remnants of Sohma? Who was in charge of the empire now? What if the groundlings still wanted to fight? Even if the Sorabito were able to demand their independence now that the empire was leaderless and vulnerable, things would not be easy. All that anger and prejudice didn't go away overnight.

There were so many things she wanted to know. Was the *Orihime* OK? Were Tomoe and Sayo OK? She could clearly see that they were injured, dried blood coating their clothes. What about the survivors of Sola-Ea? What about Himura?

Yet, as each question flickered to the front of her mind, Kurara found that she didn't care. She could not imagine a future without Haru, and so the future did not matter. Even if the Sorabito and the groundlings tore each other apart, even if the yuurei killed everyone, or all the shikigami in the world went mad, Kurara could only stand there, paralysed by her grief.

"Haru is gone. He burned to ash as he fell from the city." Tomoe's face fell. Even Sayo looked pained.

"Kurara…"

She didn't want to hear their condolences. Didn't want to see the looks of pity on their faces as they told her how sorry they were. She shoved Tomoe away. It was a testament to how terrible she must have looked that Sayo did not yell at her for it.

"Kurara!" Tomoe called after her again.

As Kurara walked off, she heard Sayo whisper, "Give her some space."

A flash of guilt lanced through her. She owed Tomoe and Sayo more than this. Though they had spent a long time apart, it felt as if the three of them had gone through the wastelands of Yomi together. They were friends. Comrades. Kurara knew that they would leave again soon; once things had calmed down, they would return to the *Orihime*. They might never see each other again.

Kurara stopped.

"Tomoe. Sayo."

Both girls looked up at her.

"I'm sorry."

To her surprise, it was Sayo who spoke first. "We know. Don't worry. Go and deal with what you have to."

Kurara nodded. As she turned away, she spotted Captain Sakurai moving through the crowd. Their eyes met for a moment. Sakurai bowed for a brief second before disappearing into the crowd.

The people had dispersed to oversee other matters. Giant golden tree aside, there were more important things to deal with: injuries to attend to, letters to send, ships to repair, people who had lost homes and families who needed comfort. Without their leaders, it seemed everyone had come to an unspoken decision to deal with their own problems before trying to make more trouble. Even Sohma, it seemed, had decided not to cause a fuss. Kurara did not know how long that would last, but she was grateful for the break.

As she made her way around the back of the Star Tree, a sudden jolt of electricity alerted her to an approaching

Crafter. She whirled around to meet them, only for her mouth to fall open when she saw who it was.

"Himura?"

Why are you alive when Haru isn't?

She knew it was unfair, but she could not help the ugly thought that rose to the top of her mind. No matter how hard she tried, she could not be like a lotus, rising above the mud and darkness of her own thoughts. No, she dragged that filth with her and fed on it through her roots. She was nothing but terrible thoughts and bitterness. Haru was gone, Himura was still here and the world was awful and unfair.

"So this is a Star Tree," he murmured. "It's beautiful."

The trunk shone like gold, the leaves as dark as night and speckled with silver. Something in Himura's expression softened. She didn't like how he was looking at her as if she might crumple like paper at any moment. Shouldn't he of all people know how strong paper could be?

"Kurara..."

"Don't touch me!" she snapped when he reached out a hand towards her. His touch would be like fire. It would burn every part of her to cinders. "Was there something else I could have done? Haru was suffering, wasn't he? If I had never let him absorb those yuurei, his core would have been fine! Then he wouldn't have been forced to sacrifice himself!"

"Forced?" said Himura. "I thought you knew Haru better than anyone."

"I do!" She did.

"Then you should know that you could never have forced him to do anything he didn't want to do."

Kurara glowered at him. That was not the answer she

wanted. She had hoped that Himura would tell her that she was right, that she had failed and everything was her fault. In that moment she absolutely despised Himura. His stupid face. His stupid expression as he stood there, breathing and being alive when Haru was not.

A dying star fell from the heavens, and from that star grew a tree. Haru was her star and from him the Star Tree had grown. *"Nothing is gained without sacrifice,"* Tsukimi had said. Well, was it worth it? Would she trade the lives of every shikigami out there for Haru? Kurara was so afraid of what the answer might be that she did not dare to dwell on the question for long.

Himura reached into the folds of his clothes and pulled out a shikigami core. "This is Mana's. It sacrificed itself to save me. The only reason I'm here is because of Mana."

"So what?" she hissed. "Are you trying to say that our losses are the same? You still have Mana's core. I have nothing!"

"You have the tree. This is Haru, isn't it?"

Kurara whipped around to stare at the Star Tree and its towering branches spreading through the sky. That was … not something she had considered before, that his soul had been transformed; that in birthing the tree, something of his essence had been left behind inside it; that his ashes were perhaps embedded deep inside the Star Tree.

When stars died, their lights continued to shine through the galaxy years after they were gone. Maybe it was all just wishful thinking. Maybe there was nothing left of Haru, and the tree was just a tree, but it eased her aching core to think that *something* of him remained.

"Let's create a new body for Mana and set it free," said

Himura. "And after that, let's keep setting more shikigami free. Are you really going to throw away everything now that you've reached your goal?"

Would she throw it all away after coming this far? Would she let Haru's sacrifice go to waste? If she didn't continue, then what was the point of everything she had done? What would be the point of all the lives that had been lost – all the suffering – if she didn't see this through? It was something Suzaku would have demanded from her, but for once, the ghost of the phoenix inside her head was silent.

Himura's ofuda floated past her ear like dandelion seeds on a breath of wind. They curled around her, inviting her to join them. There was an unspoken language in paper, and Himura had always been more eloquent when he spoke through his ofuda.

Kurara lifted her hand and her fingertips unravelled. Her ofuda swirled around Himura's and through the dappled light shining between the leaves of the Star Tree.

It was a hello. A goodbye.

Himura let her cry as their ofuda twirled around them both, though Kurara had not realized that she was crying until she felt his arm on her shoulder, offering comfort and a solid anchor against the storm of her emotions. His eyes, grey as thunderclouds, were soft, promising a brighter future once the rain had passed.

"Let's build a new world, Kurara. Together."

EPILOGUE

SOMEONE had once told her that the mind was like a bucket. Memories were drops of water, slowly filling up that bucket, the water level rising with each passing year, until at last there were simply too many drops to hold. It was natural to forget some things – even humans with their limited lifespans could not remember absolutely everything about themselves.

Kurara had always wondered if perhaps her bucket was somewhat larger than everyone else's.

Spring brought a certain air of festivity to the town. Hoshikuzu was a new settlement, built in the aftermath of the war by the combined efforts of the Sorabito refugees from Sola-Ea, the Crafters that had been stationed there, and the groundlings from the nearby villages.

Sometimes, Kurara wished that she could not remember how different this place had once been, that she could forget all about the death and violence that had led to Hoshikuzu's creation, but she knew that memories were precious, no matter how painful they were. Besides, she had tried giving up her memories once and it had not worked out well for her. Best to let them float away naturally like leaves on the surface of a gentle stream.

As she made her way down the main street, a jumble of Sorabito and groundling accents wove together into a chorus of impatient shoppers and eager street vendors trying to flog their wares. The cherry trees were in full bloom, shedding their tear-drop petals over the stone roads, and the street lamps were festooned with banners proclaiming special sales on everything from mechanical birds to lace skirts, from fresh crabs to the latest wines imported from across the world.

"Lady Priestess, would you like to try our freshwater eel? I'll sell you one box for fifty ko. How about it? Just for you, Priestess!"

"Oh, Holy Priestess, please honour my business by buying some hair ribbons! I'll give you some for free if only you tell everyone where you got them!"

People called to Kurara as she passed. Some even bowed as she walked by. Kurara gave them all a wobbly smile and a wave. It was impossible to go anywhere in the town without someone noticing her – the long white scar that stretched from the corner of her mouth to the middle of her cheek was small yet it always managed to draw too much attention. It was like a giant electric sign saying, "Hi! I'm the priestess in charge of the giant tree over there!" Kurara didn't think she would ever get used to the townsfolk treating her like some special being. Having people look to her for guidance like she knew what she was doing was more terrifying than anything she had ever known.

She hurried towards the shrine, trying not to be rude, but also doing her best to avoid making eye contact with anyone. Her steps quickened as she reached the main temple. It was a grand building five storeys tall with an offering box at the top of its steps and a tiled overhanging roof.

Behind the shrine, the Star Tree towered over everything, its golden branches and dark leaves swaying in the wind. Several smaller buildings were built around the trunk: a dormitory for the shrine maidens, a private food hall and audience chamber, and Kurara's own home, with a koi pond in front of the porch that was full of plump fish.

Her gaze darted around the temple grounds. There were quite a few people visiting today; they always came in higher numbers whenever a festival rolled around – mothers giving their children bronze coins to toss into the offering box, couples bowing before the golden trunk of the Star Tree, young students praying for happiness or romance or academic success or whatever it was that children wanted these days. Kurara had tried telling everyone that neither she nor the Star Tree had the power to make wishes come true, but that had not stopped the worshippers coming.

"Ah, there she is!" A familiar voice sailed through the air.

Kurara turned to see Tanaka, one of the temple's very first shrine maidens, making her way towards her. Tanaka was a Crafter. The wolf shikigami she had once owned had left as soon as it was free, but Tanaka had stayed to help with the shrine.

"You have a guest, my lady."

"How many times have I told you to stop calling me that?" said Kurara.

"Seventy-five times, my lady."

Kurara sighed. Before she could ask who had come to visit, a tingle of electricity danced across her skin, alerting her to the presence of another Crafter.

Himura came up behind Tanaka, carrying a small brown sack over his shoulder. Kurara could not remember the last time she had seen him – time slipped away from her more and more as the months passed – but something inside her chest unfurled at the sight of him.

After the Star Tree had bloomed, Kurara had thought she never wanted to see Himura again, but he kept coming in and out of her life like a persistent rash. Each time he visited, he brought a core in need of repair, a shikigami who wanted to be free, a Crafter who wanted to work at the shrine. She did not know when she stopped feeling hurt and angry at the very mention of him and started looking forward to his visits. Himura was one of the few people she could talk to about Haru without having to explain who Haru was and what he had meant to her.

"Well, look at you, Miss High-And-Mighty Head Priestess." Himura gave her an amused look.

"Please. If anything, I'm more of a negotiator." Kurara sniffed.

She and her shrine maidens were often called on to act as go-betweens for shikigami-Crafter pairs. Some Crafters came to them wanting to free their shikigami because they assumed that their shikigami would be grateful and nothing would change, but that was never the case. Even among the kinder masters, there was a lot of resentment. A lot of pain. Though the pair might decide to stay together, things would never be the same. It took work to mend a relationship that had been built on inequality.

Work that Kurara was willing to put in, no matter how long it took. They would never go back to the turmoil of the past. Never. It was one of the few ways Kurara could give meaning to Haru's sacrifice.

"I'd say that makes you more of a glorified therapist," said Himura.

"Well, Tanaka's much better at that part than I am."

"Not at all!" cried Tanaka. "My lady's technique of punching Crafters when they try to force their shikigami to stay with them is very effective as well."

Kurara blushed. "I only punched a Crafter once!"

Himura laughed and the burn marks on his face and arms stretched across his skin. He had always seemed like a great oak standing through a storm – reliable but immovable, his heart anchored to a single goal like the roots of a tree. Some of that stubbornness remained, yet now he appeared lighter somehow, as if some great weight had been lifted from his shoulders.

Above, an airship left a trail of white vapour across an otherwise blindingly blue sky. With a glance at Kurara, Tanaka bowed and made herself scarce, leaving the two of them alone.

"Is that for me?" Kurara pointed at the sack. She did not have to look inside to know that it was filled with shikigami cores that Himura had collected during his travels.

"Always." Himura handed her the bag as he updated her on his journey across the country, retrieving lost cores and persuading Crafters to let their shikigami go. There were still wild shikigami out there that needed to be hunted down and stopped before they could hurt anyone, except now hunts were carried out with the aim of subduing the beasts and shipping them or their cores to Kurara.

With each shikigami that was turned over to her and freed, some of the emptiness Kurara had felt after Haru's death lessened. She wondered if Haru would be proud of her.

"I saw Tomoe and Sayo while I was in the capital. They were recruiting a bunch of groundlings to fly with them on their new ship. It's called the *Suisei*. They were heading to Estia with ten feet of dried seaweed sheets and one hundred jars of pickled plums in their cargo," said Himura as he glanced up at the Star Tree's leaves.

"Groundlings? Why groundlings specifically?"

"Tomoe says exposure is the best way to challenge beliefs. She is still working with parts of Sohma. Well, at least, she's working with the people who haven't completely jumped onto the whole blood-purist, the-ground-is-the-root-of-all-evil train."

"Well, if you see them again, ask them to stop by. I could do with a few jars of pickled plums." Kurara grinned.

They walked slowly around the edge of the tree, trading stories. Not all of Himura's news was pleasant. A dying empire was a violent one. The board of ministers who had taken over Mikoshima after the deaths of the imperial family were clinging on to their colonies with brutal force. The most radical parts of Sohma were still alive and well, and anti-Sorabito protests shook the capital as people clamoured to either take the newly independent sky cities back by force or shoot them all down.

There was still much work to be done. Kurara did not think there would come a time when there was ever some part of the world that wasn't bleeding, but at least here she could make a difference, however small.

As they walked, she glanced at the roots of the Star Tree, burrowing deep into the earth, tangling around rocks and the bones of ancient creatures until they drilled down to the centre of the earth. She stopped, pressing a hand to the trunk to feel the strange warmth that sometimes pulsed through the rough bark. She was sure that Haru, or whatever was left of him, was embedded somewhere deep within the Star Tree, watching over her even now. At first, she had thought that she was just looking for anything to help her cope with his loss, but the more time passed, the more she felt his presence everywhere: in the leaves, the trunk, the sap that she and the other shrine maidens siphoned off and offered to the shikigami.

Even if he was well and truly gone, this tree was Haru's legacy, and through legacy one had eternity.

"How long will you be staying this time?" she asked, turning back to Himura.

"Only a few days."

"A few days? You should at least stay until the spring festival is over. Buy some candied fruits! Make a donation to the shrine – all the money goes to feeding the koi fish!" She smiled. It was a lot easier now. Back when the Star Seed had first bloomed, she had difficulty even getting out of bed.

She did not really remember much of those days, lost beneath a black haze of grief.

"Actually," said Himura, "I have a request."

A request? Kurara paused, waiting for whatever Himura wanted to say next.

"Has anyone asked you to turn them into a shikigami?"

Of all the things Kurara had expected him to say, this was not it. She sighed and rested her back against the rough warmth of the Star Tree.

"A few. Becoming a shikigami now is essentially a ticket to immortality – of course there are Crafters who want that. We've even had a few people try to steal the sap for that exact purpose."

Not that it would do them any good. The ritual was complex and comprised of many parts – the sealing circle, the burning, the chant to bind the soul to the ashes, and then the marks that needed to be painted on the core – the only people who knew the ritual step by step now were Himura and herself, and she knew Himura would never tell anyone.

"It's not something to be taken lightly. People shouldn't dive into it without understanding what it really means, but I'm not against it necessarily."

Himura nodded. "That's good, because I would like to become a shikigami."

"*What?*"

For the first time since Kurara had met him, Himura blushed.

"Perhaps not today, or even this year, but one day I would like to become a shikigami."

"OK, but *why*?" She stared at him in disbelief. Eternity

was an endless sea. Would he be able to stand the ebb and flow of the years washing over him while others were swept away?

"I am human," said Himura. "One day, I will die. If you'll have me, I'd like to stay with you for as long as you continue to walk this earth. With *both* of you." He glanced up at the tree again.

Kurara drew a shaky breath.

"You say that now," she said, "but if you become a shikigami, you won't have any memories of your time as a human. It's not like you'll be exactly the same person you were before. Staying with me might be important to you now, but if you become a shikigami, you won't remember any of this."

"I won't remember, but my soul will be the same. Besides … you shouldn't be alone."

I'm not alone, she wanted to say. She had Tanaka and the shrine maidens. Tomoe and Sayo visited from time to time, and sometimes Captain Sakurai and the crew of the *Orihime* stopped by. Even if one day those people disappeared, swallowed up by the passage of time, she had the shikigami.

But it wasn't the same as Haru. The two of them had always been together, and now she was just one – a single star in the night sky, shining alone.

"You'll never replace Haru."

"I'm not trying to," said Himura gently. "I don't want to be Haru, and I don't want to take his place inside your heart."

"Then why?" she asked with a hint of bitterness.

"Because I want to see it too. This peaceful future that both you and Haru wanted."

Kurara stared at him. She couldn't imagine Himura as a shikigami; couldn't imagine him as anything other than what he was now – human, so painfully human.

Memories were important. If Himura became a shikigami, he would forget everything: Tomoe and Sayo, the crew of the *Orihime*, Akane, Captain Sakurai, Kurara, Haru, and…

"What about Mana?" The snake wasn't here now, but she knew that the two often partnered together when Himura went on shikigami hunts.

"No matter what I do, Mana calls me a fool."

Kurara frowned. Did he really understand what he was giving up?

No, of course he understood. No one knew the cost of becoming a shikigami more than he did.

She looked at him, her smile soft and bittersweet. "Very well. In fact, I think I already have a new name for you. For when the time comes."

Himura placed his hands together as if in prayer.

"Then I will strive to be worthy of that name."

GLOSSARY OF TERMS

Crafters – People who can control paper at will.

Hakama – Clothing tied around the waist, which falls to the ankles.

Katana – A type of sword with a curved, single-edged blade, wielded with two hands.

Kimono – Clothing made from straight cuts. Wraps around the body and must be tied and folded securely in place.

Ko – The common currency of Mikoshima.

Kohane – A type of aircraft commonly used for transport, fighting and scouting.

Levistone – Fuel that powers airships and sky cities. Highly flammable.

Mochi – A snack made from glutinous rice.

Obi – A sash worn with a kimono.

Ofuda – Paper used by Crafters. Though traditionally one should write a blessing or prayer onto ofuda, many Crafters these days skip this step.

Qipak – A type of aircraft typically used for short flights. It resembles a small rowing boat with wings.

Senbei – Rice crackers.

Shikigami – Creatures made from paper. Kurara and others recently discovered that they have the souls of former humans inside them. A Crafter can bind a shikigami to their will with a blood bond on the shikigami's core. Without a master, shikigami eventually become violent.

Shoji – Traditional sliding doors made by placing paper across or between wooden frames.

Sorabito – Literally: Sky People. A group of people who are born on one of the seven sky cities. Considered second-class citizens by the empire.

Suzaku – The name given to a famous shikigami that dwells in Southern Mikoshima.

Tanto – A short sword usually compared to a knife or a dagger.

Tatami – A type of mat made from woven rushes and other materials.

Yōkai – Supernatural, spirit-like creatures.

Yomi – The underworld.

Yuurei – A soul from inside a shikigami core that has turned into a monster. Yuurei is both singular and plural.

PLACES

Crescent Bay – A city on the edge of Mikoshima, near the coast.

Kazami – An underground settlement created by Crafters during the Great War. Built to confuse invaders with long, labyrinthine tunnels.

Sola-Ea – One of the seven sky cities remaining in groundling control. The Emperor sets up a base and builds a levistone cannon there.

Sola-Il – The first sky city ever built. It is considered the Sorabito's founding city.

Sola-Re – Tomoe's hometown. During the war, Sohma takes over the city.

The *Hotei* – Prince Ugetsu's warship.

The *Kujiraza* – A former levistone transporter ship, which is taken over and used by Rei as a warship in the battle at Sola-Ea.

The *Midori* – A floating restaurant made of banquet halls and private rooms built by groundlings. The place where Haru and Kurara worked before it was destroyed.

The Mountain of the Falling Star – A huge mountain once struck by a meteorite. Haru and Kurara once built a home on the slope.

The *Orihime* – A Sorabito ship dedicated to hunting shikigami. A place Kurara once considered home.

Zeka – A city to the south of Mikoshima.

ACKNOWLEDGEMENTS

The ending of a series is always a strange time. I would like to thank everyone in the previous acknowledgements of *Rebel Skies* and *Rebel Fire*, but also, once again, many thanks to my agent Lina Langlee for continuing to champion my work. Thank you for keeping me sane and not letting me fall down anxiety spirals. To all my friends for their emotional support, as well as to the 22 Debut Group. (Also for keeping me sane. It was a group effort.)

Many thanks to Amir Zand for the amazing cover art once again and Tomislav Tomic for the incredible maps and inset art. Thank you to the good folks at Walker Books: Ben Norland, Rosi Crawley, Rebecca Oram, Jackie Atta-Hayford, Denise Johnstone-Burt, Kirsten Cozens, Jenny Bish, Rebecca J Hall and many more. A big thank you to my editors, Gráinne Clear, Annalie Grainger, Jenny Glencross and Clare Baalham. Thank you to the excellent translators and publishers who have brought the series to a whole new audience in languages I can only dream of speaking one day. I'd also like to thank Susan Momoko Hingley for being my excellent audiobook narrator and bringing this world to life.

Thank you to all the teachers and librarians who recommended this series to their students or their readers, for inviting me to talk, and for their unbridled enthusiasm for spreading the love of reading. You are all superheroes! Thank you to the book bloggers and reviewers for posting about the Rebel Skies series, as well as for all your messages of encouragement. I am very social media shy but I see you and I am immensely grateful. And, of course, thank you to the booksellers and bookshop owners for giving this series a chance to live on your shelves. I can't tell you what an honour it is to see your own book sitting there with other books.

Finally, many thanks to you, dear reader. Thank you for coming along with me on this adventure and stepping into this world. I hope that we will meet again someday.

May we all be worthy of our names.

———————o———————

ABOUT THE AUTHOR

Ann Sei Lin is a writer, librarian and book nerd with a love for all things fantasy. Though London is now her home, she spent several years in Chiba, Japan, living in a rickety apartment block next to a railway station, where the rush of the midnight train would make the walls shake. When not writing, she is often studying, gaming, or trying to make that origami rabbit for the one hundredth time.

———————o———————